FATAL ELIXIR

Also by William L. DeAndrea from Walker and Company

Written in Fire

FATAL ELIXIR

A Lobo Blacke/Quinn Booker Mystery

WILLIAM L. DEANDREA

WALKER AND COMPANY
NEW YORK

First published in the United States of America in 1997 by
Walker Publishing Company, Inc.

Published simultaneously in Canada by Thomas Allen & Son Canada,
Limited, Markham, Ontario

Library of Congress Cataloging-in-Publication Data
DeAndrea, William L.
Fatal elixir : a Lobo Blacke/Quinn Booker mystery/William L. DeAndrea.
p.   cm.
ISBN 0-0827-3289-5 (hardcover)
I. Title.
PS3554.E174F38 1997
813′.54—DC20   96 42461
CIP

Printed in the United States of America
2 4 6 8 10 9 7 5 3 1

FATAL ELIXIR

1

SINCE THERE WAS a lady within earshot, I suppressed the profanities that sprang to my lips when heavy pieces of headline type slid off the galley I was carrying and smashed like an avalanche into my right instep.

Still, it was not a pain that could be contained in silence. I emitted a noise, something between a wail and a yelp, then hopped to a chair near the composing table and grabbed for my aching foot.

Rebecca Payson came running in from her station behind the business desk in the anteroom.

"What's the matter, Quinn?" she asked. The concern in her voice and in her blue eyes was a comfort in itself.

"He dropped some type on his foot, Miss Rebecca," Merton Mayhew said helpfully. Merton was fourteen, and he worked part-time at the newspaper, setting type, cleaning up, and sometimes writing. He enjoyed the work, but that wasn't what kept him around. He had an enormous crush on Rebecca, and if she had spent most of her time at the livery stables, he would have developed an enthusiasm for shoveling muck. Merton didn't know, as most people in town didn't know, that when I had first met Rebecca she was a Lady of Temporary Affection in a house a few days' ride south of here, in Boulder, Wyoming. Her affection for Lobo Blacke had proven to be permanent and, nursing him back to health after the back-shot that had paralyzed him from the waist down, she had thrown over her former life and continued to care for him. She called him "Uncle Louis" now, and I think most people actually did believe she was his niece.

She bent over to look at my foot, as though the pain of it would somehow be visible through my boot. She brushed a wisp of tawny hair back from her forehead and said, "Does it hurt?"

People do ask the most foolish questions. I wondered if she thought the tears in my eyes were for the beauty of the scene, but I simply said, "Yes, quite a bit."

On the far side of the room, Clayton Henry looked up from his worktable. He was irritated, as usual, and his side-whiskers bristled with indignation.

"I *do* wish you people would be more quiet. How am I supposed to finish this woodcut for Saturday's *Witness* in the midst of all this clamor?"

Henry was the latest addition to the staff of the Black Hills *Witness*. He was a perpetually frustrated man because he could not live up to his own standards. It was not enough for him that he was undoubtedly the best violinist, the best painter, the best engraver, and, since the murder last winter of his mentor, Edward Vessemer, the best photographer within five hundred miles. Henry knew he was not the best in the world at any of those things, and he despised himself for it. Lobo Blacke had caught (and killed) Vessemer's murderer, with Henry's help, and the man had grumpily agreed to stay and work on the *Witness* as photographer and woodcutter.

"I'm sorry, Mr. Henry," I said. "The next time I severely injure myself, I'll try to do it so severely that I lose consciousness in the process." I put my foot back on the floor and winced as I did so. It continued to throb, and by now, I fancied I could see the pain through the boot.

"That won't do any good," Henry said. "People will only fuss around you all the more, and splash water on you. Just try to be more careful."

"I will," I said. "Thank you."

Sarcasm was lost on him. He sniffed and went back to his work.

That was when the door to the inner office opened and Lobo Blacke wheeled himself out. He was in a bad mood, too. There had been a lynching to the east, in the Dakota Territory not too far from here, and the ex-lawman was writing an editorial about it. He'd shown me a first draft last night, scrawled in his large, untidy hand.

"There is nothing we appreciate," he had written, "better than a good necktie party. It has the double virtue of removing vermin from our community, and of providing moral example to our youth. But both of these virtues are removed when the hanging is done outside the law. Even if you lynch the right man, he will have kinfolk saying that he could have proved his innocence in a trial, and a hanging is something you don't want second-guessed, because that clouds the moral issue.

"Furthermore, when a group of citizens catches somebody and strings him up without a trial, they are depriving one or more hardworking government employees of their living wage. So we urge the citizens of Wyoming Territory, a wiser and more temperate breed than our neighbors to the east, by all means exercise your right and duty as citizens to bring in outlaws of all kinds. But *bring* them *in*. Collect the reward, and let the professionals take it from there. A rustler hanged by a judge and jury is just as dead as one who's had a bucket kicked out from under him.

"True, the process of the law takes more time, but that's all the better for all those concerned to ponder the frailty of human nature. And when he finally does dangle, it will be much more likely to be the right man at the end of the rope."

It seemed pretty good to me, and I didn't know why he'd spent most of the morning in his office trying to improve it, but he had been, and he wasn't too happy about it.

He wheeled himself around to me, and saw the pain on my face. "Booker, you clumsy oaf, what have you done to yourself this time?"

"Try not to be so overcome with sympathy," I gasped in reply.

"He dropped a galley full of headline type on his foot," Merton said helpfully.

"And made an ungodly noise in the process," Henry added.

"Thank you, too. God bless you, Rebecca."

"Don't be silly, Quinn."

"Well, I'd better have a look at it." With a groan, I got my foot across the opposite knee and grabbed the boot, bracing myself for the pain of yanking it off.

"Don't do that," Blacke said.

Now *I* was beginning to get irritated. "And why not, pray tell?"

"Because once you take the boot off, it will swell up like mad and hurt worse. Furthermore, if you've broken it, yanking off the boot might do you a serious mischief."

Speaking of mischief, there was a flash of it in his gray eyes.

"And we couldn't have that," he went on. "There's room for only one cripple at this newspaper, and the post is already occupied. We'd better have Merton's father have a look at that before we try anything."

He was right, of course. The town of Le Four, Wyoming Territory, was extremely fortunate in having Merton's father, Hector Mayhew, M.D., Ph.D., in residence. Most communities the size of Le Four had no doctor at all, let alone one with Dr. Mayhew's credentials. I had been amazed, when I had first come here five months ago, to find in the middle of the prairie a doctor who had not only heard of Pasteur's germ theory of disease but of Lister's carbolic treatment to prevent sepsis. It was a proven fact that Dr. Mayhew's patients avoided infection much more frequently than did those of any other practitioner within reach, certainly any closer than Cheyenne. As a result, gunshot victims came from far and wide, and Hector Mayhew prospered while continuing to enjoy the small-town life he preferred for his family.

"I'll go get Dad," Merton offered.

"I'd rather you'd help me get to him," I said. "I don't want to distract people around here anymore."

"Excellent idea." Henry didn't look up from his work.

"Do you think you can make it?" Blacke demanded.

"Let's see." I struggled to my feet; or rather, to my left foot. The right one was too sore to put any appreciable weight on.

Merton came around and put my right arm around his shoulders and took some of my weight. He was a tall lad, and very thin, but strong enough to help. With his support, I thought I could make my way the hundred yards or so down Main Street to the doctor's office.

I decided to go without my suit coat, and the warm May weather outside made me glad I did. "Le Four" means "the oven" in French, but the forgotten fur tappers who named this place must have done so in the summertime. Since I had arrived, temperatures had ranged from cold to bitter cold. The vernal equinox came and went, and a month went by, and still nothing that could be even vaguely described as spring appeared. It was only during the past week that the weather had truly broken.

Spring came late to Le Four, but it came enthusiastically, and all at once. In the five or six days since the air had first softened, the earth had become fragrant, the prairie around us had thrown up some brave flowers, and the sparse trees were already in bud. The grass that had been brown and coarse (when not covered by snow) in the winter was greening nicely. Soon the cattle would be munching contentedly on it.

Very little of this could be seen from Main Street, of course, but there were other signs of the season. No visible breath, for instance. The absence of overcoats and capes, letting the women of the town be seen in their colorful finery. More goods from stores displayed on the boardwalks in front of them. This made walking a little more of a challenge for an invalid such as myself, but it was still nice to see signs of life. As a New Yorker, I liked to see some bustle. It made things more alive.

It also, I hoped, boded well for the newspaper. Since the murders last January, there had been very little in the way of news in these parts. Births—usually of humans, but frequently of calves—were common front-page stories. I must admit that circulation did not seem to suffer from a lack of news. In the wintertime, in the absence of more robust amusements, just the twice-weekly appearance of something new to read, however vacuous, was a great boon to the citizenry.

As Merton and I made our way down the boardwalk, however, we came upon something that promised a remedy to both conditions. A young man in a swallowtail coat and a flattopped derby hat was posting bills all along the street. Printed in black on bright yellow paper, they read:

THE GREAT MEDICINE SHOW!!!
Dr. Theophrastus Herkimer
(creator of *OZONO*, miracle medicine of the ages)
PRESENTS

Well, actually he intended to present quite a lot—dancing, music, fire-eating, juggling, prestidigitation that had astounded the crowned heads of Europe. Actually, it was unclear whether the whole extravaganza was what had astounded them or just the prestidigitation.

Merton wondered the same thing.

"I don't suppose it matters much," I told him. "Judging from what I've seen out here and back east, the crowned heads of Europe are an easily impressed bunch."

The young man gave his most recent tack a few more taps with the small hammer he carried, then turned to me and said, "You may scoff now, but when you see the show you'll change your tune." He was a handsome fellow, about halfway between Merton's age and mine. Young enough so that the glossy black moustache he supported seemed stuck on rather than grown. It bristled with the earnestness of his defense of his product.

I fought to keep amusement out of my voice. "I beg your pardon; I meant no offense. Am I addressing Dr. Herkimer?"

"No," he said. "I have the honor to be his assistant and apprentice. Joseph Feathers is my name."

Had I been wearing a hat, I'd have tipped it, as he did his. Instead I bowed, as well as I could, forcing Merton into a bow at the same time.

"I am Quinn Booker, and this is Merton Mayhew. We represent the Black Hills *Witness*, whose office is just a few doors down. I would be quite pleased to interview you for our columns. At your convenience, of course."

"Thank you. I was, in fact, going to go there presently, to see about the purchase of advertising space."

"We have it to sell," I assured him. "And please see me about that interview. I see by the flyer that Dr. Herkimer plans to arrive in town on Saturday. That is the day of our next publication."

The grin under the moustache was self-effacing and sly at the same time. "That is no accident, Mr. Booker. The doctor's zealous in reaching the maximum number of people with the miracle of Ozono. Forgive me a personal remark, but I can't help noticing that you are limping rather badly on your right foot, and that the young man is assisting you. Gout, perhaps? Gravel? Rheumatism?"

"Actually, no," I began.

He waved a hand to cut me off.

"It doesn't matter. Whatever the ailment, Ozono never fails to give relief. See me, and I'll arrange for you to receive a complimentary bottle. You will see for yourself what a benefactor to mankind Dr. Herkimer truly is."

"I see that you truly believe in your product."

"Dr. Herkimer's product. And one must believe the evidence of one's senses and experience, you know."

I told him I'd talk to him later. He smiled, nodded, shook my hand, and pressed one of his bills on Merton.

He looked at it as we walked on, muttering from time to time. "Cancers, asthma, phistic, ulcers, hemorrhoids, male and female complaints, flatulence, incontinence, bruises, sores, chilblains, constipation—this stuff could put my father out of business!"

"Sure it could," I said. "If it worked."

We walked on a little way, and the warm air and the exercise had loosened my damaged foot enough so that I could walk just holding on to the hitching railings that ran along the boardwalk.

"Come to think of it, that must be wonderful stuff."

Merton was puzzled. "Why?"

"Because we were just *talking* about it, and my foot feels better."

Compared to the claims made in the handbill, Dr. Mayhew's big buff, black, and red sign was almost sedate. All he promised was "prescriptions expertly compounded" and "gunshot wounds a specialty."

As we entered the foyer of the doctor's house, the bell rang, and we could hear Mayhew's voice coming from another room. Much to my surprise, the usually amiable medical man sounded harsh and impatient.

". . . And you must realize, Mrs. Simpkins, it would be unethical for me to prescribe for your husband, sight unseen. If he refuses to come to me, or see me if I call, there is little I can do."

Mrs. Simpkins's voice was much quieter, and wavered a little, the way the voices of very old people sometimes do. "Yes, I quite understand, Doctor. I—I'm sorry to have wasted your time. I was just hoping . . ."

Mayhew was a little calmer, but not much. "Yes, I know it can be difficult. But please try to persuade your husband to take serious medical advice. There is nothing I can do otherwise—I am, alas, no miracle worker."

Merton made a face. "I was afraid of this," he whispered. "Dad always—"

He cut himself off as Mrs. Simpkins came into the room. She was a small, slim lady with bright blue eyes that seemed sharp even without the aid of spectacles. She wore a dark gray bonnet over snow white hair, and she managed a sad little smile for us.

"Good afternoon, gentlemen. Merton, my, how you are growing. In a few more years, you'll be taller than your father."

"Yes, ma'am."

"So nice to see you both," she said, though I'm sure she hadn't the slightest idea who I was.

Mrs. Simpkins had been Le Four's schoolmarm for years, teaching generations of the town's young people. Then, about the time Merton was born, and she was just about sixty, she'd married Big Bill Simpkins, the second-biggest rancher in this area, a widower with a grown son.

Gloria Simpkins was still active in town charities and activities. She still directed the students' annual Shakespeare play each summer, and she was a founding member and chairwoman emeritus of the Le Four Home Health Visitors. She'd had to slow down a little in recent months because Bill Simpkins was starting to feel his age (he was nearing eighty) and he needed more care. "Charity begins at home," Gloria Simpkins never tired of reminding me during our conversations. I went out of my way to talk to her because I'd read so much about her in the *Witness* morgue and found her fascinating.

A few seconds after she was gone, Dr. Mayhew came in. He was very tall, perhaps six feet five, and so thin as to seem a poor advertisement for his own medical skills. But his grip was as strong as Lobo Blacke's, and his voice boomed.

Especially now, when he saw the bill in Merton's hand and said, "Get that foul thing out of my house!"

2

HE CALMED DOWN some after Merton scooted from the house. At least he stopped yelling. He grunted and gestured me into an examining room, helped me up on the table, and asked me what the trouble was.

When I told him, he seized my booted foot and began squeezing in various directions.

"Does this hurt?" he asked.

I took a sharp breath. "Yes."

"Good, good. How about this?"

Thick, gelid sweat appeared on my forehead. "Yes."

"Good, good. How about this?"

A red curtain highlighted by silver flashes appeared before my eyes. I expressed pain in something other than words. Not to put too fine a point on it, I screamed.

"Excellent!" the doctor said. He sounded closer to happy than at any time that afternoon.

When my panting subsided, I said I was glad to have been able to please him; it was a comfort to know my suffering wasn't in vain.

"You should be pleased, too," he said somberly. "I believe no bones are broken, and I don't think we will have to cut off that handsome boot."

With that, he grabbed heel and toe and pulled it off. It hurt like fury, but I managed not to scream again. Gingerly, the doctor peeled off the stocking and examined my foot, probing more gently this time.

"No," he said. "No broken bones, just a nasty bruise. Cold compresses for the next few days. Keep the foot elevated as much as possible. Take ten drops of laudanum in cold water if you are unable to sleep because of the pain. And be more careful of how you carry things."

"I'll try to be."

"And stay off the foot for a couple of days. Unless, of course, you get hold of some of the miracle of Ozono. Then you can do acrobatic dances at the opera house, apparently."

"Aha," I said.

"And what, precisely, do you mean by 'Aha'?"

"Well, the reason I had your son help me limp over here was something other, believe it or not, than to deliver him to a scolding. I wanted to get out of the office for a few moments because the people there had become amazingly grumpy, and I sought you out as pleasanter company in my time of affliction. At least in your case, I can see what's bothering you."

Mayhew smiled in spite of himself. "It's not hard to fathom, is it? Had you been in town longer, you would have known ahead of time that I would feel this way."

"Happens every time a medicine show comes to town?"

"Those quacks drive me to distraction. They—"

He brought himself up short, then rubbed his bony chin. "No," he said. "At least, they don't do it alone. It's the people of the town. Winter and summer, day and night, I put my hard-won expertise at their disposal, reducing their fevers, setting their broken bones, delivering their babies, traveling miles in the dead of night.

"Sometimes, I get so weary I fall asleep, and trust to the horse to find his way home. Many's the night my wife has sacrificed her own sleep to have a hot bath ready for me on my return so that I can soak the ache of cold from my bones.

"Then one of these . . . charlatans comes to town, with a tambourine and a scantily clad girl, and some cheap conjuring tricks—"

"And a medical miracle," I offered.

"Oh, yes," the doctor said. "We mustn't forget the medical miracle. Some foul-tasting herbs that couldn't cure anything, let alone cancer or ulcers.

"And those are the better ones. A mixture such as I've described might actually be of some small use as a liniment, and probably wouldn't do any actual harm if imbibed—unless, of course, as happens all too frequently, the victim is someone whose internal organs are already damaged by overindulgence in alcohol.

"The worst of them might as well be peddling prussic acid."

"That bad?"

Mayhew frowned. "Well, no. I don't know of anyone who has actually died from using any of this nonsense. But I do manage to get hold of a bottle of each of these patent medicines and run an analysis, so I know what I'm dealing with if one of my faithless patients gets sick from it. Do you know what I found in one called Dr. Eliza's Miracle Nectar?"

"I couldn't begin to guess," I said.

"Silver nitrate. Silver nitrate!"

"Is that bad?"

"It's very bad, Booker. Silver nitrate is a useful substance; it has its place in the pharmacopoeia. It is useful in cauterizing exuberant granular tissue, and much less painful than cauterization by fire. It can seal off the growth of external ulcers, and treat shingles. But if it's taken internally, crystals of silver build up in the subcutaneous fat and turn the skin a deep indigo blue.

"Fortunately, I was able to warn the people in town, and for once they listened to me. All but Harold Collier."

"He didn't listen to you?"

Mayhew shook his head impatiently. "I didn't get the warning to him. Harold lived—still does for all I know—on a tiny freehold about forty miles north of here, up near the Montana line. He'd come to town about twice a year—it was two days' ride, after all—but he was well liked, and seemed levelheaded. No one knew he'd bought a case of the evil stuff and brought it back to his place. and took it for every ailment he got and many he imagined."

"Didn't he see himself turning blue?"

"Of course he did. But since he was well supplied with the 'sovereign remedy for every known ailment,' he took it for that, too.

"Finally, he came back to town, hooded and gloved, and came to this office in the dead of night, begging for my help. But there was no help to give him. The process is irreversible."

"What's happened since?"

"I have no idea. That was the last time anyone around here has seen Harold. He begged me to keep his secret, and— Oh, my Lord, I have just told it to a newspaper. Booker, I beseech you, please don't—"

"How many years ago was this, Doctor?"

"Four—no, five."

"Then it hardly qualifies as news, does it? However, there might be a story in your battle against quackery in general. Would you mind giving a formal interview on the topic, say tomorrow?"

"But Blacke always sells advertising to these fakes!"

Now I felt a little irritable. "That is unworthy of all concerned, Doctor. Louis Bowman Blacke was a deputy U.S. marshal for twenty years, and earned a reputation for being absolutely incorruptible. He has carried that integrity into the newspaper business. It is true that anyone with something to say may buy space in the *Witness* in which to say it. But it is also true that advertisers have no effect on the editorial content of the newspaper. I would not work there if that weren't true."

The doctor sighed, a sigh drawn way up from inside his lanky frame.

"Yes, Booker, you are undoubtedly right. I beg your pardon once again."

"Don't mention it. But consider this. Saturday's *Witness* will carry the advertisement for this Dr. Herkimer—" I had a sudden thought. "Do you know him, by the way? Has he been here before?"

"Not under that name. Some of them change their names every time they have new labels printed. And I'll tell you this: If it's this Dr. Eliza, I'll know him again. And I'll do something about him. *Doctor*." He practically spat the word.

That would make a story, too, I thought.

"Saturday's paper will have the advertisement, because it's paid for. And it will carry an article about the coming of the medicine show, because that is news. It would be good for the paper, and it would be good for the townspeople, if we carried a dissenting voice in the same columns."

"It might be," Mayhew conceded. "It might also do more harm than good."

"What do you mean?"

"I mean, Booker, that the people want *so much* to believe in these quacks. And though they madden me, when I calm down, I can't really bring myself to blame them."

"Because although there have been physicians since ancient times, medicine as a *science* is still in its infancy. After all the eons, it is only in the second half of this century that Semmelweiss and Pasteur have gained even an inkling of the cause of sepsis. There is so much more to learn . . . which in practical effect means there is so much we—I, as the only doctor around—don't know.

"Booker, you are from a great, sophisticated city in the East, you have been to university, you are the only person around here I would dream of confiding this to. Too much of a doctor's job, more than half of it, consists of facing diseases and disorders of which you know little and can do nothing.

"At those times, the practice of medicine is reduced to making the patient as comfortable as possible and soothing his fears in order to give the body the best possible chance to cure itself."

"And someone comes along," I offered, "who says, 'Yes! I can cure you!' "

"Exactly. Exactly. Whatever you have, I can cure you with the miracle in this little bottle. And because disease and pain are so terrifying, they force themselves to believe. They even force themselves to believe the cure works. At least for a while. Then they ask me why I can't offer remedies like that. Some of them even try to console me for my failure to have developed a miracle of my own."

He slapped a fist into his palm, making me jump.

"It's the worst kind of fraud, Booker. It preys on our most basic fears for profit, but worse than that, I will never know how many people have died that I might have helped if only they'd trusted me instead of some foul-tasting tinted alcohol. How many parents have all unknowing let their children die or become feebleminded with a fever that none of these miracles could have helped, but that a competently administered cold-alcohol bath could? Even one would be too many, and I am certain that there have been far, far more than one."

"All the more reason for the article I mentioned."

"They won't listen. They'll just think I'm jealous." He rubbed his chin again. "And perhaps I am, at that. Jealous at the trust a mountebank can earn with a tambourine that I can't acquire even after years of hard work."

It occurred to me that the doctor was making things bleaker than they were. It wasn't that they didn't trust him. It was just that sometimes they were in the market for miracles rather than medicine, and as he'd said, he didn't keep miracles in stock.

Mayhew helped me struggle back into my boot and loaned me a handsome black cane with a silver handle to help me get back to the office. I thanked him, asked him to think about that interview. He said he would, and I left him and hobbled on home.

3

"OF COURSE HE'S heading this way, Blacke," Sheriff Asa Harlan said. "Wouldn't you be headed this way in his place? It's only natural."

As almost always happened in the presence of Lobo Blacke, the sheriff was agitated. His voice was hoarse and loud, and his bald pate glowed red. He was making pleats in the hat that usually covered it. The rabbit-fur–like hair of his gray fringe and moustache was bristling.

I knew for a fact that Harlan was brave, and one of the best shots in the territory. I also knew that he was stupid, with a deep, profound, angry ignorance that went clean to the bone. Harlan was stupid enough not to notice he *was* stupid, most of the time. Blacke, however, seemed to take delight in pointing it out to him, in person and in the pages of the *Witness*. Since for various reasons I'll get into later Harlan couldn't do much about Blacke, he tended to avoid him and everything associated with him.

For the sheriff to be here in the *Witness* office in the middle of the day was news in itself.

"No," Blacke said distinctly. "I would not be headed this way in his place. Far from it. I would probably be hightailing it north across Montana to try to get to Canada as soon as I could."

"It's only natural for him to want to come here."

"It's only natural for an *idiot*, Harlan. Paul Muller is a thief and a killer, but he's hardly an idiot."

The sheriff was on the verge of figuring out that Blacke had called him an idiot yet again when I cut in.

"Paul Muller? Isn't he in jail?"

"Well, he busted out last night. Killed a guard doing it," the sheriff said. "Just got the wire. Came here to try to get your boss to use his precious newspaper to warn people that he'll be coming this way."

"I'll run a story on the breakout, Harlan. Just don't tell me what to say in it."

"Talk about idiots," the sheriff said. "You're one of the reasons he'll be headed here." Harlan squinted and turned to me. "And what the hell do *you* know about Paul Muller, Booker? When he went to jail, you were still going to So-ciety cotillions in New York."

The truth was, at the time Paul Muller went to jail six years ago, I had withdrawn from the Society life my grandparents had planned for me and was living in the hinterlands of West Seventy-second Street, freelancing occasional articles for Mr. Pulitzer's *New York World*, but making my living primarily by turning out dime novel potboilers about the West, which at that time I had never seen. I frequented the library, watched the wire services at the newspaper, and (to admit an embarrassing fact) read the work of other dime novelists in order to evoke the West of my fiction.

I even based a few of my villains on Paul Muller, a daring and ruthless bank and train robber, though I remember finding his name impossibly dull. I think I called him Buck Murdo, or some such concoction. My heroes shot him to death (in fair fights, of course) with some regularity.

And I must admit he helped me prosper. I finally made enough money to visit the West in person. And it was then, in Boulder, Wyoming, flat on his back in a hotel bedroom, being nursed by a prostitute everyone then called Becky, that I met Lobo Blacke. He had been set up, ambushed, and paralyzed for life.

I wangled a meeting with Blacke and made him a business proposition. He and I would collaborate on his memoirs and split the proceeds. It took some persuading, but Blacke agreed. He had come to realize that if he was going to maintain any sort of independence, he needed some sort of income.

So for seven weeks, he talked and I asked questions and took notes, and the result was *The Memoirs of Lobo Blacke as Dictated by Himself*, now in its twenty-second printing, and still selling very briskly, thank you. The book has made us both quite comfortable in financial terms, but there was more we both wanted.

For me, the money was a mixed blessing, since without the encouragement of financial need, my indolent nature was all too ready to drift back into the kind of idleness I'd fled from in the first place.

For Blacke, the royalties from the book enabled him to move to Le Four and establish the *Witness*, the better to try to track down evidence against the man he was sure had masterminded the cowardly attack that had crippled him. We shall have more to do with the man in question later in this narrative.

In any event, Blacke found he needed help in turning out the paper (and doing the investigations the journalistic enterprise provided an excuse for), so he sent for me. That, at least, is the reason he gives. I suspect, though, that his shrewd brain divined that I was going stale in the metropolis, and he got me out here to see if curiosity wouldn't do for me what poverty once had. His plan had succeeded in at least one way—these days, I was hardly ever idle.

"I know enough about Paul Muller," I told the sheriff, "to be tempted to agree with you."

Asa Harlan had opened his mouth to argue with me before

the meaning of my words penetrated his brain. He stood there with his jaw open while I turned to Blacke.

"Muller was your last big arrest before you got shot." There was a time when I might have tried to be more circumspect in my language, but I had learned that anything but direct speech about his condition infuriated Blacke. "I've never seen the territorial prison, but from what I hear it's no garden spot. Why shouldn't Muller be coming here to get revenge on you?"

"Because he's not stupid, and revenge is a stupid man's game."

"I've heard you say that crime is a stupid man's game."

Blacke cocked his head and looked up at me appraisingly. "That's an annoying habit you have, Booker, tripping a man up with his own words."

I grinned.

"But this is different," Blacke said. "If he gets caught this time, he won't get off with just a robbery charge. He'll hang by the neck until he's dead for killing that guard."

I shook my head. "I don't think it would hurt to accept the possibility that his desire for revenge has grown stronger than his instinct for self-preservation."

"It's been known to happen," Blacke conceded. "But I'm not going to cower in front of the guy, either."

"Oh, come on, Louis," Harlan said, "you ain't never cowered in your life, and nobody's gonna think you're starting now."

Blacke twisted a finger in his ear and blinked his eyes a couple of times. "I must be on the way out, Asa. I thought I just heard you say something nice about me."

"Huh. I still think you're a grandstanding showboat with a chip on his shoulder who don't know how to make the right friends, but anybody can tell there ain't a drop of yellow in you."

The sheriff wiped the back of his hand across his moustache, as if to remove any flavor of his endorsement of Blacke's courage from his mouth.

"Besides," Harlan said, "I said you were *one* of the reasons to think he might be coming here. There's another one. Bigger. Nobody but me and Lucius knows it."

Blacke's eyebrows went up. "Oh? And now you're going to share it with us, are you?"

"Hope to kiss a pig's ass if I do," the sheriff declared. "This isn't no business of yours, and especially it's no business of a newspaper."

Blacke sighed. "Asa, Booker and I both pledge our word of honor that we won't print a word of what you tell us. Isn't that right, Booker?"

It went against every instinct I have as a writer. Why bother to learn something if you aren't going to publish it? I almost blurted out an angry *No!* before I got a look at Blacke. I knew that crafty look. The skills and instincts that had seen him through the decades of dealing with outlaws had spotted an angle. I could see that Blacke felt it was more important to know this than to publish it.

That was good enough for me. "Oh, absolutely right," I said. "Word of honor." I raised my right hand as if under oath.

Harlan narrowed his pale eyes. "And you won't tell nobody by word of mouth, neither."

This really was important. The sheriff was thinking hard today; ordinarily, he never would have come up with that one.

"You promise, you two?"

We both said we did.

Harlan wiped his moustache again. "I don't rightly know if I should. I'm inclined to tell you, because you might think of something to do that could help me out, but—"

Blacke slapped a hand onto the arm of his wheelchair.

"Goddammit, Asa. You've already admitted I'm brave and smart. Why don't you go the whole hog and admit I'm honest, too."

"I never said you wasn't honest."

Blacke was going to bellow, then thought better of it. He spoke very quietly and earnestly, as though to a child.

"Then, if I'm honest, you can depend on me keeping my word, can't you?"

Harlan smiled a little. "Yeah, I guess I can at that. All right, then. There's not only you here, you know. Muller's got a wife and a son here in town. That's why I said it was only natural for him to be heading this way. If you had a wife and a son you hadn't seen for six years, and the man who kept you from seeing them, all in the same town, wouldn't you want to go there?"

"Who are they?" Blacke asked.

"Well, hell, Blacke, you're the guy who kept him from seeing them."

"I know that." Blacke's voice was still quiet. "Who are the wife and son?"

"Oh, it's the dressmaker, out north of the station on Railroad Street. Goes by the name of Mrs. Murdo. The son's called Buck."

4

THE NEXT DAY, Friday, dawned even more glorious than the day before, the earth ever softer and greener, the sky blue, and the air filled with soft warm breezes. It was a terrific morning for a horseback ride, so I had decided to take one.

I have been riding since childhood, eastern style. My father, Colonel Bogardus Booker, is an instructor at West Point, and he began preparing me for a military career nearly as soon as I could walk. Unfortunately for him, by the time I was old enough to start a military career, I felt as if I'd already *had* one. Things were still strained between us.

But my father's training had cured me of something else, the need to prove my manhood by mastering a "spirited" horse. To me, the prancing, dancing, pawing, and rearing constitute nothing more or less than an engraved invitation to a broken neck.

My idea of a proper mount approximates an armchair with legs, and a horse of Blacke's, an eight-year-old mare named Posy, suited me fine. She would walk along at a respectable clip, and would canter or even gallop if you urged her strongly enough, but to see her standing in the stable, you would wonder whether to ride her or to have her embalmed, unless you could see her jaws move contentedly at some hay.

That morning, Posy and I were clopping along toward

Bellevue. Bellevue was an incongruous gabled mansion placed on a corner of Lucius Jenkins's vast ranch, far from any place the sights or smells of the raising of cattle could be expected to reach.

Jenkins had built the place to please his wife, Martha, a large, handsome woman with henna-red hair who had been a dance-hall girl when Jenkins had married her, and was now the undisputed social queen of northeast Wyoming.

Jenkins was possibly the richest man in the entire territory. He ran cattle *and* sheep (an unheard-of—practically sacrilegious—combination in this part of the country), grew winter wheat and sugar beets and horseradish, and anything that would thrive during the short growing season of the northern plains, and had started mining iron ore and coal.

I thought he was a financial genius. It was very unlikely that the bottom could drop out of all these markets simultaneously; his wealth and power were protected from all sides.

Jenkins was bald, and lately (since his wife had read something in a magazine to the effect that it was the coming thing back east) clean-shaven. He was of medium height, slim but not at all fragile looking. His happiness did not appear to match his wealth—to me he looked like a man constantly struggling to swallow something sour. Perhaps it was the high-collared Sunday suit his wife made him wear all the time. Perhaps it was the frequency with which he lost to Lobo Blacke during their twice-weekly checkers matches.

Perhaps he saved that sour look for me because he suspected (correctly) that I was friendlier with his daughter than he'd like.

Lobo Blacke was convinced that Lucius Jenkins was a genius of a different kind, as well.

Years ago, Jenkins, too, had been a federal marshal, a cool and shrewd mind who originated many of the tricks that later made a legend of Lobo Blacke. Just the kind of cool, shrewd mind that could plan huge and successful robberies after he married an ambitious woman and turned in his marshal's badge.

That much was suspicion. What was fact was that Jenkins had bought land and livestock, made improvements, built a mansion, without *ever borrowing a penny.*

From the earmarks of the crime he was investigating when he was shot; from the fact that he had begun to grow suspicious of his old friend; and from the strange, half-hostile, half-solicitous way Jenkins had behaved toward Blacke since the ambush, Blacke had come to the conclusion that Jenkins had set the ambush that crippled him.

He had come to Le Four, and was constantly searching for evidence that would send his old partner to the gallows.

Jenkins was aware of this; neither would talk of it to the other. The continuing cat-and-mouse game was fascinating to watch, especially since it was sometimes hard to tell which was the cat.

So there Blacke sat, in a town owned almost entirely by his friend-turned-enemy, armored only by his status as a beloved legend of the West, his owning of a newspaper, and his wits.

And it was the wits that had sent me out here.

AFTER ASA HARLAN had left, Blacke wheeled himself into his private office and closed the door. I perched on the edge of his desk and let him talk.

"We have to find out about that woman, Booker," he said.

"Well, I can tell you one thing already."

"What's that?"

"She's read my stories."

"Oh?"

I told him how I'd named my looking-glass figure of Paul Muller "Buck Murdo" when I'd fictionalized his exploits.

"Now," I said, "it may be coincidence that she's going by the name of Murdo and calling her son Buck, but I don't believe it."

Blacke rubbed his chin. "I don't either," he said. "Although I suspect it's more likely Muller was the one who read your work."

"You really think so?" I said.

He looked at me. "Yes, I really think so. God, Booker, you're vainer than he is. He's just the sort to enjoy having a character made after him, and you're popping your buttons because a Real Life Western Outlaw might have read your books."

"Popping my buttons," I said with dignity, "is overstating the case somewhat. As I know, and you have pointed out, western dime novels, including mine, are such total balderdash that I'm continually amazed anybody with any real knowledge of the West ever reads them."

"Merton Mayhew soaks them up like a sponge."

"I know. He asked me to write to New York for back numbers so he could read my work. The other day he solemnly told me his three favorite writers were Shakespeare, Edward FitzGerald, and me."

"I've heard of Shakespeare."

"Oh. You'd like FitzGerald. Especially his translation of the *Iliad*. He has a way of depicting the ancient Greeks in such a way—"

"How does this happen? I'm trying to discuss strategy to catch one, maybe two killers, and we wind up discussing the ancient Greeks."

He'd started it, but I really wanted to discuss catching a murderer or two, so I simply apologized and asked him to go on.

Blacke harrumphed. "All right, then. Harlan told us why he thinks—if you can call what goes on in that bony head of his thinking—that Muller will be heading back here. I'll tell you why I thought he wouldn't be."

"You said 'thought.' Does that mean you've changed your mind about it?"

"Let's just say, with the family in the picture, I'm not as sure as I was."

"I ought to go have a talk with Mrs. Murdo, once I know a little more about her."

"Good idea. But how does Harlan know this Mrs. Murdo is Paul Muller's wife? Do you think she showed up in town, dropped by the sheriff's office, and told him?"

"Mmmmm. It doesn't seem likely, does it?"

"You bet your behind it doesn't. Harlan found out the way everything that sticks in his head gets in there. Lucius Jenkins told him."

"And Jenkins knows because he used to plan jobs for Muller. Is that what you're getting at?"

"That's exactly what I'm getting at. Muller made a lot of money and a big rep pulling some of the best-planned jobs I've ever heard of. I told Harlan he was smart, and I know he was— smart enough to carry out to perfection the plans of somebody brilliant like Lucius Jenkins.

"And ruthless enough to tie up the loose ends, after."

Blacke went on to tell me about Muller's last job, the one he went to jail for. Dressed in business suits, Muller and Dakota Larry Preston went in the bank, got the manager, pulled guns on him, and got him to empty the vault into ash barrels, where the money was covered with ashes and trash. Meanwhile, Nig Jackson, a Negro outlaw recruited specially for this job, had waylaid the bank's porter and shown up for work in the man's uniform. He quite calmly rolled the barrels out to the front, where Bernie Spackett drove up in the ashman's cart, which he had stolen that very morning. Bank president, staff, and customers lined up, no shots fired, Muller and Preston strolled out the front door with smiles on their faces.

"Jackson and Spackett turned up dead—Preston shot them.

Muller always tried to get somebody else to do his dirty work, got it from Lucius, I guess." Blacke leaned back in the wheelchair. "I never would have gotten Muller except for the fact that I caught up with Dakota Larry pulling a job on his own, and he wanted to talk to save himself from the rope."

"Did he?" I asked.

"Well, yes and no. He killed another prisoner in the county jail waiting for his trial, so he swung anyway."

"I love a happy ending."

Blacke squinted at me. "Booker, you are a sick bastard sometimes." He harrumphed, then coughed.

"Coming down with a cold," he said. "I hate that."

"Well, don't try any Ozono when the medicine show comes to town, or Dr. Mayhew will never speak to you again."

"Actually, I was just going to have Mrs. Sundberg make up some soup and some hot whiskey punch." Mrs. Sundberg was Blacke's cook and housekeeper. She could boil a brick and have it come out tender and delicious.

"Anyway, with what Dakota Larry told me," Blacke went on, "I was able to catch up to Muller and get him convicted of the robbery, at least. He got fifteen years. Served six, so far.

"But Muller never talked. It was like the cat had his tongue, *and* his whole throat and down to the lungs. It was easy to see he was covering up for somebody."

"And you wanted to know who."

Blacke nodded. "It was about that time my thoughts started drifting in my old friend's direction, as a matter of fact."

"All right," I said. "Fine. But why does that make you think Muller would be riding *away* from here? Seems to me he'd want to latch up again and go back into business."

"No. Lucius wouldn't have that. He's too respectable and too rich."

"Or Martha's too respectable."

"You're learning, Booker. Lucius doesn't give a hang

what anybody thinks, but that jumped-up wife of his lives and breathes for what *everybody* thinks. I think shooting me, or having me shot, was the last criminal thing Lucius did."

"He blew a wounded man's head off last winter."

Blacke waved it away. "He was protecting you from being shot in the back. Or he made it look that way in front of a hundred witnesses."

Blacke coughed again. "I'm convinced there was some sort of deal on. Lucius says to Muller, 'I know about the wife and the kid. If you keep your mouth shut and stay away from me, they'll be well provided for. If you don't, well, who knows what might happen?' "

Now I nodded. It was pure speculation, but it made sense. But then, I thought, the presence of Mrs. Murdo and son in the shadow of Bellevue, so to speak, set them up as perfect hostages for Jenkins to use to keep Muller away. I said as much to Blacke.

"I know, I know," he said. "But family ties are strong. Lots stronger than revenge. I left Missouri in '60 to join the Union and haven't been back since, but I still miss it, even though my ma and pa are dead. If I had a son waiting for me back there, I would have gotten there crawling."

I didn't say anything. I was reflecting that my father seemed to have gotten along without me very well during our long separations during my childhood, and he never seemed all that thrilled on those occasions when we *would* be reunited.

"So he might be coming here," Blacke said. "I don't say it's likely, I just say he *might*. And no matter what, maybe we can use the wife and kid to somehow get some evidence on Lucius Jenkins."

I took a quick breath through my nose.

"What's the matter?" Blacke demanded.

"Nothing. It's just that I'd hesitate to put a woman and boy in danger, no matter who the husband and father were."

"Dammit, Booker, did *I* say anything about putting them in danger?"

"No. But then, you sent me out into a gunfight when I'd been here less than a week."

"So? You won, didn't you? You did what I told you, and you won."

"Yes. I did win. Thank you."

"All right, then. Let's just find out as much as we can find out before we get all huffy about anything. I'm not fixing to put anybody in danger."

"Not even me?"

"Ah, well, you. You're a grown man. You can always say no, can't you?"

"You only say that because you think I never will. I might surprise you someday."

"With all the warning you've given me? Nah." Blacke clapped his hands together. "Come on. Miller could steal a horse and be here day after tomorrow, if he rides hard. Let's get to work."

SO THERE I was, working.

I fixed Posy to the hitching post and walked up the front steps of Bellevue.

A butler in livery opened the door. His name was Pierre. At least that's what Martha Jenkins called him. He was a Chippewa from eastern Manitoba, and he'd learned his English from French-Canadian fur trappers. Martha Jenkins had been enchanted with his accent when she'd first heard it, had taken him out of the canoe and into a warm house. If he had to wear a monkey suit and be polite to strangers in return for a comfortable living, that was fine with Pierre.

I was the only person in town in a position to do so, but I never had the heart to tell Martha Jenkins that Pierre's accent was farther removed from the accents of Paris than the accent of Five Points in Manhattan is from Park Avenue.

Since no one was looking, Pierre had a smile for me as he took my duster and hung it up.

"Good morning, Monsieur Booker. I will tell Madame dat you are 'ere. But I dunno if she will 'ave time to see you. She is watching the maids packing 'er."

Martha Jenkins was going on a trip. That was interesting.

"Actually, I am here to visit mademoiselle."

"She is packing also. But I will tell dem you are 'ere."

5

IN MY PRIVATE thoughts, I called Abigail Jenkins the Princess of the Prairie. Despite her small size, there was something regal in her bearing, and her dark eyes could flash wittily, imperiously, or (as I had come to know) passionately.

She swept down the stairs and came up to me.

"Mr. Booker," she said. "What a pleasant surprise. I was afraid I wasn't going to have an opportunity to say good-bye."

She gave me her soft hand, expecting it to be kissed. I obliged. It made her smile. If Pierre hadn't been within earshot, she would have laughed out loud. It was her way of parodying her mother, who had developed the assumption that hand-kissing was the ultimate in sophisticated relations between the sexes.

"I was out for a ride and thought I might just drop in. I had no idea you were going anywhere."

"Neither did I, before Father told us last night. We're going to New York!"

"You'll like it," I said. "And New York will love you."

"You're too kind, Mr. Booker. Come, let us sit in my father's study and discuss it."

"I shall write it up for the *Witness*. I warn you, our readers will be devastated to learn that the town will be without you, Miss Jenkins."

She stood aside at the door of the study in order to let me open it for her. Once inside, she stood on tiptoe, wrapped her arms around my neck, and kissed me hard, for a long time. When we came apart, she still stood with her arms around me.

"Hello," she breathed.

"Hello," I said back. "What's going on?"

"After years of Mother's nagging, Father is sending her and me to New York. The owner of a shipping firm with whom he does a lot of business has a daughter about my age, and we are to stay with them."

"For how long?"

"At least six months. But it's open-ended. Six months in New York! This is the most exciting thing that's ever happened to me."

"I think I should feel insulted."

She laughed low in her throat, a low, wanton sound that made my spine tingle.

"Next to you, dear, dear Mr. Booker. Next to you, of course. I do wish you could come with me, and be my guide. Despite my father's wealth, I am just a country girl, after all."

"You'll do fine," I said. "And I'd just be in the way. You'll take New York by storm."

"But I will miss you," she insisted.

"I'm flattered. But it's not as if you were in love with me, or anything."

"Or you with me. But I do find you a fascinating man, Mr. Booker, in a number of ways."

"Flattered again," I said.

It was true. Neither Abigail Jenkins nor I was in love with the other, but we were compatible. In addition to occasional (and quite wonderful) physical intimacy, I was the one man in town of anything like the proper age who wasn't in fear of her father or in awe of his wealth. With me, Abigail could be herself, a very intelligent, uninhibited, and lively young woman who looked on the mores of the town and her mother's airs with a wry cynicism that bordered on, but did not quite cross over into, contempt.

"You say this trip was announced to you last night?"

"Yes, Daddy got a wire. Apparently, he wanted to surprise us."

"I'll bet he did. When are you leaving?"

"Tomorrow morning."

"Short notice."

"That's why we're packing so frantically."

It occurred to me that I would like to see the wire their father got. Suppose Mr. Muller, on his escape from the territorial prison, was intent on something other than revenge on Blacke or a reunion with his family. Suppose he had a bone to pick with Lucius Jenkins. That might help explain why Jenkins, who was known to hate letting his womenfolk out of his sight, was suddenly willing to let them out of the West altogether.

"I take it your father's not going along?"

"No, of course not. Who'd watch this place? Stick Witherspoon could do it if he were healthy, but he's still not fully recovered from being shot last winter."

"I see. Well, don't talk to strangers on the way east. You never know."

She ran a finger along my chin. "I talked to you when you were a stranger."

"I beg your pardon, Miss Jenkins. We were formally introduced. By your mother."

"I wish I had time to make our good-byes more memorable," she said. "But if I'm not done packing in time, Mother will be struck down by apoplexy."

"Don't pack," I said. "Just tell her you'll buy everything new in New York. So you'll be in fashion. I came here to talk to you about clothes."

She arched an eyebrow. "To *talk* about them? Usually you just want to tear—"

"Enough of that, if you please. I'm working now, and you distract me with that kind of talk."

"Oh, yes, Mr. Booker," she said in mock reverence. "I'm so sorry, Mr. Booker." She sat in her father's chair and folded her hands in her lap like a schoolgirl, but the effect was marred by her wicked laughter. "What would you like to know?"

"Tell me about the dressmaker," I said. "Mrs. Murdo."

"Quinn! I'm not even out of town yet, and already you're gathering information on another woman. And to ask *me* about it. The *cheek!*"

I raised my right hand and said, "This is strictly business. I shall be as a monk until I see you again."

She squinted at me. "I think I was seven years old. Yes, that was the last time you could have said that to me and had me believe it."

I smiled. "I am going to miss you," I said. "But your mother may come looking for you any minute, and there are some things I have to find out, so let's be serious now."

"All right, Quinn," she said quietly. Another thing I liked about her was the fact that she knew when to drop the badinage. So many people, men and women, just don't. "What do you want to know?"

"The basics. First, what is she like?"

Abigail cocked her head, thinking about it. "Quiet, serious. Absolutely devoted to her son, though how a woman can get so wrapped up in a messy little child is beyond me."

When I had been about the age of the child known as "Buck Murdo," my mother pushed me out the window of a burning building at the cost of her own life. I said nothing.

"Yet she's got to have a little devilment in her," Abigail went on.

"Why do you say that?"

There was a little grin. "Because she makes my clothes. The ones that have such an effect on you."

"Don't you tell her what you want?"

"Yes, I do. You do that with every dressmaker. You can even show them pictures. Not all of them can give you what you want, or they don't care to, if what you want is the slightest bit daring. But Jennie Murdo has always given me what I want, and more. I don't even know how she does it, but when I put on one of her dresses, I feel even more . . . attractive . . . than I imagined. No one could indulge the devilish side of me so well if she didn't have some of the devil in herself, somewhere down deep."

"She makes your mother's dresses, too, doesn't she?"

"Yes."

"Does that mean she's got a bit of the Great Lady in her somewhere?"

"Now that you mention it, yes. Perhaps a good deal more of a genuine Great Lady than mother has. She's very dignified and respectful, but she never for a second gives the impression that she thinks we're any better than she is simply because we have money and she doesn't."

"That's what America is supposed to be all about."

"Well, I know, but most people don't act that way."

I had seen people scurrying to get out of my grandfather's way on the street; heard their voices asking for favors.

"No," I said, "they don't."

"Jennie Murdo does. It vexes mother terribly. She'd probably drop Jennie altogether, except for her being so good at what she does."

"Does Jennie Murdo ever talk about her husband?"

"She says her husband died about six years ago, but you know how that is. I think he may have run off."

"Why do you say that?"

"Because all she ever says about him is that he died. I've known a lot of widows, and they almost always tell you what their late husbands thought about practically everything. 'Oh, my Fred, he loved primroses,' 'My Sam said you couldn't trust an Indian who wears white man's clothes,' 'My Quinn, he was the best—' "

"All right. Did she ever mention how she came to settle in Le Four?"

"No, I don't think so. I think most people who come here from somewhere else wind up here because this is where the railroad tracks stop, don't you?"

"How is she going to manage now?"

"What do you mean?"

"Well, she's losing her two best customers for at least six months. That will probably seriously reduce her income."

Abigail looked genuinely surprised. "I never thought of that."

"You've been busy packing."

"Don't make excuses for me, Quinn Booker. You think I'm shallow and spoiled, and of course I am, spoiled at least. But what can I do? I can't be expected to stay in this tedious place because a woman makes dresses for me. Mother and I have recommended her to everyone in the area who can afford to have dresses made outside."

"Relax," I said. "I wasn't here soliciting charity for the woman. I just wondered if you knew whether she had some other source of income, a pension or something."

"No, Quinn. I'm sorry I haven't been of much help. And I wish I knew what this was all about."

"So do I," I said. "I'll write you in New York when I can tell you."

"I'd like that."

"And don't worry, you've been a lot of help. I'll come to the station Saturday morning and see you off."

6

IT WAS A sweet little cottage, clapboard siding, shingled roof, a white picket fence, and flowers in window boxes. I'd noticed it before, up at the end of Railroad Street, but I never dreamed it was the home of Abigail's favorite dressmaker.

The day had become positively warm, and after I returned to the *Witness* to stable Posy out back and have a few words with Merton Mayhew, I doffed my jacket for the walk back through town.

It would never do, of course, for me to appear at the door incompletely dressed, so as I pushed the little gate aside, I began to slip my arms through the sleeves.

That's when the attack came.

The first wave was the dog. At least, I think it was a dog. It made noises like a dog, and the black nose and one bright brown visible eye looked like the corresponding parts of a dog. After that, it got confusing, because there wasn't much to see but a mop of straggly white hair.

Whatever it was, the creature ran yapping at me. There seemed to be movement in the fur of the more distant end of the thing that might have indicated the wagging of the stump of a tail, but I couldn't be sure. I didn't want to take any chances, especially now that I could see the sharp white teeth in its mouth.

It didn't slow down as if to spring, or anything like that, it just kept running. It was on a perfect course to wrap its teeth around my shin, and I didn't know whether to try to kick it or flee.

I wound up jumping aside at the last second, at the same moment getting the cursed jacket all the way on, and thereby vastly improving my balance.

And the dog ignored me completely, scooted through the open gate, and headed for the railroad yards.

The next wave of the attack came from a small, sandy-haired boy in knickers, carrying a stick and a hoop. In this case, fortunately, the attack was verbal.

"Ah, mister, what did you go and let him out for?"

"I didn't mean to," I said. "I just wanted to talk to your mother for a few moments. You're Buck?"

"That's right. Who are you?"

"My name's Quinn Booker. I work for the newspaper."

His eyes got wide. "You're the one who shot Frank Hastings last year. Wow, I wish I'd seen that."

"I wish I didn't," I said.

The boy eyed me with interest. "Yeah. I heard Merton Mayhew talking about you at school. He said you were a little squeamish about it." Buck Murdo's shrug said it took all kinds.

"Anyway," he went on. "I'm sorry I hollered at you about Buster. I like to get him calmed down first before I let him out of the yard. Now I've got to go get him before he gets himself run over by a train."

"Don't get *yourself* run over by a train while you're at it."

"Don't worry about me, mister. I do this all the time. Mom's inside. You won't find a better present for your girl than one of Mom's dresses," he said, and with that he was off.

I got my jacket seated better on my shoulders, adjusted my tie and hat, and went to knock on the door.

It opened quickly, as if she had been watching out the window.

I introduced myself, showed her my card, and asked if I might come in.

"Is this about business, Mr. Booker?" she asked. The top of her head came up to the top of my shoulders. She had blond hair drawn back into a tight bun at the base of her neck, and nice blue eyes. She had managed to keep any devilment that was in her out of her own clothing, which consisted of a no-nonsense blue dress and a white apron.

On a table by a window where the light was good, I could see pieces of fabric and various arcane tools. There was a treadle-operated sewing machine next to it.

"About my business, rather than yours," I told her.

"I could not possibly advertise in your newspaper, Mr. Quinn. I have more custom than I can handle now."

That was nice to know. At least she wouldn't starve.

"No, Mrs. Murdo. It's not that. You see—this will take a few minutes. Might we sit down?"

A very pleasant smile broke the stern politeness of her face.

"Of course. Forgive me. Would you like some tea? Or perhaps some lemonade?"

"Lemonade would be wonderful, thank you."

"I've made my first batch of it this year for Buck. In the summer, he practically lives on it."

"I haven't experienced a Le Four summer yet. Thank you." I took a sip. It was cool, tart, and sweet.

When Mrs. Murdo had seated herself, I got down to business.

"Mrs. Murdo, for reasons that have to do with our own safety, the sheriff has told my employer and me something in confidence. Something, I assure you right now as we assured him, that will be neither printed nor whispered by either of us."

She swallowed, but when she spoke her voice was the same smooth soprano it had been before. "I wouldn't dream of asking you to betray a confidence."

"I'm not," I said. "It concerns Paul Muller. Your husband. The boy's father."

"I don't know what you mean," she said. She was a good liar, or she'd had a lot of practice telling this particular one. "My husband died six years ago."

"Then the sheriff is mistaken?"

"Very much so. I must see him and get this matter straightened out."

I shrugged. "It won't be the first mistake Asa Harlan's made, even in the short time I've been in Le Four. But there are a couple of things that confuse me."

"I don't know how I can help you with that. Now, if you'll excuse me, Mr. Booker—"

"You know, I never said Paul Muller wasn't dead."

I could almost hear her mouth snap shut. She took a deep breath through her nose and said, "I beg your pardon?"

"I said I'd been told that Paul Muller was your husband, and you said it couldn't be, because your husband died six years ago. How did you know Paul Muller wasn't dead? Do you know who Paul Muller is?"

"Why, no," she said. "I've never heard of anyone by that name."

"Then it's just a coincidence that you and your son are using the name a writer used for a fictionalized version of the man?"

She took a long time to speak, but she met my eyes for the whole interval. Things had changed now—she knew that I knew she was lying.

"If that's so," she said slowly, "then yes. Yes, a total coincidence. And I regret your insinuation that I am 'using' a name. It is my name by law and by right."

I smiled, finished my lemonade, and stood up.

"That's good," I said. "Very good, ma'am. Then there's nothing to worry about."

"What do you mean?"

"Nothing to trouble yourself about, really. Sorry to have bothered you."

I could see a spark in her eyes, whether of anger or fear, I couldn't say.

"Really, Mr. Booker. You come here with a bunch of veiled accusations, upsetting my entire afternoon. . . . I believe I have a right to know what you think you're doing."

I pretended to think it over.

"Well," I said after a few seconds, "I can't see what harm it will do, since it's all a mistake anyway. You see, Paul Muller is a bank robber, and probably worse, but bank robbery's what he got convicted of. He was the last man Lobo Blacke arrested before he had to stop being a marshal."

"And the sheriff thinks I was *married* to him?"

"He thinks you still are. That's the point. He thinks that with the presence of the man who put him in jail, and of his wife and son, Le Four is the first place he'll head for now that he's killed a guard and broken out of jail. Of course—"

I stopped talking because she wasn't listening. Her face went white and her eyes lost focus. She swayed a little in place. I was ready to catch her if she fainted, but she never did, she just stood there, swaying.

Finally, the suspense got to me. I put my arm around her shoulders and guided her gently to a chair. I don't know if she was even aware of moving.

I went to get her a glass of lemonade. She could have used something a lot stronger, but there didn't seem to be anything of a stimulating nature in the house except a half-full bottle of Old Chief Wakkasee's Magic Indian Elixir. I took a whiff of it, and beyond the smell of turpentine, I caught a good strong scent of alcohol.

I was tempted to give her some, but my talk with Dr. Mayhew came back to me, and I stuffed the cork back in and put the bottle away. I wasn't about to take the chance of turning this woman blue on top of all her other troubles.

So lemonade it was. I put one hand behind her head and brought the glass to her lips with the other. She sipped, sputtered, and sipped again. Then she sat blinking for a few moments.

Finally, she turned to me and said, "Thank you. Thank you very much, Mr. Booker. I—I am subject to spells on occasion, and you have been quite . . . helpful."

I had to smile. She was game. She'd had a blow that rocked her on her heels, but she was still trying to cover up.

"Spells," I said. "You mean this happens frequently?"

"Oh, yes." She pulled at the lemonade as if she needed it. "Several times a day."

"It won't do, Mrs. Murdo."

"You are being offensive, Mr. Booker."

"I know I am. I'll apologize once I stop, but I'm going to go on for a while. You don't have 'spells,' especially not several times a day. Considering the work you do, you would have sewn all your fingers together on that machine over there, or at least poked yourself, and your hands are flawless. You would have dropped or spilled things, made stains, and the place is spotless.

"It wasn't a spell, it was a shock. Paul Muller is out of jail and very probably headed this way. That news was enough to drain the blood from your face and send your brain somewhere very far away.

"Now," I said, "it could be that this was the shock of joy. Women love all sorts of men, and it could be you were transported with delight to think you'd be seeing him again. If that's the case—"

"*You shut your filthy mouth!*" she spat. Her face was as red now as it had been white before, contorted and unrecognizable. She threw the lemonade in my face. It stung my eyes. I went back to the kitchen, found a cloth, and blotted myself. I sat back down, trying not to let my clothing drip on her furniture.

"All right," I said amiably. "That's not the case. That means the shock was caused by fear. But that's why I'm here, Mrs. Murdo. This isn't a time for fear, not yet. This is a time for prudence. If we know enough about the man, we can take precautions. I'll match Lobo Blacke's brain against anyone's."

"Is Lobo Blacke genius enough to prevent my son from learning his father is a thief and liar and a murderer?"

"Ah," I said.

"*That's* what I'm afraid of, Mr. Booker. My son is a *good* boy. From way down inside, he's kind and thoughtful and loving. He loved his father so much, it broke my heart to tell him the man was dead, even after I found out what he was."

"You didn't know?"

"No, as God is my judge, I did not know. I realize that makes me seem a fool, but I never knew. I never knew until they caught him."

She told me her story. She was living with her widowed mother down in Denver, Colorado, where they ran a boardinghouse. One day, a well-dressed man with flashing dark eyes and a big moustache came and took a room. He was Ben Murdo, a salesman, he said. He traveled in ladies' jewelry, and he had a business card to prove it. He was charming and polite, and though he frequently left town for a month or two at a time, he always came back to the boardinghouse. He courted her like a gentleman, and then one day he said that he had had a very successful business trip, and he proposed.

I remembered thinking that it would be interesting to compare some of the dates of these business trips with the dates of some major unsolved bank robberies.

At any rate, they were married and happy: Mr. and Mrs. Murdo settled down in a place of their own, not too far from the boardinghouse so that Jennie could still help her mother while Ben was away.

He was away far too much for Jennie's complete happiness, but they made up for it when he was home. Then, after Ben Junior was born (his father called him "Buck"), she wasn't so alone. Ben did better and better at his business trips.

Then one day, he didn't come back when he said he would. Then she got a letter from Wyoming, saying something had happened, and he probably wouldn't be able to come back for a long time, but that he would always love her and little Buck, and not to worry about him, he would be okay. There was enough money in the bank to see her through for at least a year, and he would try to get her more and have it sent, but he couldn't promise.

That was not enough for Jennie Murdo. Leaving Buck with his grandmother, she went to Wyoming and tracked down her husband—on trial in Boulder, Wyoming, under the name of Paul Muller, for robbing a bank.

"I watched as they were leading him to the police wagon," she said. "I begged him to tell me it wasn't true. I pleaded. I screamed. I am ashamed, Mr. Booker, to remember the spectacle I made of myself.

"But he never said a word, never even looked at me. That's when I knew him for what he was. That's when I knew how I had been degraded and debased, and I vowed my son would never know the shame I have felt.

"And I will keep that vow, sir, if it costs me my life. My secret is now in your hands, yours and Mr. Blacke's."

"And the sheriff's."

"And the sheriff's. God help you if you betray it. You wish my help? Very well, you shall have it. I hope it leads you or someone to shoot down Paul Muller like the dog he is before he ever comes close to this place."

"Thank you," I said. "You won't regret it," which was a prediction I had no right to make, but it seemed to calm her down a little. "The first thing I'd like to ask is, how did *you* come to this place?"

"I knew I couldn't long deceive my mother, and I couldn't bring myself to tell her the truth. I told everyone Ben Murdo had been killed in a stage accident and had been buried in Wyoming. Buck cried for days. Everything reminded him of his father. I knew I had to get far away from Denver."

"I understand. But why Le Four? Why not St. Louis, or San Francisco, or Fort Worth?"

"Oh. I had a bit of luck. I was invited to come here."

7

"IT'S JUST AS you said, boss," I told Lobo Blacke after I'd washed the stickiness of the lemonade off myself and changed my clothes. "He arranged it, but he arranged it so slickly, you'll never be able to prove anything by it."

Blacke had just taken a bite out of a sandwich, a thick slab of ham between two slices of Mrs. Sundberg's rich brown bread. For a man who sits down all the time, Blacke gets awfully hungry. He held up a finger while he finished chewing.

"I wouldn't expect anything less of Lucius. Give me details."

"Right after Jennie Murdo got back to Denver, Jenkins showed up on a business trip. He just knocked on her door. He told her he'd had dinner with an associate of his and his wife the night before, and her dress was so beautiful, even a rough clod like him noticed it. He wanted to know who'd made it, and she'd told him, so here he was. He wanted to know how long it would take her to make dresses for his wife and daughter, if he brought them to Denver for a fitting."

Blacke grunted around another bite of his sandwich. "I doubt Lucius has ever noticed what a woman was wearing. You want one of these, by the way?"

"Maybe later," I said. "Anyway, she told him she was sorry, but she was recently widowed, as he could tell by her mourning attire, and that she was soon to leave Denver, and was not taking on any more commissions. He asked her where she was going, she said she didn't know yet, and he sold her on Le Four. A great place to bring up a son, growing town, women could vote—"

Blacke's "*Hah!*" nearly sprayed sandwich around the office. We both knew of Jenkins's threat to leave Wyoming completely if women retained the vote if and when statehood came along.

"—and he would guarantee a good clientele, and reasonable rental or mortgage terms on the residence of her choice, since he owned the bank and two-thirds of the real estate in town."

"So she came, instant hostage in case her husband got loose and had any ideas."

"Of course. But as I said, how are we going to prove it?"

Blacke shrugged. "I don't know. But it's something. We'll be able to use it someday. We've got plenty of time to think of something."

"It's nice of you to say 'we,' " I told him, "but where did all this time come from? I thought he could be here by tomorrow."

"He could have, if he'd come here. But right after Asa talked to us, I had Becky send out a bunch of wires to lawmen all around. I got a reply while you were out today. Paul Muller shot his way out of a jam in Headbutt, Montana, yesterday. Robbed a general store for supplies and traveling money. Last seen heading north."

"Trying to get to Canada. Just as you predicted."

"Comes with experience."

"So Mrs. Murdo and Lucius Jenkins can relax."

Blacke made a face. "I think it might be good to leave them nervous for a while, especially Lucius. Not that I expect him to do anything rash, like pay the widow a visit, but you never know. Of course, sooner or later, word will come through to Asa Harlan, and he'll tell Lucius that the heat is off, but in the meantime, let's just let the stew bubble."

"It's going to be tough on the woman," I said.

"Dammit, don't you think I know that? It doesn't make me happy. I just think it's the best thing to do."

"Well, I've accumulated a whole bunch of information about him. What should I do with it?"

"Write it down. In fact, write it up for the paper. We'll squeeze it into the territorial news on page four—all citizens have been requested to be on the lookout, and so forth. Don't mention his wife."

"Blacke, I may not be a legendary lawman, but I do have a functioning brain cell or two."

He gave me a lopsided smile. "All right, don't get your bowels in an uproar. It never hurts to make sure." He wheeled himself to the door to the composing room. "Get that done, set it in type, and get something to eat. Henry is out taking photos of Rebecca and Mrs. Sundberg at Grechtstein's orchard—"

"Mrs. Sundberg?"

"Yeah. So what?"

"Nothing, I guess. She's a handsome woman in her way." Her way was big and robust, handsome rather than beautiful, and each line in her face, and she had plenty, was a testimony to her battles against misfortunes. She was well worth photographing; she simply didn't strike me as the orchard type.

"Actually," Blacke said, "I think Henry took her as a chaperon."

"A chaperon?" We were back to the ancient Greeks; I was turning into Echo.

"Clayton Henry is more straitlaced than a whalebone corset, boy. He's terrified of what he calls 'loose talk.' You know and I know the idea of Henry sparking Becky wouldn't occur to anybody in this town, and even if it did, you couldn't get any sparking done in the orchard in broad daylight. But Henry doesn't want to take any chances."

"*Honi soit qui mal y pense,*" I said.

"Booker, when you do that, I come closer to disliking you

than I would have thought I *could* dislike anybody who's made me so goddam much money. What was that, French?"

"Very old French. It means 'Evil to him who evil thinks.' "

"You see? That's very good. Why didn't you just say it, instead of showing off that you learned it from a very old Frenchman. In fact, try quoting it to Henry. He'll be back in about an hour and a half. Merton's coming over then, too. We have a paper to put out."

"I hadn't forgotten."

"Just making sure," he said. "I'm going to go take a nap."

With that, he wheeled himself off toward his bedroom, which, like his office, was another corner whittled off the composing room that took up most of the first floor. I'd never been in there—Blacke was, I think, sensitive about the bars and ropes and other things he needed to get into bed, or to handle his sanitary needs. I'd only caught glimpses of them through the open door.

I wished him pleasant dreams (he snorted derisively), and he disappeared into his room.

Then I got to work. Paul Muller . . . sometimes known as Ben or Buck Murdo . . .

I frowned and crossed that last bit out.

Five feet ten inches tall . . . Black hair, brown eyes, right-handed . . . Wears gun backward for a cross-draw . . . Usually sports a moustache . . . Uses Gresham's Hot Pepper Delight Sauce on everything from grits to fried chicken . . . Has a tendency to whistle "Sweet Betsy from Pike" when concentrating.

As I wrote it down and later placed the letters in the composing stick, I realized that if Muller himself ever saw this, he'd know precisely where it came from. Nobody but a woman who loves you can possibly notice so many things about you.

It made me nervous for her; I liked her. She wasn't a barrel of laughs in the way of company, but she'd borne her misfortunes with courage and resourcefulness.

Blacke has been a risk taker all his life. He's pretty blithe about putting people in danger. I never purposefully took a physical risk in my life until I went to work for Blacke. I get very nervous, but so far, I've always gone along with him, and things have worked out all right.

As I say, so far.

I spent the rest of the time looking over what else was going into the paper. Friday was the big day for that, but I hadn't been around. I noticed that Merton had done the interview with Joseph Feathers, advance man for Dr. Theophrastus Herkimer's Great Medicine Show. It wasn't signed, but I recognized the boy's style. It was a good piece, factual and impartial.

I was just finishing up a sandwich and a glass of milk when Mrs. Sundberg, Rebecca, and Henry returned from their picture-taking session. They were all in a good mood, so much so that Mrs. Sundberg saw me with the sandwich, and instead of scolding me for meddling in her kitchen, she just smiled indulgently and said she'd better go clean up the crumbs I'd undoubtedly left.

"Hello, Quinn," Rebecca said. "It's an absolutely *lovely* day, and the orchard was so nice, with the trees in bud. Wait till you see it when it blossoms."

"I'm the sort who's more interested in the apples than in the blossoms."

"The man has no poetry in his soul." Even Henry sounded less sour than usual.

"Booker," he said, "I am a man torn. I am on the horns of a very irksome dilemma."

"Perhaps I can be of help."

"I doubt it. Despite your education and upbringing, you remain a Philistine. Still, it will perhaps help me to air my problem."

"Please do."

"In such a godforsaken place as this, when one finds beauty, one should cherish it dearer than diamonds, never let it depart.

At the same time, when one discovers potential greatness, one is obliged by sheer humanity to share it with the world."

"Perhaps eventually you'll get around to telling me what you're talking about."

"I am talking, sir, about our mutual friend, Miss Rebecca Payson."

"You mean it took you until today to discover that she's beautiful? I may be a Philistine, but I was quicker than that."

Rebecca was laughing and blushing at the same time. "Stop it now, both of you!"

Henry ignored her. "I was aware of her pleasing symmetry of face, and—begging your pardon, Miss Payson, I speak as an artist—form, and of her lovely coloration. But today, looking through the lens, I discovered *beauty*. Every pose is a poem, every movement a symphony."

"You're making fun of me."

"My dear lady," Henry intoned, "I do not 'make fun.' The camera revealed your intelligence, your virtue, your grace. You are wasted in this place, being photographed by a mere second-rate technician such as myself. You should be in New York, or better still, Paris, inspiring geniuses to masterpieces."

He turned to me. "Don't you agree with me, Booker? Your opinion is valueless to me, but it may have some weight with Miss Payson."

"I agree with everything you say."

"Quinn!" Rebecca snapped.

"But," I went on, "don't you think Miss Payson's happiness should be consulted as well?"

"Bah! What is happiness compared to Art?"

"Bah, yourself," Rebecca said. "I love you all too dearly to leave." She looked at the clock. "It's time for me to call Uncle Louis."

I grinned as I saw her go, and even Henry's mouth turned up at the corners. It was the last really happy time we were to have.

8

"THE GREAT MEDICINE Show has come to town! Come one, come all! See marvels! Learn about Ozono, the medical miracle, the marvel of the age!"

The man in the flattopped black hat and long black swallowtail coat over white pants and a silver vest was mounted on a wagon nearly as loud as the voice that boomed through the huge megaphone he carried.

The wagon was a vision in red and gold, carved in curlicues and arabesques, with sylvan scenes painted in full color on the sides, some featuring plump women veiled only by a few strategically placed wisps of cloth.

Like practically everyone in town, we'd come out of the office to see the ride-through—the show itself would begin at dusk in Grechtstein's orchard. I nudged Henry, pointed at the side of the wagon, and said, "Ah, Art."

He sniffed and refused to look at me.

The man with the megaphone, he informed us, was Dr. Theophrastus Herkimer, privy to the secrets of the great healers of antiquity, the lore of Indian tribal healers, and the science of the modern age. It was his calling, given to him in a vision by the Almighty, not to seal up this knowledge in the cold marble halls of a university, but to broadcast it to the common people of this great nation, to heal their wounds and salve their troubles, at the lowest possible cost, and that, ladies and gentlemen, was why he was here today.

I had to admit, he was good. His voice had a timbre and a rhythm that got your ear rolling along with it, to the point where you were almost writing his speech in your head for him a split second before he delivered the next phrase himself. And of course, since you'd thought of it first, as it were, you were more inclined to believe it, no matter how ridiculous it was.

His appearance also helped. Despite the sharp duds, as a native of Le Four might put it, Dr. Theophrastus Herkimer seemed anything but slick. He was short and quite fat—the white pants showed the crease at the bottom of his belly quite clearly. His long white hair was straggly, and his jowls shook like jelly as he orated.

About that time, Merton Mayhew came running down the boardwalk from his father's office, a look of intense concentration on his face. At first, I thought he was on a mission to heckle the showman, but he had something altogether different in mind. He stopped by Lobo Blacke's wheelchair and muttered a few words to him.

Blacke nodded, and Merton ran inside the office, to return a few moments later with a huge armful of freshly printed newspapers, which he began selling to the crowd.

"That boy will go far," Blacke said with pride.

"You ought to give him a raise," I said.

"I'll consider it," Blacke said, and I knew it was as good as done.

This commercial exploitation of a crowd he'd collected seemed to put Herkimer off stride. He didn't lose the thread of his oration—he was far too professional for that—but he did slip his rhythm for a couple of beats.

I smiled as I wondered if Merton knew that at one stroke, he had made some money for his employer, earned himself a raise, and gained some small measure of revenge for his father.

That reminded me to look for Dr. Mayhew, and he was easy

to spot, tall as he was. He was there, standing stock-still, with a grim expression on his face. I half expected *him* to challenge Herkimer's outlandish claims, but apparently, it was beneath his dignity as a true professional man even to publicly acknowledge the existence of a charlatan.

In any case, in a few seconds, no one in the crowd would have heard him. The women were too scandalized, and the men were angling for a better look.

Because Herkimer had caused the wagon to stop where Railroad Street crossed Main Street. The crowd oozed after it, eager to see what would happen next.

The back of the wagon opened and a woman popped out with a jingle and a flash of light as the sun caught the fine gold chains that circled her face, and looped across her stomach, and held on what little clothing she wore. I had never before seen so much of the skin of a woman whose first name I didn't know. She *was* wearing a veil, however.

Strange violin music started to play, and the woman began to dance, bangles on her arms and legs marking rhythm while her bare feet kicked up a dust storm in the street.

I was sure it wasn't an authentic eastern dance, but it was worth watching. Her skin was a smooth light brown, and supple muscles rippled beneath it. I tore my eyes away from her long enough to scan my companions. Merton was mesmerized, Blacke smiling, Rebecca impassive. A look at the crowd showed me a lot of scandalized faces, and more than one man wiping his brow or licking his lips.

Clayton Henry was hidden from me on the other side of a post. I wondered how he ranked this as Art.

It didn't last long, but while it was going on, nobody bought any newspapers.

The music stopped, and now I saw that it had been Herkimer himself who had been doing the fiddling. There was, apparently, no end to that man's talents.

With a last clash of bangles, the woman stopped, threw her arms up and her head back in a posture of ecstatic triumph, then quickly climbed back into the wagon.

The megaphone went back to Herkimer's mouth.

"Ladies and gentlemen, you have been granted a rare privilege: a small part of the Ancient Egyptian Dance of the Sun God. The storied Cleopatra changed the fate of nations performing that Sacred Ritual for Julius Caesar! It has been handed down in secret for generations—Princess Farrah is the last initiate of these mysteries! Descended from the Pharaohs, a protégé of Napoleon the Great, who became the trusted friend of the princess's grandfather during his own conquest of that fabled land of the pyramids. Princess Farrah was sent as a child to share the Emperor's exile—"

"*Fraud!*"

Herkimer had been laying it on a bit thick, and it had gotten to be too much for Dr. Mayhew. Forgetting professional decorum, he shouted it again. "*Fraud!* Napoleon Bonaparte died in 1822!"

It's hard to imagine how one can talk confidentially through a megaphone, but Herkimer managed it.

"So he did, my astute friend, so he did. And there is not a bit of fraud about it. The beauteous figure you saw performing gyrations beyond the capabilities of our most energetic youth has, in fact, been *walking this earth for sixty-seven years!*"

Dr. Mayhew knew he'd been had; he looked angry and sick.

As for me, I burst out laughing at the audacity of the man, but the sound of my mirth was drowned out by the great "*Ooooohhhhh!!!*" that went up from the crowd.

Herkimer wasn't done yet.

"Now, my friends, I will not lie to you. Her devotion to the Sun God forces Princess Farrah to keep secret the full extent of the mystic methods by which she maintains her eternal youth and beauty, even from me, her devoted friend and protector.

"But in gratitude for my having saved her life from shipwreck in a China Sea monsoon, she has given me to know a portion of the wonders of which she is mistress, and that secret, ladies and gentlemen, like all my knowledge of science and medicine, has found its way into Ozono!

"You may claim your share of the wonders this evening, at" —he took a piece of paper from his pocket and glanced at it— "Grechtstein's orchard. At dusk. One dollar the bottle, for a better life than you have known hitherto. I bid you, dear friends, good day."

With that, he took a deep bow, sat down, and had his driver gallop the horses out of town.

As the crowd dispersed and we turned to go inside, Merton Mayhew said, "Um, Mr. Blacke, is it okay if I hang around the office for a while? I don't think my dad wants anybody around right now."

"Sure," Blacke grunted. To me, he said, "Well, Booker, your first medicine show. What do you think?"

I waited until we were back inside the *Witness* office before I answered. "I'm glad the man is content just with traveling from town to town and fleecing dollars from the townsfolk."

Rebecca frowned. "Why is that, Quinn?"

"Because with his gift for fast talk, if he just settled down in a city, he could go into politics, get elected, and fleece people of millions."

"He's good, all right," Blacke conceded. "And I've seen lots of them. But his real secret weapon is the girl. She is something else again."

"I hardly think," I said, "that it is proper to refer to a sixty-seven-year-old princess as a 'girl.' "

"Hah!" Blacke guffawed. "I suppose you're right, at that. I'll show more respect."

"You should show more pity," Rebecca said quietly.

"Pity?" I said.

"Yes, pity, Quinn. Do you think, whoever this person is, that she grew up as a little girl wishing to dance half-naked in a public street and be ogled by strangers?"

"Well, I suppose not, but—"

"I don't have to tell you, do I, that I know what a woman may be reduced to in order to keep body and soul together in a world run by men, do I?"

For a moment, I was too surprised to speak. It was a tacit but ironclad law in the household that we never ever spoke of Rebecca's past life. For her to allude to it indicated a depth of feeling on the issue I hadn't suspected.

"No, Rebecca," I said quietly. "No, you don't."

"And you, Uncle Louis?"

Blacke, as surprised as I was, muttered something that seemed to satisfy her.

"Good," she said. "Now, I know that you are both gentlemen in all the ways that count, and that you would never knowingly hurt a woman, especially one who is down. Just try to . . . to expand your understanding of what a woman goes through, and your instincts will lead you to the right actions. Now, if you'll excuse me, I'll go see if Mrs. Sundberg needs any help with dinner."

She went off back to the kitchen.

When she was gone, Blacke said, "Maybe *she* ought to go into politics," but there was great pride and affection in his voice.

"She'd be a lot better than some of the characters we have running things now. I refer to the New York politics I'm familiar with. I don't know how things are in the territory."

"No better, I imagine. There's just less of us in the heap for them to get in the way of. Where are you going?"

I had looked at the clock and risen. Now I said, "I'm going to the station. I promised Miss Jenkins I'd see her off."

"Hmpf," Blacke said. "Maybe with that vixen gone, you'll expand your understanding a little."

"Not again," I said.

"Not again what?"

"Not again your trying to throw me together with Rebecca."

"Well, if you weren't such a bullheaded fool, you'd already be together."

"And if you weren't so blind, you'd see that she's in love with you."

9

SOMETHING FAR TO the west—windstorm, cattle stampede, brushfire—had thrown a lot of dust into the air, and those of us who came out to the medicine show were treated to a blood-red sunset as a sort of curtain raiser.

I was the only one from the *Witness* here. Henry thought he might come, then decided to paint in his room. Blacke didn't feel like dealing with the buckboard (which he insisted on driving), and of course, Rebecca and Mrs. Sundberg wouldn't hear of it.

I had expected that that little exhibition of ancient Egyptian terpsichorean skill would keep the women of the town away, but there were plenty of them there. Moving through the crowd and eavesdropping, I learned that the women who'd seen it wanted to have their outrage confirmed, and the ones who hadn't didn't want to be left out. I was surprised to see Jennie Murdo there, with Buck right with her. She barely acknowledged my greeting, whether because she didn't want her name broadcast at a gathering like this, or because I was stuck in her mind as the bearer of bad news, I couldn't say.

I'd made it to the station in time to see Abigail off. In the light of my ever-expanding understanding, I came to see that even this rich girl had a difficult lot in life, and I told her, sincerely, that I hoped in New York she would find whatever it was she had been looking for.

In response to that, she gave me a devilish grin, wrapped her arms around my neck, and gave me a kiss dead on the mouth. In front of both her parents. For the rest of the time until the train pulled out, Lucius Jenkins looked at me as if he was measuring me for a rope.

THERE WAS A small rope barrier erected a few feet past a low wooden platform that was built up to the side of the ornate wagon, which gleamed gloriously in the fading sunlight. I decided to exercise a reporter's privilege, and ducked under the rope to check things behind the stage.

I wasn't the first one to have tried that. Stu Burkhart, a bachelor with a small spread outside of town, was pestering Joseph Feathers for an opportunity just to speak to the princess. Just to say hello. There was a dollar in it for Feathers if he'd just turn the other way for a minute, but Feathers was adamant.

"You can't go in there. The final preparations are being made. No one is allowed in there."

"That's bull, fella," Stu said. The way he slurred his words made it obvious that any alcohol content Ozono might have would be superfluous. "I been here for two hours already, hopin' to get a sight of her, and I seen somebody come sneakin' out of the wagon not a half hour ago."

"You must be mistaken. A half hour ago, we were all eating by the stream over that rise."

He pointed at a small hill. You had to take the stream on faith, but I knew it was there. A pleasant site in which to eat outdoors, at that. I was just surprised that they ate at all. I thought they just lived on Ozono.

Stu thought he would get belligerent, but then he saw me. Burkhart had been one of the spectators on the day I came to town. I had had to thrash one of Jenkins's henchmen for making rude remarks to Rebecca. Having been trained in scientific combat by Colonel Bogardus Booker practically since I could stand, it hadn't been very difficult, but it had been, it seems, impressive to look at.

And an interesting thing has happened. Since that day, I've never had to fight a man with my fists. I've never even had to offer to prove it.

"Come on, Stu," I said. "Don't be greedy. You'll see her when the rest of us do. Isn't that right, Mr. Feathers?"

The dark young man grinned in relief. "Oh. Yes, absolutely." Feathers reached into his pocket and pulled out a wooden disk, painted gold, with an overlapping O-Z device painted on it.

"Here," he said, handing it to Stu. "You may redeem this later for a free bottle of Ozono."

Burkhart ignored him. "But, Booker, I'm in love. For the first time in my life, I'm in love."

"You are also," I told him, "drunk. Not for the first time in your life."

"Yeah, but I was sober when I seen her in the first place. I just been drinkin' to work up the nerve."

"Well, it worked. But you're not thinking too well."

"What do you mean?"

"Is a sixty-seven-year-old Egyptian princess really going to be happy on a small farm in the territory?"

"I'll make her happy," Burkhart vowed. "Whatever I gotta do. I'll go to Egypt with her, if I have to." He frowned. "Where is that, back east?"

"Yeah," I said. "Way, way back. Look. You can't ask someone of her stature to decide to devote her life to you when you're drunk. Watch the show, go home and sober up, and try again tomorrow. Remember, you saw enough of her to fall in love, but to her, you were just another face in the crowd."

A tiny light went on somewhere in his fuddled brain. "Oh," Burkhart said.

"You want to make a good first impression, don't you? After all, your future happiness depends on it."

Burkhart took my hand in both of his and pumped it solemnly. "You're a good friend, Booker. I won't forget this. You can be best man."

"I'd be honored," I said. Burkhart walked off, pondering. When he had staggered out of sight back around the wagon, Feathers shook my hand, too.

"Thank you, Mr. Booker. Excellent. Do you have experience in the business?"

"No, I'm just naturally gifted, I guess. Sorry I missed the interview."

"Quite all right. The young man gave us excellent coverage. Good crowd tonight."

"I suspect that has more to do with the princess than with anything that appeared in the newspaper."

He laughed. "She is quite a testimonial to the powers of Ozono, isn't she?"

"Beyond a doubt. Sixty-seven years old, and not a single gray hair."

Feathers was slightly offended. "You're scoffing again, Mr. Booker. Wait until tomorrow, when you see what Ozono does for the health of people of this town. The place will never be the same."

"With bated breath," I assured him. That probably sounded like a scoff, too, so I decided to change the subject. "That must happen fairly frequently, I suppose."

"What must?"

"Lovesick drunks trying to get a private audience with the princess."

"It wouldn't do them any good. The princess has taken a vow of silence."

"A lot of them," I speculated, "probably aren't primarily interested in conversation. No offense meant. It just seems to me you must have evolved a way of dealing with them."

"Well, yes, if talking doesn't work."

Feathers pulled his coat aside and showed me a thin canvas bag, stuffed like a sausage with sand, hanging by a little blunt hook from the armhole of his vest. He unhooked it in one smooth motion and whacked it down into the palm of his hand with a solid thump.

"Leaves no marks, only a headache that is easily treatable with Ozono."

He replaced the sandbag and smiled at me. "Now, what can I do for you, Mr. Booker?"

"Nothing much. Just being a reporter, looking around."

"Well, look away. I'd invite you inside—"

"That would be very interesting."

"But . . ." He made it three syllables. He took a silver watch from his pocket, clicked the lid. "The show is about to start." He realized he still had the wooden disk in his hand. "Would you like a complimentary bottle of Ozono, Mr. Booker?"

I took the disk. "Sure," I said. Maybe I could present it as a gift to Dr. Mayhew.

I went back around front and mingled again with the crowd, which had grown in my absence. I saw all sorts of people there: a couple of Sioux, standing by themselves; Reverend Mortensen; and a mountain-man type—could the miracle of Ozono draw a man down out of the Black Hills, some miles to the east?—dressed in fur, and with a hood up over his head, his face invisible, and his hands swathed in gloves.

My first thought was that he must be parboiled under there. My second, that this was somehow Paul Muller in disguise, I quickly discarded when I realized it couldn't be him unless he'd taken four inches off his height.

Mrs. Simpkins, the old schoolmarm, was there, no doubt looking for more hope for her reluctant husband than Dr. Mayhew could offer.

And there were more farmers, townspeople, strangers, people in traveling clothes who must have come here right off the afternoon train into town, and more.

Then Feathers came out on the makeshift stage and started to juggle flaming sticks, yelling for their attention as he did so. He didn't have the voice of Dr. Herkimer, but he held your attention. Feathers's spiel was to the effect that though they might think so, juggling flaming torches was no great achievement. Anybody could do it—who didn't mind being burned on the hands, face, body, and legs during the learning process. While he was learning, liberal applications of the miracle of Ozono healed his burns in time for the next day's practice session. Without this marvelous product, he could never have obtained the expertise with which he hoped to have entertained them now.

He caught the last torch and bowed just as he said the last word. Then he launched into the introduction of the "person you've all been waiting for—"

"The princess!" a voice yelled, Stu Burkhart or another drunk, I couldn't tell.

Feathers's dark face split again in his charming smile. "In due time, my friend, and well worth the wait. But first, one of the geniuses of our age, a benefactor of all Mankind—*Dr. Theophrastus Herkimer!*"

And, as the Lord is my judge, he got them to applaud for the man who was going to come forth and sell them snake oil and panther sweat, or whatever it was that went into his concoction.

And if I thought Theophrastus Herkimer had wrapped his eloquence around all there was to say about the miracle of Ozono, I was sadly mistaken. He went on with it for more than three-quarters of an hour, and never repeated himself once. He traced the history of medicine (and pretty accurately, too) right up to Pasteur and Lister, and made it a fascinating story of human triumph. He talked about the arcane secrets of the alchemists. He talked about how he himself had been moved to search dusty volumes of forgotten lore to find these secrets.

So good was his delivery that I was sure the shade of the late E. A. Poe would make no objection to the near plagiarism.

He presented testimonials, "sworn affidavits" from those old favorites, the crowned heads of Europe. He did a quick and energetic jig, accompanying himself on the fiddle, and said his robust health was solely the doing of the miracle of Ozono.

Then he introduced the princess Farrah, and did that weird, wailing thing with the fiddle.

The princess came out in a white robe this time. She looked like a member of Reverend Mortensen's choir, except for the jewelry on her head and arms, and the bare toes that peeked out from the bottom of the thing as she walked slowly to the center of the small stage.

Once there, she stood stock-still for a moment, then whirled around two and a half times, ending with her back to the audience. Her hair hung halfway down her back, like black silk against the white silk of the robe. Then she thrust her arms straight out to the side, pulling the robe wide open. The red of the sunset and the red of the footlight torches danced on the silk now stretched out like butterfly wings.

The audience gasped, men and women together. I may have, too. The woman hadn't done anything yet, but she had that crowd spellbound. I suppose you can learn a lot of tricks in sixty-seven years.

Slowly, she inched the open robe down her back, revealing brown shoulders worthy of a goddess. Then, when it was halfway down, she let it drop to the stage all at once, to reveal her in the same outfit in which she'd danced in town.

It was a performance impossible to describe. For each person among the hundreds there, it was as though she had somehow divined our fantasies and formless longings, giving them, for the first time, physical form.

It was not entirely a comfortable experience. I could understand the outrage of decent citizens; not because there was anything obscene about the dance but because it is unnerving to have one's mind read.

And I could understand how a lonely man like Stu Burkhart could see her do this for a few minutes, once, from a distance, and decide he was in love with her.

She ended the dance with the same posture she'd used that morning in town, head thrown back, arms upraised. Then she quietly retrieved the robe and stepped back into it, holding it tight around her with crossed arms. She walked slowly and with dignity off the stage, never once looking at or acknowledging the audience that was applauding her.

Herkimer let his fiddle drop. He announced that he was now ready to sell Ozono. He was wise. Nothing could follow that.

10

LIGHTS WERE ON in the composing room when I got home from the orchard.

Lobo Blacke had his glasses on and was reading a book. I took a look at the spine and was amused to see that it was FitzGerald's translation of the *Iliad*.

"How do you like it?" I asked.

"Wait a second." He read to the bottom of the page, marked his place, and put the book down.

"Not bad. Good blood and thunder. I borrowed it from Merton. I figured if this fellow was one of his favorite writers—along with you and Shakespeare—that he probably had a copy. It's interesting to see that these ancient heroes were just as big a bunch of fools and crybabies as men are today."

"I told you you'd like it."

"You're home late."

"Sorry, Father," I said.

"Don't try to give me any of *that* nonsense," he said. "I'm just curious about the medicine show. Did it really last until"—he craned his neck to look at the clock—"nine-thirty?"

It was ten o'clock now, so he'd given me a generous half hour to get home from the orchard. Even Posy wasn't that slow.

"Not the show itself," I said. "That was over by a little past eight. But Herkimer was there selling Ozono till well after nine.

You'll have to expect a lot of miracles around town over the next few days."

Blacke smiled.

"As for me, when the crowd broke up, I just sat on a rock under an apple tree while I tried to figure it out."

"Figure what out?" Blacke demanded. "They put on a good show; they make a good living."

"But that's the point. They put on a great show. And the people here on the prairie are starving for entertainment. That's why we do so well with the *Witness*, and you know it."

"It's a good newspaper."

"I know it's a good newspaper, and we all work hard to make it that way, but you know as well as I do we could print nursery rhymes and keep ninety-nine percent of our circulation. The *Witness* for most of them is something to rest their eyes on other than the horizon."

"Getting bored, are you? How about a beer?"

"No, I'm not getting bored. And I'd love a beer."

I went out to the kitchen and found the nightly bucket he had delivered from the saloon in town carefully placed on ice, still cool, and with plenty of head left. I got my mug from the cabinet and poured myself some.

As I rejoined Blacke, I said, "The thing I don't understand is why bother with the medicine at all? The show itself was easily worth a dollar."

"Especially to us entertainment-starved western yokels."

"I never said yokels. *I* would have paid a dollar to see it, all right? I mean why taint the commerce in something that's worth the money with a fake 'miracle' concoction that plainly isn't?"

Blacke scratched his neck. "That's a good point, Booker. I can't answer the question, but there is something I do know for a fact: Some people can't stand to make an honest dollar. If they can't trick it out of you, they'd just as soon not have it at all."

I took a pull on my beer, surprised at how good it tasted. I didn't know how the farmers and the punchers got through a day of hard physical labor in this weather. In any weather, come to that.

Blacke was reminiscing now. "I remember Five Aces Jones, down in Texas. He played poker like he read your mind; he knew cards the way I know outlaws. But it wasn't enough for him. He got so good that the thrill wasn't there for him anymore. No risk. So to put the thrill back, he started cheating."

Blacke nodded. "Worked, too. He got plenty thrilled. You never saw so much emotion in a face as there was in Five Aces just before that red-haired cowboy drilled him.

"I remember another fellow—"

I never got to hear about the other fellow, because just then there was a knock on the door of the office. Blacke wheeled himself to the front and pulled aside the curtain in the big window beside it to peek outdoors. Then he opened the door, and Merton Mayhew came in, out of breath.

"Sorry to bother you so late, Mr. Blacke, Mr. Booker, but Pa's out to the Simpkinses' on a call, and sick people are showing up at the office, and Ma and I are swamped, and Ma wants to know if Mrs. Sundberg and Miss Rebecca can come over and help nurse them till Pa gets back."

"I'll go ask them," I said. "I'm sure they will. I'll come over, too."

"You will?" Merton was shocked. There was the assumption in these parts (and most places back east, too) that nursing the sick was woman's work. Merton undoubtedly felt he was stuck doing it because he had to.

But to give my father his due, back in the days he thought he was raising me to be an officer, he had insisted that I learn the rudiments of nursing.

"The men in your care," he'd say in that tone he had, the tone of imparting the wisdom of the ages (as, I suppose, he was—men have been fighting since time began), "are your most precious asset. Anything you, as their commander, can do to preserve them in fighting condition you *must* do. Besides, it's good for morale. You'll be giving plenty of orders, son, that will get men hurt or killed. If you can give orders that will help relieve their suffering, or even do it yourself, the men will love you, and you will be a far more efficient officer."

As I've mentioned before, I never acquired the taste for giving orders, but relieving suffering was fine with me.

"Yes, I'll be along in just a few moments, after I talk to the women. What seems to be wrong?"

"Fever. Vomiting. Intestinal pain. It's stomach grippe, but worse than any I've ever seen.

It was no lauging matter, but I suppressed the smile that sprang to my lips. Merton at that moment sounded exactly like his father.

Then the spell broke, and he was a boy again. "Thanks a lot. I'd better get back to helping Ma."

With that he was gone, and so was I, upstairs one flight to Mrs. Sundberg's room and knocked on the door.

That was a mistake. She came to the door with her face white and her eyes terrified.

"What is it?" she demanded, half afraid to know. "What do you want?"

Then I remembered that the last time she had been awakened in what was for her the middle of the night, it was to receive the news that her husband, Ole, had been murdered by a highwayman. What I should have done was to have gone up another flight, awakened Rebecca first, than had *her* fetch Mrs. Sundberg. Cowardly, I admit, but some things just *are* women's work.

I hastened to reassure Mrs. Sundberg that the trouble didn't touch her personally but that we were being called to help our neighbors.

That was all she needed to know. The fear was gone, replaced by impatience at me for standing there when there was work to be done. She flipped her hand from me. "Go away, now. Shoo! Let me get dressed."

I was glad to oblige. When I got upstairs. I knocked good and loud on Rebecca's door. I didn't want to start ideas in her head that I was making surreptitious nocturnal visits.

She opened the door sleepy eyed, not quite awake. Her thick honey hair was done in a braid, and made a blue flannel night-gown as provocative as the bangles that the princess Farrah wore.

I told Rebecca to blink a couple of times to wake up, which she did. When I could see about seventy percent of the blue, I told her of the summons.

That popped her wide awake, and once again I was chased from her doorway so a woman could get dressed. I told her I'd meet her there, since I was already dressed, and she gave me a look but said nothing.

I took the steps down two at a time. At the bottom, I had a surprise of my own. Lobo Blacke had struggled into his jacket and was just adjusting his hat.

"I'm coming, too," he said unnecessarily.

From the defiance in his tone, I think he expected me to argue with him, so I double-crossed him. "The more the merrier." I told him to lean forward in his chair, and as he did so, I smoothed out the wrinkles in the back of his jacket that he always gets when he puts the thing on by himself.

"Stop *fussing* over me, for God's sake," he snapped. "What are you, my mother?"

"Yes," I said. "Now shut up." I threw the door open, grabbed the handles on the back of the wheelchair, and pushed him out onto the walk.

It was just a matter of a minute or so before we were at the doctor's office. Helen Mayhew let us in. She was as small and plump as her husband and son were tall and lanky, and her usually jolly round face was now set grim and tight.

"Thank God you've come," she said shortly. "Take off your coats and get to work. Yes, you, Mr. Blacke. Wheelchair or no wheelchair, you can hold a man's head while he's sick."

So now, I helped him off with his coat, and we went into the next room.

Somehow, it was the more horrible for there being no blood. Even I, a newcomer in the West, had become inured to some extent to scenes of carnage—from gunplay, or more frequently, from accidents involving cattle or horses or the vehicles horses pull.

But this was something different. The moans of the victims, sounds and smells of retching, the feeble cries for help.

Soon Mrs. Sundberg and Rebecea arrived, and we all did what we could. We placed wet compresses on fevered brows, held buckets and heads for those who needed it, and tried to find soothing and encouraging words for those who were still conscious enough to need them.

It had become obvious that some of the nine people already here, on every available table and sofa, and some on blankets on the floor, were not going to survive. Jack Hennessy, the mountain of a blacksmith, already had cold, rubbery skin; he was moribund if not already dead. Others, though still evincing a thready pulse, had their eyes closed and could not be roused.

Then there was a knock on the door. Cowardly again, I left that room of horror.

I escaped nothing. There at the door was Jennie Murdo, carrying the limp form of her son, Buck, in her arms.

Her face was a mask of anguish. She could hardly breathe through her sobs, let alone talk, but she was trying, gasping, "I gave him his medicine. That's all I did, I gave him his medicine. He has his medicine every night at bedtime. . . ."

And then she started to scream.

11

I HAVE HAD a wide and varied experience with women for a man my age, but this was the first time I'd ever been confronted with one screaming and hysterical, and I didn't know what to do.

My first mistake was to try to take the boy with her.

"What are you doing to my baby?" she screamed. *"Leave my baby alone!"*

Next I tried to reason with her.

"You came here to get help, didn't you? I just want to bring Buck to where he can get help."

"You leave my baby alone!" she screamed, followed by more screaming without words.

This was the point, onstage and in books, even the ones I used to write, where the woman is brought to her senses with a resounding slap, but I was loath to hit a woman in any event, and doubly reluctant to hit one with so many troubles.

On the other hand, this screaming couldn't be good for her. It wasn't much good for me, either.

As I stood there, agonizing over what I should do, Dr. Mayhew walked in and rescued me.

"What's this?" he demanded.

The man looked like a walking corpse, his already cadaverous face showing an expression almost too angry and too grim to be that of a living man.

I opened my mouth to speak, or rather to yell over the continuing, body-racking screams from Jennie Murdo, but Mayhew shook his head impatiently.

"Never mind, I already know. A dose of Ozono. I have just left one hysterical woman over it—Simpkins is dead. How many are in there?" He gestured with his head toward the examining room.

"Nine," I said. "The boy makes ten."

"There will be more," the doctor said. He looked at Jennie Murdo. "Sadly, I can do more for her than I can for the others."

He put his black bag down on a small table in the hallway, opened it, and drew out a bottle of laudanum. He didn't even bother to measure it. He just grabbed the screaming woman by the nose, pulled her head back, and tipped a quantity into her throat. He held her nose until she swallowed, then let go.

She was still sputtering for breath when he said, "She will quiet herself presently. Bring the boy inside when you have the chance. Try to catch her if she falls; the dose was obviously not exact."

He wasn't through the door before his prediction came to pass. I turned back to the woman to find her eyes glassy and her starting, ever so slightly, to sway. I took the boy from her and laid him gently on the floor. Then I guided Jennie Murdo to a big armchair and sat her down. I lifted the boy in my arms and brought him into the examining room.

The doctor turned away from a woman I did not know, who was whimpering and clutching her stomach. He felt Buck's throat and lifted an eyelid.

"Yes," he said. "The boy is dead. Please place him over there."

It stunned me like a blow on the head. I had spent less than a minute talking to this child, but he had been so *alive*, such a *boy* of a boy, full of energy and concern about his ridiculous dog.

I placed him down even more gently than before, near where the now-dead Hennessy lay.

Mayhew now had a tube and a funnel and was doing things to the woman's mouth.

"Mr. Booker, Mr. Blacke. I believe a gastric lavage will not come too late to help this poor woman. I believe my wife and these dear ladies are doing all that can be done at the moment. If you would oblige me by stepping across the hall to my private office for a moment, I should like to have a few words with you."

"Are you sure?" I asked. That was conscience. My feet and body were more than ready to go.

The room was dark when we got there. I let the light spill in from the hallway and saw an oil lamp mounted on the wall and another on the doctor's desk. I took out my match safe and lit them both, making the light as bright as possible. I wanted a lot of light after what I'd seen that night.

By the time I'd finished, Blacke had already wheeled himself into the room. He spun over to the wall behind the doctor's desk and was scowling at his diploma.

"Why the hell," he said irritably, "don't they write these things in English, so you can know what the hell it says?"

"It just says he's a doctor, and he should be treated with the respect he deserves."

"Anybody who's met the man can tell that."

"Why do you think he wants to talk to us?"

"Don't you know?"

"I have a suspicion," I said. "I don't like it."

That brought a bitter laugh from Blacke. "I like the delicate way you put things, Booker. I think that's what makes you such a successful writer. Seven or eight dead already, and you let on as how you don't like it. Booker, my friend, this town is teetering on the brink of destruction. Unless a lot of people use their brains, including at least one who doesn't have any, this place won't be worth living in."

I was about to accuse him of overstating the case at least as much as I had understated it when the door opened and the doctor walked in.

Dignified as ever, he said, "Gentlemen," and nodded to us. He went to his desk; I sat in the chair facing him. Blacke, of course, had his own accommodation.

Mayhew looked at us for a moment, inexpressibly weary. Then he heaved a shuddering sigh and buried his face in his hands. He sat that way for a full minute, breathing deeply. Finally he lifted his face and said, "Mr. Booker, Mr. Blacke. When this is over, if it ever is, I shall take the time to thank you and the ladies for what you have done tonight."

"We'll consider the thanks as given," Blacke said. "What do you want to tell us?"

"From the look on your faces when you left the examining room, I think you already know. My son has told me that he mentioned to you that this malady reminded him of a severe grippe. I am proud of him. That was an excellent attempt at a diagnosis from an untrained boy who lacks the depraved imagination adulthood frequently forces on one. I, who do not suffer from such a lack, have a different diagnosis, and I am positive of it."

Blacke was nodding. "Poison."

"Metal," I said. "Lead, or arsenic."

"Arsenic, without a doubt. The lavage worked; I was able to question the woman briefly before I came in here. The nausea, the gastrointestinal pain, the fever, the burning in the extremities. All the symptoms of acute arsenic poisoning were present. There is no reason to think they were lacking in the patients whom I did not get to question. Mr. Simpkins's case was the same; I was called too late to save him."

"And all these people got hold of Ozono tonight, and couldn't wait to put the miracle to work."

Blacke's lips were a thin gray line. "Good God. Booker, how many bottles of that stuff did he sell?"

"I don't know. A hundred and fifty, two hundred. I do know that he ran out at one point with twenty or thirty customers left to serve, and Feathers came out and juggled some more to keep them happy while Herkimer went in to mix up another batch and pour it in the bottles."

I scratched my head. "Now that I think of it, Mrs. Murdo was among that last batch of people."

Blacke said, "That might mean something, might not. We've got to go on the assumption that every bottle of that stuff might be deadly."

"Any suggestions, Doctor?"

"I wouldn't know where to begin. At this moment, someone might be having difficulty sleeping, or feeling a twinge of neuralgia, and pouring the dose of poison that will kill him. If only there were some way to speak to everyone at once."

"Mr. Bell's telephone is still years away from Le Four," I said.

"This is no time to worry about what's impossible." Blacke was not angry, but his voice commanded instant attention. He was the marshal again, telling his deputies what had to be done.

He turned to Mayhew. "Doctor, you and your wife stay here to deal with any more patients who turn up. Can you spare Merton?"

"Well, yes, I suppose. What can he do?"

"He can knock on doors, same as me and Becky and Mrs. Sundberg. We're going to rouse the town, recruit more volunteers, send riders out to the ranches and farms, collect every bottle of Ozono we can for you to test. We'll also find the other cases that way, maybe sooner than if we waited for the news to come to us, or stop people from using the stuff if they haven't already."

"By all means," Mayhew said. "I'll tell Merton to put himself at your disposal."

Blacke managed a smile. "I expect you know how lucky you

are to have a son like that," he said. "You may be the only man on earth I envy."

That elicited one of the doctor's rare smiles. "Yes," he said. "I know." He left.

"Um, Blacke," I said. "You seem to have left me out of your battle plan."

"I've got a separate plan for you. Maybe the toughest thing of all."

"Which is?"

"Go next door to the sheriff's office. Get Harlan out of bed with whatever whore he's got tonight, and get him out to the orchard at the gallop. Go with him. Have him arrest Herkimer and his whole troupe, and bring them in, and get them locked up in jail. Have him bring the wagon to the livery stable under guard so the doctor can take a look at what's in there if he has a chance."

"Any suggestions on how I should go about this?"

"Yeah. The quickest way. Do it at gunpoint if you have to, but get it done. You're good with him, God knows why. But every second counts, Booker."

He leaned forward, his voice even more intense. "Because this is not going to be hard for folks to put together. What time is it?"

I consulted my watch. "Just after midnight," I said.

"Then sunup's in about five hours. Folks will be getting up, and they'll be hearing about this, some seeing it for themselves. By six o'clock at the latest, Le Four is going to see its first lynch mob. *They must not be allowed to succeed.* Lynching kills the soul of a town. Goddammit—"

I jumped to my feet. "All right, I understand. If I said something to the effect that I'm honored you have the confidence in me to trust me with this, you'd call me a fool, wouldn't you?"

"Yup."

"Then I won't say it."

"Good. And don't block up the door. I've got to get out of here and knock on doors."

Merton and the ladies had already started to work, and tired, muddled, confused, angry, and horrified voices filled the night air. It occurred to me that the very act of telling everyone within reach what had happened that night would very likely accelerate the birth of the lynch mob Blacke so feared, but what else was there to do? We certainly couldn't sit tight and let the townspeople poison themselves in order to protect the man who had sold them the poison.

The buzz of voices added even more urgency to my mission. I ran down the boardwalk the few yards from Dr. Mayhew's surgery to the sheriff's office. I tried the door. It was locked. Impatiently, I pulled the cord and rang the bell outside the door. The clanging seemed loud enough to be heard in Cheyenne, but it brought no response from within.

"The quickest way," I muttered, and proceeded to take off my boot and use it to smash the glass in the door. I reached in, turned the lock, and entered.

"Harlan!" I yelled. "Sheriff Harlan!"

No answer. I went to the back of the ground floor to the iron door with the serious lock and yelled through the strap-iron window.

"Anybody back there?"

"Just me, Cap'n," said a tired voice.

"Franklin?"

"Tha's right." Franklin Warrum was the town drunk. He never did anybody any harm; Harlan locked him up from time to time to keep Franklin safe.

"Where's the sheriff?"

"Ain't seen him since he brung me my dinner. Went upstairs to his quarters, I guess. Said he was gonna turn in early."

I climbed the stairs, shouting as I did so. Just short of the top, I got a response. A croaking sort of a sound. "What the hell? Go away and leave me in peace!"

This door, at least, was not locked. I opened it up and saw the sheriff sitting on the edge of a rumpled bed with his galluses up over his long underwear.

He said, "What are you doing here, Booker?" and raised a bottle to his lips. Through the man's fat fingers, I could see the distinctive yellow and black of the Ozono label.

I sprang at him and knocked the bottle from his hands. Amber liquid spewed around the room.

"Damn you, Booker, are you crazy?"

"How much of that did you swallow?"

He clutched his stomach and looked a little woozy. "Not enough. Had too much chili at Maisie's tonight. Instead of sitting here suffering, I thought I'd try some of that medicine."

"Where'd you get it?"

"Took it off Franklin. He was out at the medicine show and bought the stuff. Cheaper than booze, you know."

"How much did you swallow?"

"Just a little. Ooooh. See if there's any more in the bottle. That chili is getting me something wicked."

"Yeah," I said. "I'll bet. You're going to Dr. Mayhew's office. He's got something that'll clean you right out."

"He does?"

"Yeah, it's called a gastric lavage. You'll love it."

I grabbed the sheriff by the elbow and heaved him to his feet. He was too heavy to carry downstairs, so I more or less dragged him. If he hadn't still been able through his cramps to take some of his own weight on his feet, I would have had to roll him down.

I stopped for a second in the office, pulled open drawers in the sheriff's desk until I found what I needed.

I pinned a deputy's badge on my vest. "Swear me in, you goddam fool. Somebody has to be arrested, and you sure aren't up to doing it."

He blinked his eyes a couple of times. "You want to be a deputy?"

"That's the idea."

"Okay, you're a deputy. Say I do."

"I do." I'm sure that wasn't the way the laws of the Wyoming Territory would have had it done, but it would have to suffice. As his first official act, Deputy Booker dragged the sheriff to the doctor's office.

12

AS I'D LEFT the town behind me, heading north toward Grechtstein's orchard, I was not a happy man. Nor an especially confident one.

I had urged Posy to a fast canter, and alone on the moonlit trail, with the heat of the day having given way to the cool of the evening, she actually seemed to be enjoying it.

But I felt all too keenly the weight of the gun on my right hip. This was now my gun, but it had been the gun of Lobo Blacke, feared throughout the West, revered as a symbol of justice, all the kinds of nonsense I used to write in my dime novels.

It had been a gift to me from Blacke himself, and that was something else that had honored me almost beyond expressing. But the last time I had buckled the holster around my waist in the anticipation of having to use it, I also had detailed instructions from Lobo Blacke in exactly what to do with it.

I don't mean shooting it. I'm actually quite a good shot, with pistol and rifle. The colonel had seen to that. I mean the hard part, the dangerous part. Knowing when to shoot; how to tell that you have no choice but to shoot. That kind of thing. My father never bothered to teach me about that—as far as he was concerned, I'd point my weapon where ordered and set it off when told to do so.

And as Posy's easy lope ate up the distance between me and the Great Medicine Show, I had to admit the notion of taking orders had never before seemed so appealing.

The best thing to do, I decided, was to dismount a few hundred yards from where they were camped, approach quietly on foot, and get the drop on them while they were all asleep. I reined Posy in and tied her to a patch of scrub just below the orchard. Then, as quietly as someone city bred could, I made my way toward the wagon.

There was a crack and a whine as a rifle bullet whizzed by close to my head. I hit the ground and rolled sideways, finding a little hollow in the earth to burrow in.

"Who's out there?" a voice demanded. Joseph Feathers. It didn't sound as if he was wearing his usual smile at the moment. "You'd better get going, or the next one won't miss!"

It was only then that it occurred to me that people who had just taken in a couple of hundred dollars in hard money wouldn't be likely to go to sleep all at once and let someone sneak up on them. I was showing little aptitude for the deputy business, and the difficult part of it yet to come.

"Joseph Feathers!" I called.

"I know who *I* am. Who are you?"

"Quinn Booker! I have to talk to you right away!"

"Booker? Why did you try to sneak up on us? Why didn't you just ride right up, like a decent man?"

"Because I'm not a decent man anymore! I'm a deputy sheriff!"

"What?"

"I'll explain when I get there!"

"All right, then, come on ahead! But keep your hands where I can see them."

That was fine with me. I was just happy to be able to quit shouting. It seems wrong, somehow, to be shouting late at night out on the prairie, even though there are fewer people around to disturb.

I kept walking forward, arms visibly open and out to my sides. When I got within ten yards of the wagon, Joseph Feathers said, "I guess that's close enough."

He was sitting on the board of the wagon as though ready to drive it off, though the horse wasn't hitched up. He had a Winchester repeater cradled across his lap, a weapon, I knew, that in seconds could put more holes in me than a player-piano roll has.

"Now," he said. "What's so all-fired important as to bring you creeping around up here in the middle of the night?"

"I came to admit you were right about something."

"Oh? And what might that be?"

"Well, first, I want to say again that I've been deputized by the sheriff this evening, so this is official, and your pointing your gun at me after I show you this badge"—I twisted it so it glinted in the moonlight—"constitutes assaulting an officer, but we'll overlook that."

"Big of you," he said. He hitched the rifle a little higher.

"I also want to say that Dr. Herkimer and the princess ought to hear this, too. They can't possibly be asleep with all the yelling we've been doing."

Herkimer's voice came from within the wagon. "We're fine where we are," it said, and I knew I had at least one other gun pointed at me. "Say your piece."

"You say you came to tell me I was right about something. Why couldn't that wait until the morning?"

"I didn't know if you'd still be around in the morning."

Feathers shrugged, admitting I had a point. "True. We usually break up camp at first light, and I ride on into the next town to do the advance work."

"That wasn't exactly what I meant."

"Well, why don't you just tell me what you do mean?"

"I mean, when you told me that after the people of Le Four had a chance to take the Ozono, the place would never be the same, I never dreamed how right you could be."

White teeth gleamed as his big, friendly smile split his face. "You've seen the results already?"

I forced myself to smile back as I walked up to the front of the wagon. "Yes," I said, "and they're breathtaking."

I reached out my left hand, as if to climb up there with him, but instead, I grabbed his rifle by the barrel and pulled hard, at the same time drawing Lobo Blacke's gun.

He never let go of the rifle; instead, he half fell, half jumped off the wagon after it. Now I didn't dare let go of it, either. I had to keep pulling to keep the opening of the barrel behind me. This locked us in a strange embrace, and soon we lost our balance and went down. Feathers kept trying to roll away from me and kept us thrashing back and forth. This undoubtedly saved my life by making it impossible for the man in the wagon to get a clean shot.

It ended when I was able to push open a space between us and bring my gun up, and jam it hard under his ribs. Feathers froze as soon as he felt it there.

"All right," I said. "Let go of the rifle."

As soon as he did, I pulled it free, sat up, and threw it into the woods. Still holding the gun in place, still looking Feathers in the eye, I called to the wagon.

"All right, Herkimer. If you've got a gun on me, you'd better get me in the head with your first shot, or Mr. Feathers will be plucked off to heaven. Or wherever it is that he belongs."

No answer. I was tempted to look at the wagon, but that would give Feathers a chance to grab for the gun, and that would never do.

So I stared at him, waiting, not even blinking. Silently, I slowly counted to ten, then again.

"Of course, if you have no great love for Mr. Feathers, then the joke is on me. And on him. Because if I don't see both of you out here by the time I count to ten, I'm going to pull the trigger. One. Two. Thr—"

They must have loved Mr. Feathers very much indeed, because they were both out of the wagon before I finished three. They came out the front, obligingly in the direction I was looking. They jumped down off the wagon to the ground.

"All right," I said. "Hold it right there."

I put my free hand on Feathers's face and held it there while I stood up and backed away from him.

"Now, before you stand up, Feathers, throw the sandbag away."

He did, and went to stand near the others.

"Come to think of it," I said, "why don't you take off your jacket, so I can see that you don't have any other surprises under there."

Once I'd eased my mind about that, I was able to take a good look at the other two. Dr. Herkimer and the princess were wearing identical white nightshirts. The style was much more becoming in her. Unfortunately, they could have been hiding a cannon under those things.

"I apologize," I said. "But in the interests of safety of all concerned, I'll have to ask you to take those off."

"That's it, isn't it?" Feathers sneered. "A chance to see her naked."

"Oh, shut up. I swear to heaven, Feathers, I'm here to save your life, and you are certainly making it a chore. Go ahead, get them off."

Since I'd already seen more of the princess's skin than of any woman with whom I did not intend to become intimate, it was no surprise that naked in the moonlight, she was breathtaking.

Dr. Herkimer, however, was no advertisement for his own product. His rubbery skin was saggy and wrinkled, and speckled with purplish spots.

"You may clothe yourselves again," I said. "I'm sorry, but it had to be done."

Herkimer scurried back into his nightshirt, but the princess merely picked hers up and held it before her. Maybe she thought it would distract me. She was probably right. I was going to tell her to put it on when Feathers spoke first.

"What is it you are here for, then? Not to give a testimonial to Ozono. And that business about saving our lives was a lie, too."

"No," I said. "No testimonials. But I haven't told you any lies, either. I *am* here to save your life. And Ozono *has* had a breathtaking effect on the health of the town. It was loaded with arsenic. When I left, nine people had died of it. There are probably more by now."

Well, the princess might not speak, but she wasn't a mute; there was plenty of voice in her gasp. As for Herkimer, he turned white and looked as if he was going to faint. Feathers caught him and held him up. There was a look of real concern on his face.

"He looks as if he could use a shot of tonic," I observed. "But I don't recommend it."

Herkimer, the mesmerizing orator, was having trouble finding his tongue.

"No. No. Nonono. It's . . . it's impossible. It can't have happened."

"It happened," I said softly. "I watched them die. The thing is, I don't want to watch you die. The first stirrings of lynching fever are beginning now. There isn't a lot of time. So what do you say we all go back to town before they can get really started, and get you safely in a place where we can guard you?"

"It's a trick," Feathers said. "He's after the money."

"Don't make me laugh," I said. "I'm the third- or fourth-richest man in town" (depending on how much Lucius Jenkins pays Asa Harlan under the table, I thought), "and I could buy and sell your little medicine show."

Feathers sneered, "Why should I believe that?"

"You'll believe it when they stretch your neck on that tree over there."

"But it's impossible," Herkimer said again. "Ozono is made only from the purest ingredients. Oh, sure, I exaggerate some, but you know, you've got to, the ru—the customers expect it, don't you see? But there's nothing in there that could ever, ever *hurt* anybody."

"There was tonight," I said softly.

"Then I've been set up. Sabotaged! I've been selling Ozono for thirty years, and never given anyone so much as a bellyache."

"I'm not saying," I told him quietly, "that you're not telling the truth. In fact, I'm sure you probably are. Lobo Blacke—you know about Lobo Blacke?"

Three heads nodded.

"Of course. Well, Lobo Blacke is going to thrash this all out, and it might be nice for you to be alive when he does it, especially if it works out your way."

Feathers was muttering half under his breath, "It's a trick, it's a trick," but I think the old man could see I was sincere. I was about to press the point home when the princess attacked me.

She was a naked wildcat, all claws and teeth, and she seemed to be in a dozen places at once. I could have shot her, I suppose, but I'd been so intent on putting the idea across that I was out to save their lives that I couldn't make the mental transition in time.

Then the princess did another surprising thing. She broke her vow of silence.

"*Run!*" she screamed in a voice so tortured it might well have come from ancient Egypt.

Feathers didn't wait to take her up on it. In seconds, he was in and out of the wagon with two sacks of money, then up on a horse tied to the back, and he was gone. By the time I managed to throw the princess off me, there was nothing left of him but echoing hoofbeats.

13

BUT THE PRINCESS wasn't gone. She was coiling for another spring when Herkimer said, "No. No, my darling. You mustn't. We must go with the man."

She looked at him as if he were insane.

"Yes, we must. Joseph has made a grave mistake in running away."

Grave may just be the word, I thought.

"We're innocent, my princess. We have harmed no one. If we run away, not only do we risk our own lives, but even if we did get away, we could never again draw a peaceful breath. We must clear our name. And the name of Ozono."

The princess dropped her head and stood there, helpless.

"All right," I said. "Back inside, with me this time. Get dressed. Touch nothing but your clothes."

They dressed as I watched. Herkimer didn't bother with vest, collar, or tie. The princess, for her part, put on a chaste gingham dress with a high lace collar that wouldn't have been out of place in Rebecca's current wardrobe.

When they were finished, I made Herkimer get their horse and hitch him up. Then I made the princess get out there with him on the board, told him to take the reins and head the wagon for town at a decent clip. I sat just inside the open doors of the wagon itself, holding the gun in my right hand and trying to assess the damage done to me by the princess with the other.

My eyes were still in their sockets, and no blood was actually flowing anywhere on my face; it just stung so much, it seemed as if there should be. I supposed I'd have to be contented with that.

I made him stop a little way down the trail while I retrieved Posy and tied her to the back of the wagon. It was a ticklish maneuver, and I shouldn't have even attempted it. A calm old horse like Posy would wander on home when she got lonely. But I didn't think about that until later. In the meantime, I was encouraged that neither Herkimer nor the princess did anything about trying to escape.

The sky was lightening to the east. That scared me. I'd taken too long at this. Blacke had said the mob would be in full flower by dawn, and that wasn't too far away.

I told Mr. Herkimer to go a little faster. He obliged, and he also got conversational.

"You seem a rather cultured man to be a deputy sheriff in this part of the world."

"Yeah," I said. "Well, I'm hoping to shrink into the job."

"Witty, too," Herkimer observed.

I decided I'd be happier chatting than worrying about what we were going to face as the sky got lighter and the sun popped up over the horizon.

"All right. As long as we're buttering each other up, I'd like to say you seem to be a rather honest man for one in your profession."

"Having known numerous others in my profession, I will take that as a compliment. But what makes you say so?"

Now that he wasn't orating, it was possible to detect the trace of an accent in his voice, from somewhere in the Southwest—Arkansas, Oklahoma, Texas, something like that. They all tended to sound the same to my eastern ears, but Blacke could tell the difference.

"You've had two pretty good chances to escape, but you haven't taken them."

He turned around a little so I could see his smile in the growing light.

"Ah, my friend, that wasn't honesty. My honesty manifests itself in the wholesomeness of Ozono. I shudder to think what some other medicine men put in their tonics."

"Silver nitrate," I suggested.

"Oh, no. Not that. That would turn a man—"

"Yes, I know. So what do you call your willingness to be brought in?"

"Practicality. A man in my field must be above all a practical man. I love what I do, and I do it well."

His pause seemed to invite a comment. I obliged. "Superbly."

"Thank you. But as I'm sure you can appreciate, my livelihood depends almost entirely on attracting *notice*. If we became fugitives, the only way we could even hope that the mob or the law wouldn't catch up to us would be to abandon this wagon, and our entire life. And my princess and I love the life I lead."

"You might still be convicted of something, you know. This is a mighty angry town."

"And properly so." He bowed his head. "Dear Lord, have mercy. But do I not have your promise that the great Lobo Blacke is going to lay the blame for this horror where it truly belongs?"

"I said he'd work on it. And what's wrong with Feathers? Does he lack your love of the business, or does he not have any faith in Blacke?"

The old man sighed. "Joseph is young and headstrong. He's learned he can't trust everyone, but he has yet to gain the deeper wisdom that life is impossible unless you know when to trust someone."

"And I'm that special someone, am I?"

Again the smile. "In the circumstances, trusting you seems like the practical thing to do."

"It certainly is your best chance," I conceded. "I don't suppose Feathers's idea of practicality would include circling around and setting up an ambush?"

I was surprised when I heard myself say that. It was the first time this whole night that I had thought of any possible problem before it actually occurred.

"Oh, dear Lord, I hope not," Herkimer said, and he sounded sincere. But I reminded myself that while Herkimer might be the most honest medicine-show man walking the earth, that still didn't say much.

Well, I told myself, I hope you're satisfied. Now you've given yourself two things to worry about. And worry about them I did. I worried myself sick about them for the next twenty minutes. Then we ran into the mob, and I stopped worrying about Joseph Feathers.

They were just at the north fringe of town, on Railroad Street, not too far from Jennie Murdo's cottage, a little way below where the street itself peters out to the north trail.

And mob was the word for them. I saw guns, but they didn't even seem to have a rope. It was still a murky, predawn light, so I couldn't make out any of the faces of the crowd, but I knew it would include some people I'd seen and smiled with every day for the past five months.

I grabbed Feathers's Winchester repeater—I'd had the old man retrieve it while he was hitching up the horse—holding my pistol dead on him and making him hold the rifle only by the barrel.

Then I said, "Stop the wagon. You two get in back here."

They showed no hesitation about obliging—more practicality, I supposed—and I replaced them at the reins. For reasons of morale alone, I snapped the reins and let the horse pull us on a few yards. Then the mob confronted the wagon directly.

A tall gangly man was at the front of the mob.

"Come down off the wagon, Booker. We got no quarrel with you."

Stu Burkhart. Of all people. I never would have imagined him a leader of men. Stu seemed sober enough; maybe he'd gotten a look at what the arsenic had done and been shocked sober. I've heard it can happen.

"Unfortunately, you're making it a quarrel. Stand aside, all of you."

I hadn't expected that to work, so I wasn't disappointed.

"We're going to get at those killers whether you like it or not!" came a woman's voice I didn't recognize.

"They've got to pay, Booker, and you know it." That from Stu again.

"Listen," I said. "Does anybody know how Asa Harlan is?" "Real sick." "Sleepin'." "Doctor said he might make it."

"Well, look at this badge," I said.

"Asa Harlan pinned this badge on me just after he took sick," I lied, "and told me to bring these people in. Bring them *in* to the sheriff's office, to be locked up. Not hand them over to a crazy mob. Crazy with grief, maybe. But killing folks before you know all the facts will just make this worse."

"We've got all the facts we need!"

"We mean to have them, Booker."

"If you mean to have these people," I said quietly, "you're going to have to kill me first."

Stu Burkhart was just as quiet. "If that's the way it's got to be, Booker."

For effect, I raised the Winchester to my eye and sighted down the barrel at the bottom of Stu Burkhart's neck. I didn't need to do it. I could hardly have missed from that distance. But I wanted the people at the back of the crowd to see me.

I raised my voice. "Whoever's going to shoot me had better get me in the head." What the blazes, I thought, it had already worked once tonight. "Because a shot anywhere else, and I'll ventilate him right here. And you folks behind him might find it healthier to stand aside. That's good. Now, if innocent people have to start dying, Stu, you and I can be the first."

This worked for a while. Unfortunately, I couldn't think of an end to it. Some of the mob were perfectly willing to sacrifice Stu and me and an unspecified number of others to get to the "low-down poisoners" in the back of the wagon.

The sun was well up now, and I could feel it hot on the side of my face. Sweat was beginning to gather in my hair, and I wondered how long I could keep this up.

Then I heard hoofbeats and the creaking of a buckboard being driven too fast. It reined in as close behind the mob as I was in front of it.

"All right, Booker," said the welcome voice of Lobo Blacke. "Nobody's gonna do anything now."

"That's bold talk for a cripple!" came a voice from the crowd.

Blacke's voice was deadly. "Who said that? I don't care. Go for your gun. I'll find you in the crowd and kill you before you clear leather."

There was not a sound.

Blacke grunted. "So leave the bold talk for men with the tripes to back it up."

There was grumbling.

"There'll be no lynching," Blacke said. "Simple as that."

"You all ought to be ashamed of yourselves!" said the voice of Rebecca Payson, and I was so startled I took my eye away from its bead on Stu Burkhart. There she was on the buckboard next to Blacke, standing now, yelling at them like a firebrand at a temperance meeting.

"*Ashamed* of yourselves," she said again. "Before Mr. Booker went out to fetch these people, he spent half the night with me, tending the sick. Mr. Barr, he talked your wife through the worst of it; the doctor says she's going to live. Mrs. Paiswenden, the last gentle touch and kind word your husband ever knew was Quinn Booker's.

"And now, you threaten to kill him because he stands in the way of your committing a wicked, evil act that none of you would even consider if you were in your right minds!"

I wanted to kiss her. While they were thinking that over, Blacke broke in. "And think about this. Now that Harlan is laid up, Booker is the law around here. I spent most of my life seeing that the law was enforced, and I'm not stopping now."

Since he had his hand on his gun butt, this impressed even more of them.

"All right," I said. "Now, break this up and go home." Much to my surprise, they started to do so. I was beginning to believe I would get through the night alive, after all.

"Except for you, Stu. I want you to stroll yourself down to the sheriff's office. It's about a seven-minute walk—you can have ten."

"Why the extra time?"

"You can leave your gun somewhere for safekeeping on the way."

Stu made an ugly scowl and I thought he was going to say something, but I didn't give him the chance.

"Just don't make me come looking for you." Then I snapped the reins and brought my prisoners off to jail.

i

14

MY LONG NIGHT wasn't over until eleven o'clock in the morning. I left the keys to the jail, and a whole lot of guns, with Stick Witherspoon, Lucius Jenkins's top hand, who'd been forced out of his bed by recovering arsenic victims over at Dr. Mayhew's. Stick, as you may remember, took a bad leg wound last winter, and still wasn't just right.

I went back to the *Witness* office, took a bath, had a late breakfast, then collapsed in my room for a two-hour nap. When I went downstairs, I found Blacke engaged in his twice-weekly checkers game with Lucius Jenkins.

That was Blacke, always probing, always looking for a way through Jenkins's defenses. With all that had been going on, I personally would have been just as glad to put a long-term project like hanging my old friend on the back burner for a while.

I sat down at my desk and began to write up the story for Wednesday's paper; we might even put out an extra.

I hadn't even dipped my pen in the ink when Blacke said, "What do you think you're doing?"

I told him.

"Afraid not, lawman. Your place is down the street."

"What are you talking about?"

"Like we told the crowd this morning, Booker. With Asa out of commission, you're the law in this town."

"Nice job this morning, by the way," said Lucius Jenkins without looking up from the checkerboard. Sunlight through the window gleamed on his bald head. "I never did think a man should be hanged without a court's say-so."

Blacke shot him a look, but there was nothing to read on Jenkins's face.

"Thanks," I said. "And very droll, Blacke. But I'm not a lawman or anything like one. I just had Harlan deputize me so that I'd have some authority to get the job done."

"Listen, Booker." Blacke was using his "I've-got-no-time-for-nonsense" tone of voice. "You may know you're not a lawman, and I may know it. Lucius knows it now, too. But to the people of this town, *you are the law*. If you try to put the badge down, that mob will be right back at the steps of the jail. And this time nobody will be able to talk them out of it."

The sick, hollow feeling inside me told me Blacke was right. "But Harlan might be sick for *days*."

Jenkins was nodding solemnly. "Maybe weeks. Doc Mayhew says there's no doubt you saved his life. Sheriff asked me to thank you."

"Yeah," Blacke said dryly. "Lucius is a real Christian. Visiting the sick."

"Good. He can come and visit me while I try to play sheriff."

My face must have made an eloquent display of all I'd been feeling, because suddenly the two men at the checkerboard laughed, and for a second, you could think they were still just friends.

"You just better hope this poisoning distracts the other unfriendly elements around here, or Le Four is likely to experience a real crime wave."

Blacke was still smiling. "It's not as bad as all that, Booker. Lucius, as the town's leading citizen, and I, as the owner of the local paper, have wired to Cheyenne to have a federal marshal sent out here and take over until Harlan's back on his feet. Should take five days or less."

"It's better than weeks," I conceded. I wiped a spot of now-useless ink from my hands and stood up. "I guess I'll work out life as a lawman as I go along," I said.

"Don't be a martyr," Blacke told me. "You can still have your meals here. But of course, you'll have to sleep over there."

I was glum. "I thought so. Have you seen Harlan's quarters?"

"No, Booker. I don't get upstairs much anywhere."

"Well, in this case you haven't missed much. The place is a pigsty."

"Not anymore," Blacke told me. "While you've been shirking your duties in slothful slumber, Becky and Mrs. Sundberg have been over there giving the place an overhaul. You won't recognize it."

"That'll be a help."

"Oh," Jenkins said. "To do everything legal, I've set it up with the town clerk to put you and Stick Witherspoon on the payroll as full-time deputies. I'll stand for the wages."

"Thanks. But do you think Stick is up to it? Full-time, I mean? With that limp, and all?"

Blacke said, "Sure, he's probably glad to have something to do. And don't worry about the limp. There was a fellow Lucius and I knew back in Dodge, had a deputy with a limp. He did fine. What was his name, Lucius?"

Jenkins scratched his big black moustache. "Damned if I remember. Doolin? Something like that."

I left them, went back upstairs to my room, and packed some personal things. When I came back, the game was over, and they were still reminiscing.

I said good-bye, put on my jacket and hat, and reached for the doorknob.

"Wait a second," Blacke said.

"What now?"

"You should be wearing something you're not, lawman."

For what seemed like the hundredth time in the last fourteen hours, I pointed at the star on my vest.

"Not that," Blacke said. "The gun."

"Oh," I said. "Right."

I unlocked the drawer in which it was kept and buckled the evil thing around myself again.

"If you get a chance," I said, "I'd like for you to come by and pay me a visit later. I think we ought to have a talk."

"I'll be there," Blacke promised. He was putting the pieces back on the checkerboard when I left.

In the short walk down the road from the *Witness* to the sheriff's office, I already felt like a fraud. By the time I'd rung the bell, and Stick Witherspoon looked at me through the peephole in the new wood panel that replaced the glass I'd smashed, unlocked all the locks, moved the chair from under the knob, and let me in, I felt like an absolute fool.

I helped Stick lock up, and by that time I couldn't feel any stupider, so I walked around to the sheriff's desk, sat down, and put my feet up.

Stick grinned at me. "You're a lot prettier sight back there than Harlan is, that's for sure."

"Shut up," I said cordially, and his grin widened.

Stick comes by his name honestly. He's about average height, but he seems a lot taller than he is because he's so skinny. The bullet that hit him in the leg smashed the bone there mostly because there wasn't much else to hit. He was the top puncher around, though, or he wouldn't have been top hand for Lucius Jenkins. He was good-natured in a cynical sort of way, and with his straggly light hair and moustache, looked boyish, even though he was past forty.

"How are the prisoners?" I asked.

"They're fine. I threw Franklin out of here, like you said. He was hungover and wanted to sleep some more, but I booted him."

"Sure," I said. "No sense a poor drunk burning up if the mob comes back and tries to torch the place."

"You really think that will happen?"

"According to the great Lobo Blacke, not as long as Quinn Booker, Legend of the West, is upholding the law around here."

"It's funny when you say it like that."

"Good," I said, "because it's downright terrifying if you say it or think of it any other way. Quiet so far, then?"

"In a manner of speakin'."

"What do you mean?"

"Since you talked to Burkhart and I chased Franklin, nothin' from the outside's come by. But those two ladies . . ." He wiped his forehead. "I want to tell you. Before they even went upstairs—they're still there, by the way—they took a look at the cells, curious I guess, about the poi—I should say the *accused* poisoners—and they get a look inside.

"Well, right away they turn on old Stick, as if I ever been in this building before this morning in my entire life, and Miss Rebecca says, 'Mr. Witherspoon, this place is not fit for human habitation,' and the other one just makes a face, and before you know it, I'm playing musical chairs with the prisoners, leadin' them from cell to cell while the ladies scrubbed.

"I had them cuffed and leg-ironed the whole time I was moving them around, but they took it nice as pie. Doc Herkimer, he just says he quite understands, and the princess, she don't say anything, but she gives me a smile."

"Yeah?" I said. "I'm jealous, Stick. I didn't know she could smile."

"Oh, yeah. Gives her a whole different look, maybe not as . . . different . . ."

"Exotic?" I offered.

"Yeah, not as exotic, but a whole lot more human."

"Well, treasure it, Stick."

"Oh, I will."

"Have you had anything to eat?"

"Well, the ladies brought me some pie."

"Go get some lunch. We'll get the money back from Lucius Jenkins later. I'd send you over to the *Witness*, but anybody who could feed you over there is here."

"Sure thing, Booker. If I'd known this lawman stuff was so interestin', I might have taken it up long ago."

We rendered the door passable, checked the street, and I let him out. Then I took a look at the prisoners. They were asleep in their freshly scrubbed cells. They were well and truly scrubbed; the smell of lye soap could almost make your eyes tear. That might have accounted for the heavy snoring coming from Dr. Herkimer. The princess, for her part, was curled up on her cot (fresh linen, too) with her knees up and her hands together up under her head. Forget her being sixty-seven years old; she looked six *or* seven.

Let them sleep, I thought; they'd had a rough night.

I went upstairs and heard the bustle before I got there. The living quarters for the sheriff was a blizzard of mop and broom, of suds and fresh linens. Mrs. Sundberg was down on her hands and knees, scrubbing the floor. Rebecca was standing on a rag that had been placed carefully over the seat of a chair, washing high up on the wall.

"What are you doing here?" Rebecca demanded.

"Apparently, I live here now," I said.

"Not for another two hours, you don't," she said. "It will take that long for all this to dry and air, won't it, Mrs. Sundberg?"

"At least," said the woman on the floor.

"We thought you'd still be asleep," Rebecca said. "How much sleep did you get?"

"About two hours."

She sniffed. "Uncle Louis should have sent you right back to bed."

I laughed. "Instead, he sent me right back over here."

There was silence for a moment. Then I said, "Rebecca?"

"Yes, Quinn?"

"Stop scrubbing for a moment. Come down from the chair. Of course, you can stop, too, Mrs. Sundberg."

She waved a brush at me. "I don't stop a job till it's finished," she said. "It's the only way to get anything done."

Rebecca came down from the chair anyway. "Yes, Quinn?" she said primly.

"Well, I just want to thank you—both of you—for what you're doing here. For what you've done for the prisoners."

"You're quite welcome. But there's something I have to say to you, Quinn Booker."

"Wait just a second, okay? I also want to thank you for what you did for me this morning."

"I just told the truth."

"To a bunch of armed madmen. Who had every intention of killing me. I know it made a difference, and I'm really grateful."

"Well, I live in this town, too. I'm not going to let them act that way if I can possibly do anything about it. Now, about what I wanted to tell you."

"Yes?"

"You can't possibly expect a woman to stay in a cell like that."

"It's the only kind of cell I've got."

"She has no privacy! It's indecent."

"You sound as if you have an idea."

"Yes, I do. There is another small room on the floor above this one. The windows are barred, as are all of them. If you and Stick Witherspoon, and Uncle Louis, can figure out a way to secure the door, then she can be here in decency. After all, these people haven't actually been charged with anything, have they?"

"Not by the law. The idea of the cells was to keep them handy while Blacke and I are looking into this, and even more, to keep other people out. You know, the armed madmen."

"Then you're not going to go all masculine and stupid about this?"

"I'll take a look at the room. If it's suitable, you can give it the treatment."

"Oh, we already have."

"That's what I like about being a sheriff. You get so much respect."

"You are getting respect," Rebecca insisted. "We respected your decency and intelligence and we went ahead."

"Maybe I ought to pin the star on you," I said. But I went up and checked the room, and it was fine. I went back and told Rebecca that Stick and I would rig up some sort of lock and move the princess right after she woke up.

Stick had gotten back from lunch by the time I got back, and was waiting patiently outside for me. I went out as I let him in. I was going out because I was a newly born disciple of Mrs. Sundberg's. The only way to get anything done was to work on it without quitting.

I went out to pretend to be a lawman for a while.

15

IN MY DIME novel days, I had written frequently of the "lonely life" of the lawman. Now I was learning that that much of my work, at least, had been true, even for such a trumpery excuse for a lawman as I was.

The badge and the gun made a difference. I had always before perceived Le Four as a friendly place, and frequently stopped in the course of my travels to pass the time of day with my fellow citizens.

Now the look in their eyes—not hostile, exactly, but wary and apprehensive—gave me to know that there was no topic suitable for small talk between us.

And I was different, too. I was scared, and trying not to show it, shooting my eyes all around me, trying, in my unexpert way, to spot trouble before it started.

The first thing to do was to find out how bad the current situation was. Dr. Mayhew was in his office, drinking a cup of coffee so powerful that it felt as if you had to push the aroma of it aside to make room for yourself inside the door. He asked me if I wanted a cup, but I told him I could get all the stimulation I needed smelling his.

"What's the count now, Doctor?" I asked.

He rubbed his eyes. I had been feeling pretty sorry for myself with my two miserable hours of sleep; I don't think the doctor had had any.

"Fourteen, Mr. Booker, and ten more very sick but recovering. Virtually everyone within reach has been warned, and under lock and key in my laboratory is a vast hoard of confiscated bottles. A sampling has shown me that only about a fifth of the bottles sold last night had been tampered with, for which thank God, otherwise this town and the surrounding area would have been an absolute charnel house."

I was puzzled about something. "Only a fifth of the bottles, you say?"

"Roughly. A little less in my sample. I tested sixteen; three held the arsenic."

"Now why would someone go through the stock, poisoning bottles at random . . . ?"

"I'm sorry, Mr. Booker, you are on your own. I am very fatigued. Habit and training allow me to carry on the mechanical tasks of my profession, but the drawing of conclusions is beyond my current capabilities."

I smiled at him and he managed a weak one in return.

"This town owes you a lot," I said. "Can I make one more demand on the mechanical tasks of your profession?"

"Of course."

"Herkimer's wagon, and therefore both his inventory and his pharmacy, if you will, are locked up in the livery stable. Would you take whatever it is you might need and go examine it?"

"Looking for arsenic, I presume."

"Of course. And anything else of interest. When Blacke and I talk to Herkimer about this, I would like to be able to cut through the claims of Ozono's being compounded according to the secrets of the ancients."

The doctor struggled wearily to his feet. He was so tall and so bony that it took a long time, and the time seemed to be filled with painful sounding creaks, but he made it, and walked with me to the door.

"I heard what you did this morning," he said.

"I suspect," I said ruefully, "that the story was difficult to avoid."

"Merton was sorry he missed it. But my point is this: I abhor lynching, and what you did was the only course open to a man of conscience."

"Thank you."

"But I also want to say that this poisoning is as drastic and foul an act as any that I've ever heard of, and the author of it must be found and made to pay for it."

I met his eyes. "Whoever that might be," I said.

"Of course. But if it turns out to be the medicine man, do not be swayed by his persuasiveness or by the charms of the so-called princess."

"I'm not going to be swayed by anything but facts and logic," I told him. "Besides, I'm just filling in for Harlan, remember? And on top of that, it's the jury that does the swaying around here."

Mayhew was silent for a few moments.

"I've offended you," he said.

"No, you've astounded me. Everybody around here is acting as if I've thrown over journalism to become the deputy sheriff. Nonsense. It was an emergency measure that has carried on past its time already, believe me. There's something else you can do for me, Doctor. Get Harlan well enough to be propped up behind his desk, and let me get this silly badge off my chest."

"I'll do the best I can."

"I know you will. Thanks."

Now it was time to go ask some people some questions.

I decided on the old schoolmarm, Mrs. Simpkins, first, for two reasons. First, her husband was the first to die, and second, being old and small, she was least likely to get violent.

She lived at the far end of Main Street, in a big house that Big Bill had also used as headquarters for his ranching and business interests. In a town that lacked a Lucius Jenkins, Big Bill Simpkins would have been the leading citizen, and according to some old-timers, he had been before Jenkins had settled in these parts.

Fortunately, both men realized there was enough wealth to go around in the West, and that kind of rivalry frequently ends destroying a whole town.

I say "fortunately." It might have been that. It might also have been, as Blacke once theorized, that Lucius Jenkins arrived and made things very plain to Big Bill that if Big Bill wouldn't try to get in the way of any of Lucius's empire building, Big Bill could live a long and happy life, prospering off his own lucrative, if less ambitious, ventures, and that Big Bill had the brains to agree.

She answered the door herself, but I'd been expecting that. When, late in life, one of the rich men in town had made her a bride, Gloria Simpkins had declared she'd have no other woman living under her roof, maid or cook or otherwise. She did her own cooking, and most of her own cleaning, although there was an Indian woman who came once a week to help her with the heavy stuff.

The kerchief on her head and the smudge of dust on her cheek told me that she was continuing the tradition in the face of death.

I took off my hat before I spoke. "Good afternoon, Mrs. Simpkins," I said. "I'm sorry about your loss."

She smiled lightly. I expected her face to be ravaged, but there were no red eyes or tear tracks to be seen. Her face was as white and smooth as always.

"Why, thank you, Mr. Booker. It's ever so kind of you to come and see me, especially since I know how busy you must be."

"How's that, ma'am?"

"Why, with your new job as sheriff."

It was either smile or scream, so I chose the former. "Just a deputy, ma'am, and only temporary. Though I would like to ask you a few questions, if you wouldn't mind."

"Not at all," she said. "Do come in. Mind you wipe your feet, now."

I obeyed, and walked into the most pleasant room in Le Four. There were two modes of decor in the Wyoming Territory—dirt-floored poverty, and overstuffed imitations of what people imagined rooms were like back east, with chintz and antimacassars and lace panties for furniture legs.

But this was different. This room looked like a room of the West, and I don't mean just because of the pair of horns and the puma heads mounted on various parts of the walls. There was space between the furniture, and the furniture itself had been built for comfort and simplicity. It was a pleasure to sit in one of the chairs.

As soon as I was down, though, Mrs. Simpkins popped right back up. "Where *are* my manners? What can I get you, Mr. Booker?"

"Nothing just now, ma'am. I'd just like to talk to you a little. Please sit down. I like this room," I added.

She looked around, still smiling. "Thank you. It does have possibilities. You must come back when I get some proper furniture in here."

"I sort of like this furniture," I said sheepishly.

"You mustn't fib to an old woman, Mr. Booker. You can't possibly like these monstrosities." She shuddered. "They have no sophistication. They have no elegance. My husband insisted on hanging on to them simply because they were made by his son."

I hadn't met Big Bill's son. "Oh. Is he around? Perhaps I should talk to him as well."

Mrs. Simpkins sighed. "No, he's not here. But he will be, as soon as he hears what has happened. Willie Simpkins was always one to cut in where he saw an opportunity for himself. I taught him at the school here, you know. A willful and stubborn child who was always undermining my authority, asking impertinent questions."

"I suppose it's just as well he's not around, then."

She smiled again. "Well, of course it won't do to talk ill of a member of the family, but I doubt I would have married my William if his son hadn't decided to try his luck elsewhere. He'd never mind his father, either."

I felt a sudden empathy with William Simpkins. "How old was he?" I asked.

"Thirty-three. He'd be forty-seven now. But a son must always be subject to his father's wishes, don't you agree?"

"I believe we owe all the respect we can give to the ones who deserve it," I said carefully.

She beamed at me, apparently thinking that I agreed with her.

"Very, very good, Mr. Booker," she said, as though I were an unpromising pupil who'd suddenly delivered the right answer. "Now, what was it you wished to talk to me about?"

"First, I'd like to congratulate you. You're bearing up very well."

"Yes," she said. "I shall miss my William, but at least now he is at peace. His health was failing, you know, and if this thing hadn't happened, he would have passed away, with much more suffering, before winter could come again."

"How did he come to take Ozono?"

"Well, you know, he asked me to get him some. William was very stubborn and foolish (though not as much so as that son of his) and he refused to see a proper doctor. Just would not have it, no matter how he suffered.

"And yet, he had such a weakness for these patent nostrums, he was sure the next one would do the trick. 'What do doctors know?' he used to say. 'Never met one who'd made any money. Give me what a businessman sells.'

"I had long since given up arguing with him, and, now that illness had such a hold of him, I was just trying to find something that might ease his suffering for a while. So I went up there and I watched that ... *display*, and when I got jostled in the throng for what seemed the longest time, bought the product, and came home and gave it to my William."

Her face clouded up. "I suppose it did ease his suffering, at that. It's vanity to try to fathom the workings of the Lord, Mr. Booker."

"No, ma'am," I said. "But even if the Lord used this way to end your husband's suffering, I don't think he would have sacrificed thirteen other men, women, and children of this town to do it."

"Everyone has his destiny, Mr. Booker. I grieve for the families, but I don't presume to question the Almighty's purpose in allowing it to happen."

"His purpose? No. But my destiny, apparently, is to be the deputy sheriff of this town for a few days, and I intend to question whoever put the arsenic in the medicine. And everyone who might help me find that person."

She smiled approvingly.

"We all do what we must, Mr. Booker."

"Did you see anything unusual at the medicine show, Mrs. Simpkins?"

"Well, I don't call a young woman dancing practically naked 'usual,' do you, Mr. Booker?"

I suppressed a smile.

"I meant anything that might help identify who did this. One witness has said he saw someone sneaking out of the wagon before the show, when the three showpeople were accounted for. Did you see anyone?"

She squinted her bright blue eyes and put a finger to her chin while she concentrated.

"Do you know," she said after a few moments, "I believe I did. A small figure, coming down the wagon stairs a little while before the show started. I was going to knock on the door and ask if I could simply buy some of the product and go home, but I decided against it. I'm quite timid in some matters, Mr. Booker. But yes, your witness is right. I did see someone. May I ask who your witness might be?"

"I wish you wouldn't; I'd hate to have to refuse you. Can you tell me anything more about the figure you saw coming down the stairs?"

"No, I really can't. It seemed small, and quite dark, but it was late in the day then, and the shadows were deep, so that might account for that part of it."

"Was the figure carrying anything? Looking around? Did it make any noise?"

She shook her head. "No, Mr. Booker. I truly am sorry. It was just a figure in the shadows that I saw for a matter of seconds. I used to stress to my pupils the importance of being observant, but now I find I'm no better than the worst of them. I truly am sorry."

"It's all right," I said. "At least now I'm sure the intruder did exist. Now, thank you for your time. If you should think of anything—"

Then she gave a little gasping "*Oh!*"

"What's the matter?"

"I just did."

"Just did what?"

"Just did think of something."

"That's quick results."

"I saw someone there, at the medicine show. Someone I hadn't seen in years. An old pupil of mine. That's what reminded me, you see."

"Who was it?"

"Harold Collier."

"Harold Collier," I echoed. The name seemed familiar to me.

"Harold is in many ways a tragic figure. He was a very bright and willing boy, and a hard worker. He had arranged for his childhood sweetheart to come meet him here, so that they would be married in the spring—her family had moved to Texas, you see, I don't recall her name—but over the winter, some horrid patent medicine had darkened his skin—"

"The blue man," I said. "Dr. Mayhew told me about him."

"Yes," Mrs. Simpkins said sadly. "He refused to see his sweetheart when she came. She went back to Texas. and no one has seen Harold for several years. I was one of the last people, I suppose, who spoke to him before he went into seclusion. When he showed up last night in gloves and bundled up in furs, I knew it was him. I tried to talk to him, but he pretended not to know me. I suppose that's natural."

"Why is that?"

"Because the last time I saw him, he was swearing vengeance."

16

THE FIRST THING I decided to do was nothing.

I mean, I could have saddled up Posy and galloped hell for leather (whatever that means) out the forty miles or so to the place where Harold Collier had holed up, but I couldn't see the point to it. If Harold were really as dedicated a hermit as he seemed to be, it might lead to another of those conversations that take place with the participants pointing guns at each other, and I was sick of those already.

All Mrs. Simpkins had told me was that Harold Collier's life had been ruined by a patent medicine man, and that he had (at the time) expressed a flaming hatred of the breed.

At first, I was excited to hear it, though I realized shortly that I already knew it. I also realized that I had myself seen Harold's fur-swathed figure at the medicine show. I could tell you one thing—he wasn't a "small figure" by any stretch of the imagination.

No. A talk with the blue man was definitely on my agenda, but he'd keep.

I didn't think it was Harold, anyway. It just didn't *feel* right. Sure, he could have arsenic—everybody had arsenic. The two forms of wildlife the West had in common with the East were the robin and the rat, and arsenic was for rats. But why would he pick on *this* medicine show? How would a hermit with little or no human contact even know when one was in town?

I shook my head as I took a long walk down Main Street. I just felt in my bones it was somebody closer to home.

And at that, something was going on close to home. My new home, God help me, the sheriff's office. Right out in front of it, in fact. A couple of cowboys had hold of Merton Mayhew. One, a redhead, had the boy's arm twisted up behind his back; another, wearing a Mexican sombrero, had a hand around his throat.

They weren't doing the boy any immediate harm, and they were yelling something at the door of the jail.

I ducked into a doorway. I didn't want my sudden appearance to touch anything off. Also, I wanted to hear what they were saying.

"Booker," the one with the hand on the throat was saying, "we've got the doctor's kid out here. We won't hurt him if you just open the door."

There was a response from inside, but I couldn't make out the words. I looked over the cowboys, but I didn't recognize them. Not Jenkins's men. I'd made a special effort to know the faces of all of Jenkins's punchers by sight. These guys must have been from one of the smaller outfits to the south of town.

Stick was done saying whatever he had to say. Diplomacy was obviously not one of his strong suits, because Sombrero's face turned red, and his voice got even rougher.

"Yeah? Well, I don't really give a damn *where* he is, Witherspoon. What the hell's the matter with you? You know that old bastard killed Shorty Rogers out at our place. When they kill your friend, you've got to do something about it, and we aim to!"

Sombrero nodded at Red, and he jerked Merton's arm a notch. The boy let out a yell.

"Did you hear that, Witherspoon? We got nothing against the boy, but it's gonna go hard for him if you don't open up that damn door!"

They'd gathered a bit of a crowd by this time, but the by-standers were afraid to do anything. Both men wore guns low on their hips, and they were already showing that nothing much was beneath them.

I was proud of Stick, but I knew he couldn't, just in the name of decency, listen to Merton being hurt outside.

My blood was boiling already. I forgot to be scared, but not, thank God, to be cautious. I had my gun in my hand when I stepped out of the doorway.

I didn't even say a word. I took careful aim and shot Red in the back of the leg. It wasn't that I had a heart filled with mercy. That was just the spot at which I could hit him with the least danger of hitting Merton.

Red went down, clutching his leg. He brought Merton with him, but the boy was soon up and scrambling away. Sombrero was going for his hip.

In a drawdown, he would have killed me, but if I don't have to draw, I'm a good shot. As soon as Merton was clear, I had a bead on Sombrero's chest, and he knew it. He took his hand away from his hip, empty.

"Hold them high," I said, walking toward him. Even as I did so, I wondered why I didn't shoot him. Everything that had happened since last night had boiled up in me so much, I was so mad I wanted to puke.

"You shot him in the back, Booker," Sombrero said.

"I'll cry about it all night," I said. "The scorn of such a hero as yourself will haunt me the rest of my life. Take off your gun. Slowly."

He complied. While that was going on, I spoke to a couple of onlookers.

"Drag the redhead over to Dr. Mayhew's. Tell them why I shot him, and tell him to fix this man up good. Tell him I said to use plenty of carbolic." Carbolic acid killed the invisible, tiny animals that made wounds turn septic. It could save a man's life, but it burned worse than fire.

Sombrero was aghast. "You're going to turn Red over to the boy's father? That ain't right."

"When I feel the need for instruction in moral philosophy," I told him, "I'll find a better source than you."

Sombrero said, "Huh?"

"Never mind. What's your name?"

"Fenster. Nathan Fenster."

"Well, Nathan Fenster," I said, "you were torturing a boy in order to get the chance to kill an old man."

"Somebody's got to do something."

"Oh, somebody's going to do something. I intend to do something. And I want the whole town to see it. I'm going to find out how tough you are against somebody who can fight back."

I told some of the crowd to hold Fenster while I got my gun off and handed it to Merton.

It's happening again, I thought. Give me a role to play, and Fate makes me play it out. I couldn't put Fenster in jail (couldn't risk the safety of Herkimer), but he needed to be punished. And I was sick and tired of lynch-mob mentality. Rebecca that morning had held them off with words, but that was only temporary. The town needed a lesson that could be seen and remembered and spread by word of mouth.

And who was there to provide this salutary service? Quinn Booker, Scourge of the Frontier. I would have laughed if I hadn't been so angry.

"Merton," I said. "You've got the gun. Do you want to shoot him?"

"Huh? Don't be silly, Mr. Booker."

I smiled a little. "Right answer, Merton. Go to the head of the class."

I shed my jacket and hat.

"All right," I said. "Let him go."

As soon as they did, Fenster surprised me—he ran. Ran like a fox from the hounds right down the middle of the street.

He didn't run far. I'd played in the first fifteen of rugby for Columbia University (it made a large contribution to the current shape of my nose), and I knew what to do with a running man. I chased him, dove at his knees, wrapped my arms around them, and brought him down.

When I was done, I walked to the sheriff's office in half a daze. The crowd that had gathered parted for me, in silence, just as they had when I'd had my ridiculous gunfight last winter. It's appalling how much respect a man can earn with a violent act.

Some of them murmured congratulations to me. It was obvious that they enjoyed the show. If I'd claimed I had a patent medicine that made me able to shoot people and beat them that way, I could have sold it by the gallon.

"Go home," I said, and by God, they began to. I called through the door. "All clear, Stick. Let me in."

Slowly the barricades came down, and the locks were undone, and Stick opened the door. I slipped inside, Merton right behind me. Stick grabbed him by the shoulder.

"What about the kid?" he asked me.

"I still have a message to deliver," Merton protested.

"Let him in," I said. "He's suffered already in the line of duty for it."

Stick let him in and blockaded the door again. We kept doing that until that whole business was over, but we never needed it again. Apparently, all the people of Le Four needed to return to their peaceful, law-abiding selves was the sight of their deputy sheriff acting like a madman.

"You know," Stick said, "I used to not have a lot of respect for easterners, but there are places in you ain't nobody found yet."

"I hope to God nobody ever will. What have you got to tell me, Merton?"

"Mr. Blacke apologizes—"

"Stop the presses! BLACKE APOLOGIZES. There's a page-one headline right there."

"—but he's taking the liberty of inviting himself and Mrs. Murdo to meet you here at seven o'clock to discuss something of importance."

"Jennie Murdo?" I said.

"If that's okay with you," Merton concluded.

"What?" I said. I was still trying to figure out what Blacke wanted to bring Jennie Murdo here for. To confront the prisoners? To go hysterical on me again?

"How are the prisoners, by the way?" I asked Stick.

"They're fine. I moved the princess upstairs to that room you wanted me to ring up."

"Fine," I said. I turned to Merton. "Tell Mr. Blacke I will be pleased to entertain him and Mrs. Murdo at the appointed hour. Then go have your father look at your arm."

"Oh, that's nothing, Mr. B—"

"Go!"

He went. I spent the next few hours wondering what Blacke could possibly have on his mind.

17

BLACKE SHOWED UP well before seven. I'd already sent Stick back to the doctor's (I was sending everybody there today, it seemed), so I opened the door myself, took the wheelchair from Rebecca, and brought him in.

She said she'd be back in an hour and a half to take him home and left, ignoring Blacke's shouted protests that he could damn well get home by himself, he was a cripple, he wasn't a baby.

I gave him a minute to calm down before I asked, "Where's Mrs. Murdo?"

"I sent McGruder from the livery stable to pick her up in a wagon. He'll take her home, too. She's liable to be a little shaky."

"Her son died horribly before her eyes less than twenty-four hours ago," I pointed out. "She has an excuse to be shaky."

"Sure," he said, shrugging it off. "Well, *you've* had quite a day, haven't you?"

I shuddered. "I was going to kill them, Blacke. I *wanted* to kill the one. I probably would have beaten him to death if Merton hadn't stopped me."

"No you wouldn't have."

"How do you know?"

"Been there myself, too many times. There's a line a good man doesn't cross, no matter how hard he's pushed."

"I wish I were as sure of it as you are."

"Let me worry about that. All it means is that you weren't cut out to be a lawman."

"That's what I've been saying from the beginning!" I shouted.

Blacke was nodding. "And for once you were right."

I wasn't about to rise to that kind of bait.

"Any word on when the marshal is supposed to get here?" I asked.

"He's supposed to ride out tomorrow. Be here in a few days. I heard something else, though, in reply to my wire, and that's what this is all about tonight."

"Thank you," I said. "Thank you from the bottom of my heart."

"What for?"

"It's going to be such a relief to know what *anything* is all about around here lately, I may faint."

"Before you do that, why don't you fill me in on what you've been up to today?"

"I thought you knew."

"Only the spectacular stuff."

So I filled him in on everything from the Sundberg/Payson cleaning frenzy to my talk with Mrs. Simpkins to the last little details of my excursion into wanton violence.

Blacke rubbed his chin. "I don't know if you noticed this, boy, but you've got hold of a good indication these people are innocent."

"What do you mean?"

"Rebecca's attitude. She's a real good judge of people. And while she'd want any prisoner to get decent treatment, I don't think she would have gotten so intense about it if she believed these people could have poisoned half the town."

"It's hard to believe anybody could, but I think I know what you mean. I suppose I should have picked up on that. Of course, you know Rebecca much better than I do."

"Whose fault is that?"

I wasn't about to get started on that topic again. Fortunately, a knock came on the door, giving me an excuse to let the matter lie.

I figured it was a fairly robust knock for a woman the size of Jennie Murdo. Cursing the lack of a peephole, I yelled through the door and asked who it was.

"Hector Mayhew. I've got that information you wanted."

When I'd let him in, he kept talking as though there'd never been a pause.

"I would have had this a lot sooner," he said, waving a small wad of paper with tiny hen-scratch writing all over it, "if you hadn't spent the day filling my surgery with customers."

Blacke smiled. "Did you use a lot of carbolic on Red's leg?"

The doctor ventured one of his own rare smiles. "I used carbolic," he said, "in copious amounts. I daresay, it will be only the bravest and most foolhardy microorganism that ventures anywhere near the vicinity of that man's leg in the coming weeks." The smile vanished. "Seriously, Booker," the doctor said, "thank you for what you did for my son."

"I would have done it for anybody," I said. I *think* I was telling the truth. "It was just an added pleasure that I was able to do it for Merton."

"Well, thank you anyway. You are rapidly becoming in my son's eyes a bigger hero than Ulysses."

I felt embarrassed. "Maybe you should have the boy fitted for spectacles," I suggested. "Anyway, Doctor, what did you find out?"

"It's all here," he said, attempting to hand the papers to me.

Blacke said, "No one can read your writing, Doctor. It's just a good thing you fill your own prescriptions."

"You'd like me to report this orally, then?"

"If it's not too much trouble," Blacke said.

"A phrase, Mr. Blacke, should be added to the Hippocratic oath, forswearing for the physician the right ever to find something 'too much trouble.' For a doctor, the concept simply does not exist. However, if I am going to do this, I would prefer to do it in the presence of Herkimer himself. Is that possible?"

"I could get him," I said. My voice was tentative. It was just possible that Dr. Mayhew had gone over the edge of sanity along with me and practically everybody else in this town, and planned to produce a derringer and shoot Herkimer dead as soon as he saw him.

I hesitated in order to give Lobo Blacke's legendarily keen lawman's instincts a chance to work, and to tell me not to fetch the prisoner. However, either those keen instincts had sniffed out nothing wrong or they were taking a nap, because Blacke just sat there with a look of bland expectation on his face.

"Right," I said. "I'll go get him."

Herkimer was sitting on his bunk, not looking at much of anything. He didn't even seem to notice me as I came by.

"Mr. Herkimer?" I said. I wasn't about to call him "Doctor" with Mayhew in the building.

He jumped. "What? What? Oh, yes, Mr. Booker. I'm sorry. I was daydreaming."

"Put on your boots and come along with me. Somebody wants to talk to you."

"What do you mean? Where are we going? Mr. Booker, please don't—"

"Listen. From the time I got to your camp, before sunup, and friend Feathers let off a rifle shot at me, I have been risking my life all day to keep you safe. With that much invested in you, I'm not about to let anything happen to you now. So put on your boots and come along with me. All right?"

"How is my—how is the princess?"

"She's in a proper room upstairs. The man who was here this afternoon tells me she ate a good dinner. Since then, she's been left alone. As have you. Right?"

"Yes. No one has bothered me."

"Well, they've bothered the hell out of me. So please trust me the way you did this morning, and do what I ask."

"Yes, I will. I'm sorry, it's just that I've nothing to do all day but think about those poor people who died, and realize the people are all blaming it on *me*."

"We'll get you something to read. Take your mind off it. Come on."

He was ready now, and I brought him out. He blinked in the brighter light of the office proper as I made introductions.

Dr. Mayhew hardly waited for me to finish.

"Dr. Herkimer," he said sternly. "I have just one question to ask you."

Herkimer was shrewd. He had noticed, as had Blacke and I, that Mayhew had called him "Doctor."

I wondered what that could mean, but it took only a second before I found out, because Mayhew went on to add, "Where did you qualify?"

Herkimer said, "I don't know what you're talking about."

"You know very well what I'm talking about. I have spent most of the day examining your wagon, wherein you make up your Ozono, as well as analyzing the Ozono recovered from those who bought it yesterday. Dr. Herkimer, I state to you categorically that the substance you call Ozono could only have been formulated by a qualified physician, or a pharmacist at the very least."

"Wait a minute," Blacke said. "You're telling me this character is a real doctor?"

"I have every reason to believe so. I also believe," he said, turning to Herkimer, "that I owe you an apology. I began the day convinced that through some combination of evil, ignorance, and carelessness, you caused the death of fourteen innocent people. I no longer believe that. The man who formulated Ozono could not possibly have done such a thing."

"Why?" Blacke wanted to know. "What's in the stuff?"

"In short? Medicine. Good, wholesome, effective medicine in moderate doses. Would you like to hear more detail?"

"Would I understand it?" Blacke asked at the same time I said "Yes."

Blacke shot me a look. "Oh, yeah, I forgot. Dr. Booker of New York."

"I'm interested," I said.

"Ozono is based in neutral grain spirit—liquor, in other words—which helps the patient sleep. It contains oil of cocillana, which soothes the throat, tincture of opium for narcotic and anaesthetic effect, powdered willow bark, which is known to reduce fever. Shall I go on?"

Blacke looked at me.

"No, that's enough," I said primly.

"There is," Mayhew said, "none of the chalk, none of the turpentine, none of the other worthless or worse ingredients I have found in all the other patent medicines I have tested. I would not hesitate to prescribe this product to patients of my own."

Herkimer seemed to grow and change color as he heard that, as if growing back into the spellbinder he'd been the first two times I'd seen him.

"That's quite a testimonial, Doctor," he said. Even his voice was coming back. "Do you mind if quote you in the future?"

"Relax," said Lobo Blacke. "We're still trying to determine if you have a future."

Herkimer visibly deflated once more.

"So, Doc," Blacke went on. "Why don't you tell us what you're all about."

"I—I am a medical doctor," Herkimer said.

"My God, man," Mayhew exploded. "You say it as if it's something to be ashamed of."

"No. I have my share of shame, but that is not part of it. I qualified in Indiana in '58. I have never been stricken from the rolls, so far as I know."

"But why, man?" Mayhew demanded. "Why do you degrade yourself with this charade of a life?"

"Because it is lucrative, Dr. Mayhew. Because I have reasons for wishing to lay by a quantity of money before I die. I was never successful at building a practice. I have never been able to have the rapport with an individual somehow that I can attain with a group."

"And so I created Ozono, confident that whatever fantasies I might spin to sell it, it was at least a product that would do those who took it good. And now look what has happened."

Blacke was nodding. It was easy to see he was enjoying this. "Yeah," he said. "Someone added arsenic to the formula." He turned to Mayhew. "How? In the powdered willow bark?"

Mayhew goggled at him. "How did you know?"

I sometimes think that Blacke lives for moments such as those.

"It stands to reason. I know enough about arsenic to know it doesn't dissolve in liquids, even alcohol. If the poisoner put it in the willow bark—that doesn't dissolve either—it would be harder to see. And since everybody who bought and took the stuff didn't get sick, it's obvious it had to be in one of the components of the stuff, to go into that extra batch Herkimer had to make when he ran out."

Herkimer put his face in his hands. "I thought of just closing up shop, business had been so good. But I didn't want to lose that last knot of customers. If only I hadn't listened to my greed—"

"Then people in the *next* town would be dead," Blacke said. "And a whole lot more of them than there are here. And you might not have found law enforcement so dedicated to stopping lynch mobs as Mighty Deputy Booker, here."

"Very funny," I said. "But now that you mention it, how could the poisoner have known that Herkimer was going to whip up another batch?"

Herkimer's eyes went wide in surprise. "He couldn't have. I didn't know myself."

"Then maybe," I said, "the poison was intended for the next town."

"Could be, Booker," Blacke said. "Herkimer, where were you going next?"

"We hadn't decided. We never decide where to go next until we determine how much distance we want to put between ourselves and the next town."

"That's practical," I conceded.

Blacke said, "So the poisoner just didn't *care* where or when people started to die. Which brings us right back to a lunatic."

"A smart one," Mayhew pointed out. "As you yourself have said, he knew where to put the arsenic for best effect."

"A very smart one. You want to ask anything, Booker?"

"Yes," I said. "We've got two witnesses who said they saw a small, shadowy figure in a cloak or something like it, sneaking down from your wagon before the show. Did you see or hear anything?"

"No, but—two witnesses? Are they reliable?"

"I believe them," I said. "One's our retired schoolteacher, widow of the first victim. The other was the leader of the lynch mob that met us outside town this morning. I don't think either one of them would lie to *save* you."

"But then . . ." It took a moment to get the words out, they were so big. ". . . I'm in the clear. I'm in the clear."

"It would be reasonable doubt in a court of law," Blacke said. "But, God help us, a court of law isn't what we're worried about here. It's going to take a lot more than a shadow to be settling things for good around here."

"Yes, but at least now I can *hope*."

"That you can do," Blacke said reassuringly. "Just don't hope for too much, too soon. There are complications that even the heroic deputy here doesn't know about."

"And it's high time," the heroic deputy said, "that he did."

18

IT WASN'T UNTIL almost a quarter after eight that we heard McGruder's buckboard pull up in front. Dr. Mayhew had gone home to check on his patients and, if possible, get a little rest. A happier Dr. Herkimer had been led back to his cell, refreshed with the hope that the Great Lobo Blacke was on his way to proving his innocence to the satisfaction not only of the law but of the whole town.

I went to the door and began the rigmarole of opening it. Jennie Murdo, all in black, was waiting patiently there. I stood aside and let her in.

She was like a walking corpse. There was no spirit in her eyes, none in her voice when she said, "I almost didn't come, you know. I had decided not to."

"Thank you for changing your mind," Blacke said.

"Mr. McGruder wouldn't go away. He just sat outside and waited. And I realized it didn't make any difference. If I stayed, if I came. If I let you tell me whatever mysterious thing you have to tell me, at the end of it, my son will still be dead. Because I killed him."

"He was killed," Blacke said, "by whoever it was who put the poison in the patent medicine. Not by you. You couldn't have known."

"I should have known."

"How?" I asked.

"A mother should know. I should have taken some of the medicine first."

"Then you'd both be dead," Blacke said. A little brutally, I thought. "It works that fast, you know."

"There's no reason for me to live." There was still no emotion in her voice.

"Your husband doesn't have that problem," Blacke said.

"What do you mean?" Jennie Murdo demanded.

"News of your son's death caught up with him at Buffalo Butte, and—"

"Where is that?"

"Montana. Three days' ride north and west of here. Two if you ride hard, and I expect he will."

"He's coming here?"

"Yes."

"How do you know?"

"He said so. He'd been riding with the Gabus brothers, Sam and Elmer, when they'd seen a paper in Buffalo Butte, who picked up the story from the wires. He saw his son's name and told the brothers he was heading south to 'kill the bastard' who'd killed his son. Soon after he left them, a posse caught up with the Gabuses. They talked. The sheriff there, who's an old friend of mine, figured I'd want to know, and he wired me."

"I see. And what has this to do with me, Mr. Blacke?"

Blacke leaned back in his chair.

"The other day, Mrs. Murdo, you told Booker here that you wanted your husband gunned down on sight. Now that he's on a mission of revenge over his boy—and yours—maybe you don't feel the same way about things."

"Mr. Blacke," she said. "My attire proclaims my grief. My other feelings are my own business."

"Mrs. Murdo," I said, "from everything I've heard about your husband, I never got the impression that he was any great shakes as a detective. If he blows into town intent on killing somebody, he is almost certain to get the wrong people."

Suddenly a little light went on in her eyes. "You mean he didn't—the man you have in jail didn't—"

"I'm not saying that. I am saying there is cogent reason for thinking he may not have. We all want the real killer, and we all want what vengeance the law, I repeat, the *law*, can afford. We don't need Paul Muller riding in here with blood in his eyes. Who knows how many other innocent people may wind up dead."

That reached her. The idea of more innocent people dying brought some humanity back into her outlook.

"No. We most certainly do not need that. But what can I do? If I had any influence on the man, he would be the husband I thought he was instead of a robber and a killer."

"It's possible," Blacke said, "even likely, that he'll try to establish contact with you when he first gets back here. He doesn't really know how you feel about him, does he?"

The realization surprised her. "No. No, he doesn't. Oh, my Lord, if that man thinks I have been sitting around waiting for him . . . But how would he know I'm here?"

Blacke made a wry face. "Someone would have told him," he said, the someone, of course, being Lucius Jenkins, letting Muller know the bargain guaranteeing a decent living for wife and son in return for silence was being kept.

"Now, if he turns up," Blacke said, "don't make him mad. Just string him along, then make sure Mr. Booker knows what he's up to."

"I—I can do that."

"There's an alternative," Blacke said.

"What do you mean?"

"Well, my conscience won't stand for my letting you agree to this before I tell you it could be dangerous. Very dangerous."

"Whatever he has done, Mr. Blacke, Paul has never hurt *me*."

"He was supporting a double life in those days. In any case, you don't have to do this. I have some friends down in Boulder—"

"Colorado?"

"No. Wyoming Territory. They'd take you in and watch you until this blows over."

"I see." She took a deep breath. "No, thank you, Mr. Blacke. That won't be necessary. My life is not so dear to me anymore. I shall risk it, gladly, if it will help to save others. I ask only one thing in return."

"Name it," Blacke said.

"It must come from Mr. Booker."

"Yes?" I said.

"You must never rest until you find the person who did this. You must find the evidence, and this person must be hanged!"

"I'll never draw a peaceful breath until I do," I said. As I did, I realized to my horror that what I'd said was the absolute truth.

"Very well," said Jennie Murdo. "Is there anything else you wish of me?"

"That's it for now," Blacke said. "Mr. McGruder will take you home. And thank you."

"No, gentlemen. Thank you. You have given me something I haven't had—a reason to go on living, at least for the next few days. Mr. Booker, I will let you know as soon as there is anything to tell you."

She rose and pulled on her black lace gloves as I let her out.

Blacke and I sat there looking at each other until we heard McGruder's whip.

"This, I take it," I said, "was the complication I didn't know about yet."

"That's it." He seemed rather satisfied with himself.

"If that marshal doesn't get here before Muller does, I'm going to kill myself."

"What the hell, if the marshal doesn't get here before Muller does, you probably won't have to."

Blacke saw my face and started to laugh. "Oh, don't worry so much, Booker. I haven't got you killed yet, have I?"

"Not through lack of trying."

"Come on, I'll get you through this."

"If you don't, I swear I'll come back and haunt you."

"You're doing fine, so far. But I've got to ask you something urgent."

"Yes?"

"What the hell does *cogent* mean?"

"Forceful. Compelling."

He smiled and shook his head. "It's so damned educational just to *know* you, Booker."

"You, too, Blacke," I said. "You too."

19

BLACKE AND I had just finished discussing my agenda for tomorrow (although I much rather would have discussed steps taken to ensure my personal safety, to say nothing of my life) when Rebecca came and took him home.

I locked up (I was so sick of that door) and decided to go upstairs and go to bed.

First, I checked on Herkimer, who was once again asleep. Another indication that the old man was innocent. Nobody who'd just poisoned fourteen people to death could possibly sleep as much as he did.

Before retiring, I knocked on the princess's door. "You all right in there?"

In reply, a piece of paper slid out from under the door. At first glance, it might have been Egyptian hieroglyphs, but a closer study revealed it to be crude English letters reading "please come in."

"Now what?" I muttered. I told the door to wait a minute, I went down to Harlan's room, transformed by the magic of Rebecca and Mrs. Sundberg into a room fit for human habitation, and got rid of my gun belt and my vest, hat, and jacket. For all I knew, the princess was fixing to jump me again, and I didn't want to have a weapon handy for her to grab. I also wanted freedom of movement if she had to be suppressed.

Back upstairs with the key, I knocked again and told her to get back across the room, over by the window. Then I undid the big padlock Stick Witherspoon had fixed and lifted the heavy oak bar that crossed the door.

The princess was standing by the windows, still in the demure dress she had put on that morning. The problem was, on her, nothing could be demure. She stood, lit by the single lamp, looking like all the allure and mystery of the East; for a moment, I could almost believe all the cock-and-bull stories Herkimer told about her.

She smiled at me, put her hand on her heart, and then pointed it, open, at me.

"You want to thank me?" I said.

She nodded, then pointed out the window.

"You saw me deal with those two idiots this afternoon?"

Again she nodded.

"Well, you're quite welcome. Anything else before I go to bed?"

She came toward me. I was wary, but it didn't seem like an attack; whether it was or not depends on your definition of the word. What she did was grab me by the shirtfront, pull my face to hers, and kiss me on the mouth. It began gently, but soon warmed, then burned into something I wouldn't soon forget. It lasted a long time, as kisses go.

When it broke, I caught my breath and said, "I've never kissed a sixty-seven-year-old woman before. If I'd only known."

The princess rolled her eyes and shattered her vow of silence into a million pieces.

"Oh, *dang* it," she said with a nasal twang that instantly explained the vow of silence. "I'm twenty-two years old, my name is Daisy Herkimer, I was born in Oklahoma, my mamma was a full-blooded Cherokee, that crazy old man downstairs is my daddy, and I've wanted you ever since I laid eyes on you. Now kiss me again."

I kissed her again, and again and again. It was remarkable to hear that down-to-earth voice coming from that exotic face and body. Remarkable and exciting and very endearing.

Daisy Herkimer hadn't stated explicitly to what extent she wanted me ever since she first set eyes on me, but she soon made that clear enough, virtually clawing the shirt off my back and freeing herself from the dress.

Naked, she was more than a princess. She was an empress. A goddess. Eagerly, she pulled me to the bed and fastened her mouth on mine.

I know it was wrong. Like it or not, at that moment, I was the law in that town, and it was no part of my duty to be making free with the person of one of my prisoners, no matter how eager she seemed to be to make free with mine.

But I was also a young man who was tense, enervated, and scared. I never realized until it started to happen how much I needed a woman; how much I needed this woman.

I would worry about the ethics of it later. For now, I would let nature take its course.

And what a glorious course that was, all the peaks and valleys of her, the smooth dusky skin over the strong dancer's muscles, the voluptuous little mound of softness at the bottom of her belly. And her hands and mouth were restless, too, delivering countless caresses and scratches and kisses and bites, each one raising the excitement to a new level.

Then it was time, and I began to merge with her.

And stopped halfway.

I pulled my head back in astonishment. Her black eyes were very bright.

"What's the matter?" she said.

"You're a virgin!"

At that, she wrapped those strong legs and arms around me and squeezed hard.

"Not . . . any . . . *more!*" she said triumphantly. After a sharp little gasp, she spent the rest of the time alternating between wild laughter and shuddered moans.

Finally, sweat dripping from my hair, I collapsed alongside her.

"Goodness," she said.

I started to laugh. "What's so funny?" she demanded. "Are you making fun of me?"

Gently, I kissed her neck. "I wouldn't presume to make fun of you, Princess. It was a laugh of joy. You are unique in all the world."

She narrowed her eyes at me. "I'm still not sure you're not making fun of me," she said. "But I wish you wouldn't call me that."

"Unique?"

"No. Princess. It's so boring, you couldn't begin to know. Mope around all day, don't smile, don't laugh, don't say nothing. It's like being a statue. The only good part is the dancing."

She pursed her lips in thought. It was certainly true that Daisy Herkimer was a lot more animated than the princess Farrah.

"Course," she mused, "I think I just found me another good part. Can we do that again?"

"In a while," I said. "Men don't bounce back as quickly at this stuff as women do."

"My mamma mentioned that. Told me how wonderful being with a man could be, too. Don't think she built it up enough, though."

"Some mothers don't want to raise expectations that high."

"Mmm," Daisy said. "I love my daddy, but I miss Mamma."

At that moment, I remembered Daddy, sleeping locked up in a cell downstairs. I had just deflowered the man's daughter under the same roof. I was thinking that if I had any decency, I'd horsewhip myself.

Trying to get my mind off it, I asked her to tell me how it all happened.

"How what all happened?"

"How your father went from regular doctor to medicine show man. How you went from being a half-Cherokee American beauty to an Egyptian princess."

"You really want to know that?" Her tone implied she didn't believe it. I assured her I did; she shrugged her lovely shoulders and told me.

It was simple enough, the way she explained it. Her father had done some medical missionary work among the Cherokee, who had been moved from their homes in the East to Indian territory in Oklahoma.

"Well, the medical part went okay, but the religious part didn't work too good, because he took up with my mamma, and she had Joe and me."

"Of course," I said. "Joseph Feathers is your brother. I should have realized."

"Why? You've been kinda distracted since you learned I wasn't sixty-seven years old." She kissed me a few times, providing more.

The children were only a few years old when Herkimer had to go back to his sickly wife in Indiana. He kept in touch over the years, wrote and sent some money, but he never got back to his true love and his children until after his white wife died.

"Then, give him credit, he come on down lickety split," Daisy said. "Trouble was, Mamma died when he was on the way. With her dead, he didn't want to hang around there anymore. Can't blame him, neither did I. He talked about bringing us back to Indiana, but Joe talked him out of that one, too."

"He did? How?"

"Well, I think he was right. Let me tell you something if you don't know it, being from the East and all. Ain't nobody likes a half-breed, not the white and not the Indian."

"Lobo Blacke's best friend was a half-breed. A Blackfoot Swede named Ole Sundberg."

"Yeah? I'd like to meet him."

"He died last winter. His widow was the older woman who was cleaning up this place."

"Yeah? She looked white."

"She is white. I don't think either one of them ever gave it a second's thought."

With long fingers, she combed back a lock of the liquid blackness of her hair. "Well, maybe not *everybody* feels that way. You seem to like me okay." She planted her tongue firmly in her cheek.

"You don't act like a woman who was a virgin less than an hour ago."

"I tell you, Mr. Booker—"

"I think you can call me Quinn."

"Quinn, I ain't been *thinking* like a virgin since I first laid eyes on you. Outfoxing Joe, bringing us into town—"

"Then why did you try to claw my eyes out?"

"Family loyalty, Quinn. You may have been my dream man, but I still thought you were fixing to hang my daddy."

She smiled warmly. "Anyway, when you faced down that crowd, and again when you dealt with those men out in the street, I knew you were a real hero. This is the happiest day of my life."

Time to head that sort of talk off.

"So your father didn't bring you back to Indiana."

"No. Maybe not *everybody* hates half-breeds, but enough do, and Daddy wasn't going to take us back to his hometown just so's we could be outcasts there.

"He also realized that money makes a lot of difference in this world, and that a half-breed who could buy her own house and hire a maid would have a better time of it than one who had to depend on what God gave her."

"You certainly can't complain about what God gave her."

"You're sweet. But someday, I really *will* be sixty-seven, and then what's gonna happen?"

"Anyway, that's when Daddy decided to get out of regular doctoring and into the medicine show. We've done all right. Couple more years, I'd be able to buy that house. It's a hard life, but it sure is interesting. When I don't have to remember about being that stick of a princess, I mean."

"Only now," I said, "it's gotten too interesting."

"Oh, Lord, I know what you mean. All those people, losing their kin, blaming it on Daddy. I hope you can't blame me for wanting to put it from my mind."

"Not really," I said. "I don't much enjoy thinking about it myself. But bear with me for a few minutes. A couple of witnesses have reported seeing someone sneaking out of your wagon before the show. Someone small, in a long coat like a duster, or a cloak or something like that. Did you see anything like that?"

"Nope, I was out walking in the woods after supper. I have to tell you that since Daddy don't want anybody to hear my voice, that wagon gets to be like a prison cell sometimes."

She giggled.

"What's so funny?" I demanded.

"This is more my idea of what a prison cell should be. The company is so much nicer."

"Where did your brother go?"

"Why do you want to know that?" she asked. All traces of the giggle were gone, and she was suddenly suspicious.

"It would be a good idea to find him. As long as he's at large, he's in danger. To say nothing of riding around with all that money on him."

"You won't put him in jail?"

"Not if he didn't do anything."

"Then I think he's probably going to try to find some way to get to Minneapolis. That's where Daddy keeps most of our money, in the Proctor Bank there."

That was nice to know. I'd send a wire in the morning.

I kissed her on the cheek. "You're a good girl, Daisy."

"Hell," she said, "I can think of a better way to thank me than *that*."

Then she said, "You ready yet?" with a little tinge of impatience in her voice that sent shivers down my spine.

Fortunately, I was ready, thereby preserving my status as dream man for a little while more, at least.

Daisy was ready to take it more slowly this time, enjoying each experience for itself, instead of thinking of them as hurdles to be crossed on the way to a goal. The goal having been reached, she was more than contented to enjoy the scenery (as it were) en route this time.

But it was frantic again by the climax. She was so energetic that I held her tight and rolled her on top of me. "Oh!" she said, but she adapted to the situation with enthusiasm.

When we were done, she put her mouth close to my ear and said, "You're full of surprises, ain't you?"

"You, too, Daisy," I said. "You too."

20

LOBO BLACKE'S HOUSEHOLD probably eats breakfast later than any establishment within twenty miles of Le Four. The reason is simple, though unacknowledged. Blacke needs his sleep.

It was lucky for me that morning, though, because once I handed over the guardianship of the sheriff's office to Stick Witherspoon (who had greeted me by telling me I looked chipper this morning) and walked out to the telegraph office at the railroad station, by the time I got over to the *Witness* building, Mrs. Sundberg was just dishing out the flapjacks and bacon and potatoes and pouring the coffee.

I took my place, wished everyone a cheery good-morning, and dug in. I asked Blacke how the paper was getting along without me.

"Fine," he said. "Got along without you before you got here, remember. We'll publish on Wednesday."

"Good," I said. "Because I think I'm going to devote the day to riding out to check on Harold Collier."

Blacke stuffed a rasher of bacon into his mouth and nodded while he chewed.

"Tolerable idea, I suppose. What's your thinking?"

"Well, he's the only person we know with even a ghost of a motive. I mean, it wasn't the right medicine show, but he may be that crazy."

"Somebody turned me blue, I'd be crazy. At least in a wheel-chair, they get used to you and stop staring after a while."

"All right. And he was definitely there at the show. I saw him, Mrs. Simpkins saw him. Stu Burkhart thinks he saw him."

"Burkhart would say anything," Blacke said. "Something else, Booker. Harold's a freak now, a loner. People like that tend to do a lot of watching, and a lot of times, they see something interesting."

It was something I hadn't thought of.

"Hmm," I said. "Maybe I ought to haul him into town and let you have a go at him."

"Not necessary yet," Blacke said. "Just sound him out. Like I said, he may know something. Besides, I've been doing a lot of thinking since our talk last night, and I think I might just be starting to have a glimmer."

"Oh," I said. "That's nice. A glimmer of what?"

"Just a glimmer, Booker. A bright spot in the darkness. Gonna have to check a few things before I'm ready to talk about it."

We'd been down this road before. Over the time I'd been with Blacke, I'd learned he wouldn't tell you a thing before he was ready to.

"Okay," I said. "Good luck. Don't make me read about this in the paper."

Much to my surprise, he found that hilarious. He had to clap a hand over his mouth to keep from showering the rest of us with a mouthful of coffee.

"Uncle Louis, control yourself," Rebecca said. She was half upset, half amused.

"I'm sorry," Blacke said, though he didn't sound sorry. "It's just that Booker is beginning to sound just like a lawman."

"No chance," I said. I patted my lips with a napkin, sat back, and patted my stomach. Folks had a tendency to do that after one of Mrs. Sundberg's breakfasts. I think it was an instinctive attempt to tamp the food down into a more compact shape.

"If you've got a couple of minutes," I said to Blacke, "I'd like to talk to you out in the composing room before I get going."

"Sure." Blacke wheeled himself away from the table.

"Unlike you," I said when Blacke had settled himself at his place at the checker table, "when I get information, I share it." This drew only a grunt in reply, so I simply went on to tell him about the Herkimer family's relationships and backgrounds, and of the possible destination of Joseph Feathers.

At that, I got another grunt.

"My," I said. "Aren't you charming this morning."

"I'm thinking," he said. "And just to show you what a sport I am, this time I will share it with you. With Muller coming down from Montana as fast as he can, and Feathers heading for Minneapolis as fast as *he* can, given the times they left, I make it about seven to three they're going to meet somewhere on the road."

"Ouch," I said.

"Yeah. It could be very ugly. And there isn't a goddam thing we can do about it, so we might as well forget it."

Blacke looked at me skeptically.

"So you got the princess talking, huh?"

"She wanted to talk."

"Anything she said surprise you any?"

"Well, yeah, it did, but it shouldn't have. I should have figured something was keeping her with the medicine show. I know for a fact that there are theaters in New York that would pay her two hundred dollars a week just to go onstage and stand in one spot, let alone dance the way she can. Places a lot closer to here, too. She must have had offers. Family loyalty explains a lot."

I scratched my head. "I guess it was natural skepticism. Herkimer just doesn't strike me as the type who could captivate an Indian beauty and father two children by her."

"Oh?" Blacke was amused. "And just who *is* the type to captivate an Indian beauty, Booker?"

"I don't have the slightest idea what you're talking about."

"Really, Booker, it's no use. It's like you've been dipped in gold paint, it shines out from you. It's getting to the point where Rebecca can't even bring herself to be disappointed in you. You may be horny as a billy goat, but you're a happy, innocent billy goat."

He shook his head. "If people back east are all like you, no wonder it's so crowded."

"Are you through?"

"Sure," he said. "Let me know what you find out from Collier."

"I'll do that," I said.

About halfway to Harold Collier's place, the fun of the trip was gone, as far as Posy was concerned. I warned her we had a long day's ride ahead of us, but I guess to her a long day's ride was just a couple of hours.

In any case, I let her take it easy, drink in the streams, eat some grass when she could find it, and we got to the Collier place about noon.

There wasn't a sign of life about the place. I still hadn't learned much about farming or ranching (and, truth to tell, I never much wanted to), but I expected with the sun high in the sky like that on a pleasant day, I would have found him outside somewhere, doing chores.

There was a neat little cabin at the top of a small rise, the ideal place from which to cut me down with rifle fire, not that I had reason to suspect him of any such intention. It had just been that kind of a week.

I forced myself to ride straight up to the cabin and tried to control my imagination-fired nerves.

I stopped Posy about fifteen feet shy of the door, walked her the rest of the way to the railing, tied her, then went and knocked on the door.

I got no direct response, but there was noise inside, like the scrabbling and chattering of some large rodent. I put my ear to the door, and I thought I could make out hoarse whispers of "No, no, go away, go away."

"Mr. Collier?" I yelled through the door.

Still no answer.

"Mr. Collier, please. I know you're in there, and I have to talk to you."

"Go away! I don't bother anybody, and I'd like the favor returned. What call have you got to come here disturbing me? I don't bother anybody!"

"I know you don't, Mr. Collier."

"Then go away!"

"But I'm afraid I do have to talk to you. My name is Quinn Booker, and I'm a deputy sheriff in Le Four." I wondered if I would ever get to the point where I could say that without feeling like a fraud.

"I don't believe you," he said. It was a nice enough voice, or it would be if the tension ever came out of it.

"If you open the door, I can show you my badge," I said.

Silence for a few seconds. Then, "I'll open the door on the latchstring. You hold the badge up to the crack. If you try to break in, I'll slam the door. I'm pretty strong, you know. And don't try sticking your foot in the door, or I'll crush it for you."

I sighed. "I won't put my foot in the door. I don't want any rough play, Mr. Collier, I swear I just want to talk to you."

The door opened enough to show a thin black pencil line between itself and the jamb. I unpinned that ridiculous star from my vest and held it up to the crack.

"Okay," Collier said. "You're a deputy sheriff. I'll talk to you. We can talk just like this."

I was trying to keep my patience. This man, after all, had faced trials.

"I think it would be better if you let me in, or if you came out here," I said.

"No!" he shouted. Then, more quietly, "I don't want you to see me."

"Mr. Collier, it doesn't matter if I see you. I've spoken to Dr. Mayhew, and I know all about your condition."

"He had no right. It's bad enough I'm a freak—blacker than any slave—without the doctor making sport of me."

"He was not making sport of you. He spoke in utmost sympathy, and a desire to prevent others from suffering your fate."

Collier gave a strangled laugh. "Was that before or after they began dying like flies?"

"Now who is making sport of the misfortunes of others?" I asked quietly.

The laughter was suddenly cut off. I heard a click and a squeak and the door swung open.

Collier was just two white eyes in the darkened cabin. "Come in," he said.

I stepped forward, and now I could see that he was carrying a gun, but he held it loosely, pointing at the ground, and he turned his back on me, placing it negligently on a table as he did so. He sat with his back toward a curtained window. The only light in the room sneaked in around the edges of that curtain.

I took the other chair, facing him.

"What do you want?" he asked.

"I'm trying to find out how and why those poor people died."

"They got bad medicine, same as I did."

"Not quite," I said. "You got medicine some ignorant quack put together, neither knowing nor caring what was in it. The people who died got medicine that was deliberately made deadly."

"Deliberate or accident, I'm still a monster."

"You were at the medicine show," I said. "All bundled up. I saw you there."

My eyes were adjusted to the gloom by now, and the streaks

of sunlight sneaking through showed brightly on some of the
blue of his face. His lips split in a silent snarl.

"Are you trying to say *I* poisoned those people?"

"No, although I think the real poisoner would like me to
think so."

"What's that supposed to mean?"

"Why did you go to the medicine show?"

"What are you driving at? Dammit, tell me!"

"As soon as you answer my question. You haven't been
seen off your own property for years. Suddenly you're at a
medicine show, the sort of venue one might think you'd be
eager to avoid."

"You *do* think I poisoned them. Get out of here! Get out
of here now!"

I pushed my hat back on my head. "I'm afraid that if I go
now, you'll have to come with me. Because I really need an
answer to that question."

"Oh, sure," the blue man sneered. "Take me with you. Drag
me through the streets. Let the town laugh at the freak."

"They might do worse than laugh," I said. "The last time I
brought anyone to town they tried to lynch him. I don't want to
have to go through all of that nonsense again; I've just about got
the fools calmed down."

"I don't care about your troubles, Mr. Booker. I've got
enough of my own."

"If you could stop feeling sorry for yourself for ten seconds
and use your brain, you'd realize you can only help yourself with
an honest answer to my question."

I don't know if he ever used his brain or not. It did take him
just about ten seconds to say, "Well, for what difference it
makes, I got a note."

"A note?"

"A message. Walker, the grocer, makes up a parcel for me
once a month. I leave some game on the stump for him, and he

leaves me my goods. This time there was a note in with the goods."

"Do you have the note?"

"No, I don't. Made me so crazy I burned it. But I couldn't get it out of my mind. I suppose now you don't believe I got it."

"It would be nice to have seen it, that's all."

"Well, wait a second."

He got up from his chair and walked over to the table where the gun was. My spine crawled, and my fingers itched to go for my own gun, but I sat tight. Collier rattled through an untidy stack of papers and came out with a slightly crumpled white square. He brought it to me.

As I took it from him, his hand touched mine. Blue skin didn't feel any different from any other kind.

"Here's the envelope it came in, for what it's worth. There's no writing on it."

"That's a point in your favor," I said.

"It is?"

"Sure. If you were framing something up, you'd have *something* written on here, to make it look good."

Collier nodded soberly. "I suppose I would have, at that."

I didn't know if I actually believed that, but since I wanted him comfortable enough to talk to me, I was glad to have said it.

"What did the note say?" I asked. "What did it look like?"

"What do you mean, what did it look like?"

"Was it Spencerian copperplate?"

"Huh?"

"Fancy handwriting? Pen or pencil or something else?"

"It was pencil. No fancy handwriting, either. Just plain old square letters."

"Did the paper match the envelope?"

"Folded over once, it fit just perfect inside."

"Okay, what did it say? The exact words as well as you can remember."

"I remember. There wasn't that much to it. It said, 'The man who made you the way you are is coming back to town.' Then it had the place and the date."

"It said that?" I demanded. "It specifically said the man who made you the way you are was going to be there?"

"That's what it said," Collier told me. "So I went. I don't know why I went, but I did. I left my gun home. I figured if I was going to kill the son of a bitch I'd do it with my bare hands. I guess. I don't really know what I was thinking."

Collier started laughing at some private joke. I could see that the inside of his mouth was blue, too.

"Anyway, it was a wasted trip. It wasn't the man who'd sold me my poison, or anyone like him. I hung around for a while, in case the note meant to say he would be in the crowd, but he wasn't. So eventually, I went."

"Did you see anything?"

"Like what?"

"Some people claim they saw someone sneaking out of Herkimer's wagon before the show began. Did you see anything like that?"

"No. I wasn't paying much attention to the wagon, I was concentrating on the crowd, and cursing myself for a fool, exposing myself for no reason. I wish I knew who wrote me that note."

"Can't you guess?"

"You mean, you can?"

"Sure I can," I said. "It was from the killer."

21

"MY," CLAYTON HENRY said without looking up from his worktable, "I may be missing some of the vestiges of civilization in having come here, but none of the decadence. This town is another of the sinful Cities of the Plain, isn't it?"

I walked around Henry to see what he was doing. He was preparing a woodcut from the photograph he'd taken of the first of the funerals held today. No doubt as the law in town, I should have been there, but Blacke had gone, and he was worth three of me, any day.

Blacke covered a belch with his hand and said, "One thing you're not missing is good food. Damn, but that Kate Sundberg can cook. Somebody's going to come and marry her away from us someday."

"Just don't invite anybody to dinner. Look, Blacke, I admire Mrs. Sundberg's cooking as much as you do, but as a topic of conversation, it lacks body. What do you think of my theory?"

"That the killer sent the note to get Collier out to the medicine show? Sure, it's obvious."

He held up two big hands and started counting reasons off on his fingers. "Collier is known to have reason to hate at least one medicine man; it's not that big a jump to thinking he hates them all. Two, this town treated the man rotten when he had his trouble, running from him as if what he had was catching, especially that little jilt he was supposed to marry, so you might suspect he hates the town, too. And three, just from what you've told us here tonight, the man is not holding real tight to his wits. It would be mighty tempting to believe he'd be willing to wipe out as many as need be in one big blast of revenge."

"But of course, to make any of that believable, he's got to *be* there. So the note gets him there. Insurance, in case the medicine show people don't get lynched in the first wave of enthusiasm."

"Yes," I said, "but this means that the killer planned this for *days* ahead of time. This wasn't the work of a madman—"

"I've been saying that all along," Blacke said.

"—but of someone who plotted and connived to kill all those people. And for a reason. A specific reason."

"Exactly," Blacke said. He clapped his hands together and dropped them back in his lap. "Find the reason, and you find the killer."

"But it . . . it's *monstrous*," I said.

Clayton nodded in satisfaction. "Just as I said. Sodom, Gomorrah, and Le Four. Who knows what else is going on in this seemingly boring little town?"

"We could do without that, Henry," Blacke said. He turned to me. "Of course it's monstrous. To us. But not to the person who did it. That person had what seemed to him—"

"Or her," Henry said. "I've always thought the devil must be a woman, you know, and this was a very devilish scheme."

"Or her," Blacke conceded. "He or she had a compelling reason for doing this, no matter the lives that would be lost."

"I can't imagine it," I said.

"Oh, come on, Booker. Didn't the villain in one of your dime novels plan to dynamite a whole town just so he could rob the bank in the confusion? He would have killed scores of people, and you imagined *that*."

"Well, of course I did. But that was melodrama. That was a

villain as black as Mephistopheles. It was only a story. This is real life. Someone from the town we live in had to have done this, and we *know* there aren't any villains from melodrama living in Le Four. Not even—"

"Quiet," Blacke snapped.

I shut up. I had forgotten that Clayton Henry didn't know of the special place Lucius Jenkins occupied in Lobo Blacke's attentions.

"Sorry," I said.

"Yeah." He was still scowling under his brows at me. "You have to watch yourself, Booker. For instance, you should never take it for granted that you really know anybody. Look what happened to me."

I was about to reply when I saw that the scowl was still there, but Blacke's attention wasn't. He had a tendency to chase a train of thought, forgetting everybody else in the room. It could be disconcerting, but it frequently got results.

As it did this time.

"Booker, you say Collier swears the note to him was written in pencil?"

"Well, I didn't make him swear to it, but he was sure that it was."

"Well, then, let's see something. Get that envelope, will you?"

When I handed it to him, he asked Henry for a pencil.

"What sort?" the artist demanded.

"Henry, I'm really not in the mood, okay?"

"Blacke, you wound me. I'm not being difficult. There are many kinds of pencils. Hard, for outline work. Soft, for shading. Charcoal for sketching, even colors wrapped in wood for ease of handling. And those are just the artistic applications. I'm sure other disciplines have shaped the tool for their own purposes."

Blacke muttered an apology. "That's what happens when you ask an expert," he said. "I'd like the use of a soft one, I guess."

Henry handed over a large green cylinder. Blacke took it and stuck it behind his ear. Then he wheeled himself around the composing room. He grabbed a sheet of newsprint, returned to his checker table, and folded the paper up into a thick pad.

Then, methodically, he began shading in the blank envelope with the pencil.

"Of course," he said quietly as he worked, "you've already realized, Booker, that it's hopeless to try to find out how the note got in the parcel. They sit there in the store, labeled, anyone could have slipped it in here in town. And anyone with access to a horse could have left the message while the thing waited on the stump."

By now, the whole front of the once-white square was blackened in. Blacke picked it up and regarded it closely.

"Mmmm," he said. "Nothing here."

He turned it over and repeated the process on the other side.

"You see, Booker, when people use a pencil, they sometimes press hard enough to leave an impression on the sheets beneath. And sometimes, when somebody's dashing off a note, they pick out the envelope and the paper, and just fling them down on the desk, one over the other, and start to write. It's a long shot, but we've got nothing to— Hah! There it is, see it?"

He held the envelope up for my scrutiny, and I did see it, upside down across the lower right-hand corner of the envelope, little rivers of white in the leaden blackness that read:

ADE YOU THE WAY YOU A

" 'The man who made you the way you are,' " I quoted. "Well, it makes Collier's story look pretty good. I don't think he's subtle enough to have framed this up. He'd almost have to be depending on a genius like you to be there to find it."

But Blacke wasn't listening. He was still staring at the envelope.

"What's the matter?" I demanded. "You think he *did* frame it up?"

"No, it's not that. Look more closely."

I did, and for a long time, too, but whatever these ghosts of departed pencil marks were saying, I was deaf to it.

"It matches the message Collier said he got," I said. "It's in plain square letters, just as he said—"

"Are they plain square letters? Look at it, Booker."

I peered. I squinted. Then at last I saw what he was driving at.

"Well, square maybe, but not exactly plain. The line is thicker in some places and thinner in others. Like some of that fancy lettering Henry does for display ads. Only not so . . . fancy," I concluded lamely.

"May I see it?" Henry asked. Blacke nodded. I handed the envelope over. Now Henry frowned over it for a few minutes and delivered his own judgment.

"Yes, this is exactly the kind of stroke an untrained person would get in attempting to use a broad-nibbed pen. You can see that sometimes the thick strokes are the downstrokes, and sometimes the cross-strokes. A pen properly held would show consistency."

"Except it wasn't a pen," I said.

"Why not?" Henry demanded.

"Because Collier said it was pencil," I said.

"Hell with that," Blacke added. "Because a pen nib pressed hard enough on to make impressions on a piece of paper below would probably break. It would certainly squirt ink all over the place."

Henry conceded that Blacke had a point.

"Still," the artist said. "The stigmata are unmistakable. There must be such a thing as a broad-nibbed pencil. Another little mystery for you gentlemen, eh? Nothing like a little mental stimulation to speed the evening along, I always say."

He returned to his woodcut with every sign of being absolutely delighted with himself.

As for Blacke and me, we undoubtedly would have been left with the prospect of a supremely stimulating conversation about pencils to speed our evening along if there hadn't been a knock at the door.

I opened it to find Dr. Mayhew there, holding a bucket of beer.

"I took the liberty of tipping the boy and completing delivery," he said.

"Well, then, you must come in and share it with us."

The doctor smiled. "I was hoping you'd say that."

Blacke and Henry greeted Mayhew warmly. The doctor was probably the only man in town Clayton Henry accepted as an equal.

Beer was distributed to three of us; Henry preferred to drink his own sherry.

By tacit agreement, we waited until we took that glorious first swallow before anyone spoke.

Blacke broke the silence. "What brings you here this evening, Doctor? No bad news, I hope."

"No, actually, good news. I sent three more patients home today, and I am now convinced that everyone is going to make a full recovery."

"How's the sheriff?" I asked.

"He will, too, although I believe he has the farthest road to come back."

"It figures," I said bitterly. For a while, here in the office working with Blacke as usual, I had almost managed to forget that ridiculous star on my chest. Now it felt as big and heavy as a wagon wheel. "What's so especially wrong with him? He didn't take that much of the stuff."

"No, he didn't. I'm convinced you saved his life, Booker, and I'm making sure he knows it. Unfortunately, our sheriff has a tendency to indulge in habits that are less than wholesome, and with his resistance lowered by the poison, he is now paying the price in fever and debility."

Mayhew took another pull on his beer.

"Last night, for instance," the doctor said, "he began formicating."

I had never seen a look like that on the face of the lawman who'd seen everything; a look of sheer horror.

"Right there in your *house?*" Blacke yelped.

"Of course," Mayhew said blandly.

"With *who?*"

Blacke's question was nearly a roar. I either had to leave the room to dissolve in hysterics or help the situation. For the sake of future domestic peace, but not without a twinge of regret, I chose the latter course.

"Blacke," I said, "the doctor said *form*icate. With an *m.*"

"Oh," Blacke said. "And would someone be so kind as to tell me what in blazes formmmmmmmicate with an *m means?*"

I yielded to the doctor. After all, he got us into this.

"It means," he said, "to have the false sensation that ants are crawling all over one's body."

Blacke rubbed his jaw. "I don't know, judging from Harlan's usual state of cleanliness, you'd think he'd be used to things crawling on him."

After the doctor finished laughing, he launched what promised to be a spirited defense of his patient's sanitary habits.

He was interrupted by a noise outside, something that was definitely *not* crawling. A horse, at the gallop, coming down Main Street at top speed. The hoofbeats stopped; there was a thud, and they resumed, fading quickly with distance. By the time I got to the door, all I could see was a cloud of dust at the far end of town.

22

T H E N I L O O K E D in the other direction and saw what had made the thud. A body lay in front of the sheriff's office, half on and half off the boardwalk there.

"Doctor!" I yelled, only to discover that the man was right behind me. "You're going to be needed."

Heads were peeping out of windows as Mayhew and I ran across the dirt street toward the body. Despite the doctor's longer legs, I got there first.

I rolled it over and saw what I expected to see—the face of Joseph Feathers.

"He's dead, of course," the doctor said. "Strangled."

I appreciated the "of course." It didn't take a medical degree, or even such layman's knowledge as I possessed, to tell that. The livid mark on the neck, the popping eyes, the protruding tongue, the bluish tinge added to Feathers's already dusky face. It was there for everyone to see.

There was also a note, pinned to the soiled white shirt. It said: THIS IS THE FIRST. I patted the body down, not the pleasantest thing I've ever done, and found nothing of interest. There was no sign of any of the money he had been so zealous to protect from me.

A voice behind me said, "You know what this means," and I jumped a yard in the air.

Blacke had materialized on the scene with Rebecca, as always, behind the chair.

"I realize that this means Muller is probably around. Does it mean anything else?"

"It means we have to be extra careful, and it would help to catch the real poisoner as soon as possible."

"Thank you," I said sincerely, "for saying 'we.' I've been getting mighty lonely in this job. As for the second thing, didn't you hint the other day that you knew who the real poisoner *was*?"

"I might have given that impression, yes."

Mayhew was still doing doctor things with the corpse. Then he stood up and said, "I'll have a couple of men bring the body to my office for autopsy." He stood there for a few moments, then added, "I would certainly like to know your thinking on this matter, Blacke."

"No, you wouldn't," the ex-lawman said flatly. "Not only wouldn't you believe me, you'd probably want to lock me up. And you'd probably talk Booker here into doing it."

I sniffed. "I'm tempted to lock you up until you talk."

Blacke grinned. "Becky would cut off your ears."

I decided not to risk it. "All right, all right, have it your own way. You always do, anyway. Rebecca, don't let anything happen to him until he talks, okay?"

"I won't let anything happen to him," she said with a smile. Then she brought a hand to her mouth.

"What's the matter?" I said.

Blacke craned his neck to try to get a look at her.

"Look at us," Rebecca said scornfully. "Laughing and joking as we stand over a corpse. What a bunch of ghouls. Are you really that jaded. And, God forbid, am I?"

Blacke reached over his shoulder and patted her hand. "No, darlin', we're just too big to cry or to yell about how scared we are. The doctor and Booker have things in hand here. Let's go home."

They left; soon, the doctor's body-carrying recruits arrived, and I went inside. I felt awfully inadequate for somebody the Great Lobo Blacke had announced had things "in hand."

Stick Witherspoon let me in. "I was coming out," he said, "but I saw the three of you out there, and I figured it'd be just as well to keep the door locked."

"Yeah," I said. "I just wish you'd kept it locked."

"But then you couldn't have got in just now—oh, I get it. Getting to you, huh?"

"It got to me days ago, Stick. Have you eaten anything?"

"Oh, sure. Mrs. Sundberg brought me a fine dinner, said Blacke told her he'd be keeping you kind of late. Uh, Booker, if you don't mind my asking . . ."

"Yeah?"

"What the hell just happened out there?"

I looked back toward the cells. "I'll tell you in a while, okay? Look, I'm taking the prisoner upstairs for a few minutes."

Stick gave a good-natured shrug. "You're the sheriff," he said.

"No I'm not," I said distinctly, and went to fetch Herkimer.

"Mr. Booker," he said when he saw me. "It's good to see you." Then he saw the keys in my hand. "What are you doing?"

"Relax," I said.

"But is it safe? If all doubts about our innocence have not been laid to rest, I think I'd just as soon stay here. This is quite a comfortable jail, actually. And I do appreciate the special care you've taken of the princess."

I didn't say anything to that.

"We're just going upstairs to see the princess," I told him. "We're not leaving the building."

At that, he visibly relaxed, but he tensed up again when I told him that the princess and I had had a long talk, and that I knew her real name and their relationship.

"Who else have you told?"

"Just Lobo Blacke. Don't worry, we won't spread it around. Unless it becomes necessary to use it to clear you."

We were halfway up the stairs by now, and Herkimer, walking ahead of me, was feeling it. He had to puff between every few words. "How could that . . . knowledge . . . be of any help?"

"I can't imagine," I told him. "But I've given up trying to predict things. If I could predict things, I'd be a gambler."

And if I had any brains, I thought, I'd be back in my rooms off Printing House Square, in New York, writing stories about the West of my imagination.

I knocked on the door and told Daisy I'd brought her father to visit her. This was designed to communicate two things—one, that everybody knew what everybody knew, and two, for God's sake, don't be naked when I open the door.

I took my time about the locks and bars, just in case, and at that, I could swear she was buttoning the top button of her dress as I opened the door.

She saw her father and ran to embrace him, saying "Daddy" in that remarkable Oklahoma voice. "I'm so glad to see you. I'm sure everything is going to turn out okay."

I cleared my throat. "Not everything," I said.

They turned to me, with the same look of apprehension on their faces. For the first time, I could see a family resemblance between them.

"Did you hear the galloping outside before?"

"I heard it," Daisy said. "I tried to see out the window what was goin' on, but you were all too close to the building."

"Someone dropped off a body in front of the jail—the body of Joseph Feathers. I'm sorry."

"It's my fault," Daisy whispered. "I let him get away. If I'd let Mr. Booker bring him in with us, he'd be okay now."

"Shhh, Princess, shhh," her father said. His voice was smooth, but his eyes glistened with tears. "Under all his smiling,

Joseph had an anger in him that wouldn't let him rest. It was the anger that hurt him, not you. Not you."

The old man turned to me. "What happened?"

"As I told you before, one of the poisoning victims was the son of an outlaw. We—Lobo Blacke and I—think they chanced to meet."

"But that means . . ." Herkimer didn't want to say it. That was all right with me, because I didn't much want to hear it.

But he pressed on and got it out. "That means the outlaw you mentioned is around here somewhere. And that he'll be coming for the princess and me. I don't care so much for my-self—"

"It's permissible to care for yourself," I told him. I once had someone determined to kill me, and I couldn't think about any-thing *but* myself.

Herkimer shook his head. "I'm an old man who's lived his life foolishly. But the prin—my daughter must be protected."

He stood up and threw out his chest. A hint of his spellbind-ing public voice returned.

"In fact, I shall turn myself over to this man's vengeance in return for a promise to spare my daughter."

"Daddy!" Daisy screamed.

"You'll do nothing of the kind," I said. I wondered why I was so angry at him for this gesture. I suspected that some part of me was tempted to take him up on it.

"I've had too much trouble keeping you alive so far to let it go to waste now. Come on downstairs, Dr. Herkimer. I've got a busy day tomorrow."

23

IT WAS EVEN busier than I had anticipated.

The first thing I did when I got up that morning, after shaving and dressing, was to go check my prisoners.

The princess greeted me in a sedate quilted robe. It occurred to me that Rebecca must have helped fill out the prisoner's wardrobe with some things of her own.

"I just stopped by to see if you were all right," I said.

"I'm fine. I had a little trouble going to sleep last night, but I'm all right now. Dad was right about Joe. I loved him, but it wasn't a happy life he lost, and it never would have been, either."

"Anything I can do for you?"

"Well, right now, you can kiss me."

She didn't give me a chance to tell her that wasn't exactly what I meant. It was a nice way to start the day, at that.

"Anything else?" I asked. "Now that that's taken care of, I mean."

Her face got grim.

"Yes," she said. "When you catch the one who did this— What the hell are you smilin' at?"

"What were you going to say?" I demanded. "String him up? Or shoot him down?"

"I don't much care which."

"I didn't think so. Just like the people who wanted to string up you and your father didn't much care, either."

"That's different!"

"How?"

"We're innocent."

"Everybody's innocent until a jury says otherwise. That's the whole point."

"You're just tryin' to confuse me! The skunk who killed my brother deserves to die."

"Sure, he does. After a trial. Anyway, the whole thing isn't worth our arguing about. In a day or two, thank God, I won't be the sheriff around here anymore, and finding the killer won't be my responsibility. Besides, if it really is Paul Muller who's done this, he'll be a lot more likely to shoot me down than the other way around."

Daisy put her soft brown hands on my shoulders. "You don't really believe that, do you?"

"I certainly do."

"Well, I don't."

"I'm not going to go out and get shot just to prove you wrong, you know."

"You'd better not get shot for any reason," she said. "I don't think I'm done with you yet."

I took her hands off my shoulders and kissed them. "You are for this morning, I'm afraid. Stick will be here any minute, and I've got work to do."

I went downstairs and had a few words with Dr. Herkimer. Despite his brave words of the night before, he had had a tougher night of it than his daughter had. His eyes were staring and rimmed with red, and his voice was a croak when he talked.

I know about losing a mother; and in a fundamental way, though he was still back up the Hudson breathing fire on prospective officers, I had lost my father as well. I tried to imagine what losing a child must be like, but I couldn't. I just knew intuitively that it must be the worst kind of grief.

By the time I finished with Herkimer, Stick was waiting patiently outside. I let him in.

"How are things at Dr. Mayhew's?" I asked.

He shrugged. " 'Bout the same. Had to tie Asa Harlan to the bed. Every once in a while, he gets to thinking he's got ants crawling on him, and he's like to beat himself to death trying to get them off."

Stick shuddered. "Grisly sight. I think I'd rather have a gunshot wound."

"You ought to know," I said.

I told him I'd be out most of the day, so he should tell me now if he needed anything, and I'd make sure to have it sent. He said he'd already done that on the way over, so everything was fine.

I told him he'd make a better sheriff than I ever would, and he surprised me. Instead of laughing it off, he rubbed his chin and said that unless he was mistaken there was an election next spring, and who could tell.

I made a mental note to tell Blacke about that. A sheriff in Le Four who wasn't in Lucius Jenkins's pocket might be a big help in furthering Blacke's plans.

And practically the first person I ran into as I walked out the door was Lucius Jenkins.

I almost didn't recognize him. Gone was the Sunday suit, the derby hat, the gold-thread vest, and the flower (fresh from his wife's conservatory) that he wore in his lapel every day, winter and summer.

Today, Lucius Jenkins was dressed like a cowboy, with a no-nonsense Stetson on his bald head, dungarees, and a work shirt with a leather vest over it.

It made a vast difference. He looked younger and stronger, even bigger. He looked a lot less like a criminal mastermind, but he seemed much more of an immediate menace.

He also seemed profoundly irritated by the largish young man who was walking alongside him. He was about my age and height, but much broader, carrying a load of muscle under a fairly comfortable layer of fat.

He had all of this stuffed into a brown suit that looked as if it had not known the touch of an iron since it had been inexpertly packed some time before.

"It's my own father, Mr. Jenkins. I have a right. At least as much as you have to be there."

"Probably," Jenkins admitted, "since I'm blamed if I know what the hell I've got to be there for. I'm a busy man."

The young man waved that off. "That's about the joint option you and Dad took on that grazing land across over in Dakota. He always said something about you getting hold of it when he died."

From this, and from a sort of unformed facial resemblance, I deduced that this was Junior Simpkins, son of the late Big Bill, unfavorite stepson of Mrs. Simpkins. It was nice to have one mystery solved, at least.

"Good morning," I said brightly.

"Morning," Jenkins said grumpily. He performed introductions. When young Simpkins heard I was the deputy, and acting sheriff, he shook my hand with enthusiasm. "I have great admiration for you, sir. I'm sure you'll bring my father's killer to justice."

I raised an eyebrow. "Wouldn't you rather I just shot him?"

"Oh, no. I'm a firm believer in the law." He turned to Jenkins. "That's why it's so ironic that I can't be at the reading of my own father's will. I know my stepmother doesn't like me; I know my father and I had our difficulties—although we had begun corresponding again, at last, a few months ago."

"Well, apparently his health was slipping," I said.

Junior looked interested. "Was it? He never mentioned that. But you see, that's exactly the sort of thing I want to know. It wasn't necessary for Wick Ploset to hint my father left me nothing. I didn't *expect* him to leave me anything. I don't need anything. I have a fine furniture business in Denver, and it's thriving. I don't have all the drive and ability of a Big Bill Simpkins, perhaps, but in my own way, I've made a success on my own, and I think my father would have been proud of that."

He turned to Jenkins again.

"So won't you please help me? I know that Ploset is your lawyer, too. In fact, my father used to say that you led him around by the pe—" Junior coughed. "That Lawyer Ploset had a high regard for your good opinion. I know that if you prevailed upon him, he'd let me in. It's a last message from my father on earth, and I . . . I just want to hear it, that's all."

Jenkins seemed to be hesitating. I put my two cents in.

"Oh, go ahead, Mr. Jenkins," I told him. "Imagine how Abigail would feel if anything were to happen to you while she was away."

Jenkins's head came up as if my words had been a gunshot. His eyes were very cold, staring at me, trying to decide how much I'd meant by what I just said.

After a good half minute, Jenkins turned to Junior and said, "All right. I'll get you in. After that, you're on your own."

Junior raised his right hand. I could see calluses all over it. That was the hand of a carpenter, all right.

"I'll sit in a corner, and I won't say a word, I promise."

"That's fine," I said, beaming. "And would you both hang around town for a little while afterward? I'd like to talk to you both about something important."

That gave them a little more fellow feeling, wondering what I had in mind now.

The answer, to tell the truth, was not much. I was trying to think like a madman who would make detailed plans to kill people wholesale. And while he could in no conceivable way be the smallish figure Stu Burkhart and Gloria Simpkins had seen coming out of the medicine show wagon, perhaps being cut out of a rich father's will might be enough of a motive for a madman to want to kill that father so much that he didn't care how many others he destroyed at the same time. I found it rather hard to believe, but I found the whole business nearly impossible to believe. If someone had told me a week ago that I'd be the law in Le Four, conversing with a blue man, sleeping with an Egyptian princess from Oklahoma, and looking for the cold-blooded cowardly murderer of fourteen people (to say nothing of the revenge-bent outlaw who'd taken his son's name from me), I would have suggested one of us be committed. So I wasn't going to let my incredulity stand in the way of what I had to do.

Junior was delighted to oblige. He was staying at Mrs. Cranmer's rooming house, the most respectable place in town. Jenkins was less than enthusiastic, said he couldn't imagine what I wanted to talk to him about, and I told him I'd think of something.

He grumbled something and said he'd probably be playing checkers with Blacke in that case. I said it was fine with me.

I tipped my hat, and let them make their way to the west end of town where Warwick Ploset practiced law, usually in the furtherance of the interests of Lucius Jenkins.

As I walked in the opposite direction, toward Railroad Street, I was trying to think of something to ask Jenkins. I knew what I wanted to find out—how he was reacting to the almost certainty that Paul Muller was somewhere around town. I just didn't know, yet, how to elicit that information without tipping him off that Blacke suspected him of masterminding the man's crimes.

I wanted to know the same things from Jennie Murdo. It was possible that Muller had communicated with her somehow. It was something I should find out.

I should have, but I didn't. Because when I got to the little cottage at the head of Railroad Street, I found the door ajar, the interior a wreck, and the place deserted.

24

WARWICK PLOSET'S OFFICE was above the dry-goods store, but it had its own stairway and entrance. I took the stairs two at a time and burst into the office.

Ploset's clerk tried to stop me, but I didn't even stop to bother to point out my badge. Since he was twice my age and half my size, I simply lifted him up and carried him in with me.

"Mr. Ploset, I'm sorry," the clerk piped up. "I couldn't stop him. He's a madman."

"Just a man in a hurry," I said. I put the clerk down.

Gloria Simpkins, in her best schoolmarm voice, said, "This is most unseemly, Mr. Booker."

"Yes, ma'am," I said. "I apologize for the interruption. To you, too, Mr. Ploset. To all of you."

Ploset was a white-haired man who was convinced he should have been a judge. At least, he always pursed his lips judiciously before he said anything.

It cost him the chance to say anything.

"We were done here anyway," Lucius Jenkins said. "Weren't we, Ploset?"

He pursed his lips, and I thought Jenkins was going to strike him.

"That's right," he said at last. "There was just the signature of the testator and the witnesses to read."

"Let's just call that done, all right?" Jenkins turned to me. "What do you want, Booker?"

"I'd like to talk to you outside."

"Fine." Jenkins slapped the disreputable hat on his bald head. "Ploset, you can go ahead and read those signatures. You don't need me. Mrs. Simpkins," he said, touching the brim of the hat. "Junior."

Down on the street, Jenkins turned and looked up at me. "I don't as a rule, Booker, appreciate my business being horned in on like that."

"Sorry," I said, but I wasn't really sorry at all. As Lobo Blacke had said when I'd popped in to tell him about Jennie Murdo's disappearance, now I had an excuse to ask Jenkins all the questions I wanted.

"Well, I'll let it go this time, because when I spend ten minutes in a room with Wick Ploset, I end up wanting to kill him. He's always making complications where there aren't any. If you wanted to leave your son a thousand dollars and all the rest of your money and property to your wife, couldn't you just say that?"

"I suppose so."

"Yeah, well, it took the lawyer a half hour." His face looked sour.

"So how about you," he barked. "What's your question?"

"Oh, I've got many more than one."

"Dammit, Booker, I don't have time for many more than one. I'm a busy man. I've got a ranch to run, and you've stolen my top kick to be a deputy's deputy or some such foolishness. I've got to get back to Bellevue."

"That's fine," I said. "I'll ride back with you and ask you on the way."

"You will, will you?"

"Sure. My horse is tied up right outside the *Witness*."

I'd anticipated the move on his part, and had Merton bring Posy around the front while I pushed on to the lawyer's office.

Jenkins narrowed his eyes at me. "And you want to come out to the ranch. My daughter's not there, you know."

I met his gaze. I wondered how much he knew, and I wondered how much he minded what he did know. This was not, however, the time to force the issue.

"I'm aware of that, Mr. Jenkins," I said. "If you recall, I was at the station to see Mrs. Jenkins and your daughter off. Have you heard from them?"

"Sure," he said. "Got a wire yesterday saying they'd arrived in New York and send more money."

I tried to suppress a laugh, and failed. Jenkins tried to give me one of his fierce, deadly scowls, but he, too, burst into laughter, and just for a second, I had an inkling into the camaraderie that Blacke must have shared with this man in times long past.

We reached the *Witness* office; I climbed aboard Posy, and we headed out of town, east toward Jenkins's spread.

"Now, Booker, what *is* your question? Or at least the first of them."

I had decided that the first of them would be very basic. "Your wife's dressmaker, Jennie Murdo. Do you know that she's gone?"

"What do you mean, 'gone'?"

"I went to the house you rent to her, to ask her a question or two, and she wasn't there."

"Hell, maybe she stepped out for a few minutes."

"I don't think so," I said. "The door was standing open and the place was a mess. I think—Blacke thinks so, too—that she either left in a big hurry or that she was dragged out of there."

We were past the edge of the town now, but so far away from it that if we looked over our right shoulders we couldn't see the cottage at the far end of Railroad Street.

Jenkins, however, did not look back. He didn't even look at me, just kept his eyes squinted and on the trail. It occurred to me, not for the first time, that Jenkins should give up the checker games with Blacke and switch to poker. There was nothing to be learned from that man's face.

Or from his voice either. He might have been talking about the weather when he said, "Well, now you've made a legend of him, nobody can contradict him, but Louis was always a bit apt to jump to conclusions, you know."

I asked him what he meant.

"A woman's just lost her only child in a terrible way, she might do anything. Brooding for a couple of days, you know, and then just running away from her grief."

"She might have run away," I conceded. "But if she did, I'll bet she was running away from something other than her grief."

Now Jenkins asked me what *I* meant.

"Her husband," I said. "He might blame her for what happened to the boy."

"Husband? It was my understanding when she came to live up here that she was a widow."

Inside, I was kicking myself for a fool. I had telegraphed my punch with the word "husband." I should have just sprung the name "Muller" on him and seen what happened. My only consolation was that he probably would have poker-faced that one, too.

Still, I couldn't just wheel Posy around and go home. I had to press on with it, no matter how hopeless.

"That's what she lets on," I said, "but she's married to Paul Muller."

Jenkins nodded as though he were thinking it over.

"That does change things."

"Yeah, it sure does. I assume you've heard about that body that was dumped in front of the sheriff's office last night."

"I've heard about it, but not much."

I took that with about a hogshead of salt. You don't get to be a man in Lucius Jenkins's position without knowing everything that happens in your town.

"The corpse was one of the medicine show people, the one that got away. He was strangled, and there was a note promising revenge 'for my son.' "

"This situation is getting out of hand," Jenkins said sourly, and for once, I believe the words and tone expressed an honest emotion.

"You don't have to tell *me* that," I said. "That's why I want to ask you this: You don't have Mrs. Murdo out there at Bellevue, do you?"

And just like that, I got another honest emotion out of the man. He turned his head to me so fast and hard that his horse started to wheel in that direction. His face was red and dangerous.

"Just what is *that* supposed to mean, Booker?" he demanded, and he wanted to know *right now*.

The vehemence of his action surprised me. One panicky brain cell wanted me to go for my gun, a move that would have certainly gotten me killed.

Then I remembered that the one person on earth whom Lucius Jenkins was afraid of was his wife, and I understood the reaction.

I managed a smile and a calm voice.

"Nothing untoward, Mr. Jenkins. Nothing like that ever crossed my mind."

"See," he said, "that it don't."

"I was just wondering if Mrs. Murdo, remembering your previous kindnesses, had asked you for sanctuary, with or without telling you about her husband. I've never met Paul Muller, but from what I've heard of him, he's perfectly capable of blaming his wife as much as anyone for the boy's death. In the servants' quarters at Bellevue alone, you'd have plenty of room for her, and ample chaperonage, too, if anyone were to find out she were there. Not that I'd spread it around, of course."

Jenkins had gone back to looking straight down the trail.

"Don't try to snow me, Booker. You and Blacke would splash it in ink all over that newspaper of yours."

"The *Witness* is the sole property of Mr. Blacke," I corrected. "And sure, we'd print it, but only after Muller was safely locked up."

"Or dead," he said. "You can't ever say somebody like Muller is safely locked up."

"That's the point," I conceded. "Anyway, you haven't answered my question."

"I haven't?"

"No. Have you given Jennie Murdo sanctuary out at Bellevue?"

"No. Absolutely not."

"Thank you," I said. "What is that?"

Jenkins had murmured something. I thought I'd caught it, but I wasn't quite sure."

"Nothing," he said. "Nothing at all."

I let it go, at least for now. What I thought he'd said was "I wish I had," but that didn't make any sense to me.

"Is that it?" he asked. "You can go back to town now, if you're finished."

It was tempting. We'd come quite a distance from town, and the landscape had begun to rise from the flat monotony of the area in and around Le Four. There still weren't any trees to speak of, but there were the occasional undulation to the landscape, some rocks, and even a defile or two along the route, including one we were heading toward now.

I knew I wasn't going to get any more out of Jenkins on this trip—it was only luck that I'd gotten anything at all—and God knew I had more to do back in town.

My indecision must have communicated itself to Posy, because she slowed down, actually coming to a stop for a moment to lower her head and bite off a piece of scrub. Jenkins, as usual, looked neither back nor to the side, but kept riding at a steady pace, just as glad, I was sure, to be rid of me.

It was that certainty that made up my mind for me. If he

didn't want me around, I wanted to be around him, if only to see if I could irritate him out of that deadpan once more.

I gave Posy a little flick with the reins and urged her forward, following Jenkins at a distance of about twenty-five or thirty yards.

I was just about to enter the defile when the avalanche started.

I suppose to a dweller of the Black Hills, or of any serious mountains, that rock slide was a pretty trumpery affair to be called an avalanche. The walls of the defile, after all, had to be less than thirty-five feet high, and the rocks raining down on us—on me, but especially on Jenkins—were no bigger than my head.

But they *were* as big as my head. And they *were* falling thirty-five feet, and this was enough to frighten me as much as any avalanche ever need do.

That frightened Posy, too, and she whinnied and reared, and I showed my horsemanship by immediately being thrown.

I scrambled out of the defile until the rocks stopped falling, and when they did, I heard a weird laugh.

"For my son, Jenkins! For my son, you lying bastard!"

Echoes made the voice impossible to locate, and equally untraceable hoofbeats followed, but I knew as I stood there that for the first time, I had heard the voice of Paul Muller.

25

I DIDN'T EVEN bother to look for Posy. When she calmed down, she'd be eating a plant somewhere nearby and would come when she was called.

Instead, I scrambled on foot into the defile, across shifting piles of stones, calling for Jenkins.

For a long time, I got no answer other than the clatter of rocks sliding away under my boots. I fell down a couple of times and earned a couple of bruises, but I don't think they slowed me down much.

I found Jenkins's horse half covered in stones, with a huge, bloody dent in its skull.

Reasoning that he probably hadn't fallen too far from the animal, I stood there for a few seconds and listened hard, then started scrabbling through the rocks.

After I'd removed five or six, I thought I heard a groan. I followed the source of the noise, and after what seemed a long time, my battered fingers touched something that wasn't rock. I dug faster now, uncovering what turned out to be the man's chest. I put my hand there for a few seconds and felt a good strong heartbeat, so I worked my way up the body and got the head free.

Jenkins was bleeding from a nasty gash in his skull. I made a hasty bandage out of my handkerchief and tied it around his head with my tie. Then I uncovered the rest of him, and, after making sure there were no broken bones, I dragged him clear of the rocks, out the other side of the defile.

He groaned again as I put him down on a patch of grass. I took it for a good sign. Dead and moribund men don't groan.

I felt him for a while, went to the other end of the defile again, called Posy, and led her the long way round to where I'd left Jenkins. It took a long time, but if I tried to take that horse through that jumble of rock, she'd be sure to break a leg. Then, not only would I have to shoot Lobo Blacke's horse, I'd have left myself horseless halfway between town and ranch with an injured man on my hands.

Jenkins was conscious by the time I got back to him. Not happy, but conscious. He was confused, the way people with head injuries so frequently are, but instead of asking, "Where am I?" he wanted to know, "What happened?"

That was easy to answer, at least superficially. "Rock slide," I said.

I got the canteen off my saddle and gave him some water to drink. Then I used some to wash some of the blood off his face, and by the time I finished, he looked as if he actually might live.

"What happened?" Jenkins murmured again.

"Shut up," I replied cordially. "I'll tell you when we get you to Bellevue. I'm going to lift you up now and get you on the horse."

He made no protest, and I went to work.

He didn't weigh anything. Everybody in Le Four spent so much time talking and thinking of Lucius Jenkins as the "biggest man in town," we tended to forget that that was a figure of speech. Right now, he was a small, thin, and injured old man.

I'm not entirely sure how I did it, but I somehow managed to get Jenkins on the saddle, upright, in front of me. I think he helped a little, which was another good sign.

In any case, I had my arms around him, holding the reins

and keeping him upright, and his head reclined against my chest. I remembered embracing his daughter in a similar, if more energetic, manner, although not on horseback. It had been a lot more fun with Abigail.

I set Posy off at a slow walk, and we made our way to that incongruous mansion on the prairie. Once there, I couldn't figure out how to get him *down* off the saddle, or dismount myself without dropping him on his head again, so I sat there outside the building and yelled for help.

It eventually came in the form of Pierre and several of the maids. We got him into the parlor and onto a chaise longue, pulled off his boots, and covered him with a sheet. A rider was dispatched to town to fetch Dr. Mayhew.

By this time, Jenkins had recovered sufficiently to call for some whiskey and to get downright cantankerous when I vetoed it.

"Damn you, Booker, this is my house."

"You've had a head injury," I said. "No booze until the doctor says so."

"I'm all right. Just a little beat up."

"Why take chances?" I said.

Jenkins eyed me narrowly and grumbled into his moustache. At last, he gave that up and said, "You promised you were going to tell me what happened."

"That's right, I did." So I told him, all of it, including the faceless taunting from above.

"I figure it has to be Paul Muller," I said casually.

Jenkins's voice was bitter. "That bastard," he said. "That miserable bastard."

I shrugged. "Like you said, someone who's just lost an only child is apt to do anything. Try not to touch that bandage, Mr. Jenkins. I'm no expert, and it may come loose."

He jerked his hand away from his head.

"You have to wonder, though," I went on.

"There's no sense wondering about what a madman does."

"Oh, I don't know. Crazy people start from a different place from the rest of us, but they usually follow the same rules once they get started."

"I've got a headache." He closed his eyes.

"You shouldn't go to sleep, either," I said.

Jenkins growled.

"Help me with this. Suppose Muller is mad with grief, or injured pride, or whatever it is. Why should he want to kill *you* of all people?"

Jenkins narrowed his eyes at me.

"And it *was* you he was trying to kill," I assured him. "He had numerous chances at me, and never bothered. And he mentioned you by name at the end, and said it was for his son."

Jenkins said nothing. I scratched my chin.

"You never so much as laid eyes on his son, did you?"

Jenkins started to shake his head, winced, then said, "No."

"I didn't think so. The only thing you ever had with either him or his family was to steer his wife to a place where she could make a decent living for herself and the boy. And even then, you had no idea of her and Paul Muller, isn't that right?"

Jenkins mumbled a reply.

"What's that?"

"That's right," he said, loud and clear.

"So how," I mused, "could he *possibly* have you on his revenge list?"

"I don't know," Jenkins said. "Could you please shut up for a while, Booker?"

"Don't go to sleep now."

"I won't."

I gave him about three minutes. Then, at last, I said, "You know what I'll bet it is? Muller's heard how Le Four is practically your own little private fiefdom, and he holds you responsible for everything that happens in it. I'll bet that's what it is."

I put a happy little smile on my face and lapsed into silence once again. This time, we sat there long enough for the afternoon shadows to have lengthened perceptibly, and Jenkins didn't take his shrewd black eyes off me the whole time.

I tried not to let on that I noticed.

Finally, Jenkins cleared his throat and said, "Booker?"

"Yes, Mr. Jenkins? I'm sure the doctor will be here before too long."

"To hell with the doctor. I'm not worried about the doctor. I want to ask you a question."

"Certainly," I said. "I've been asking you questions all day."

"How much does Blacke pay you?"

That caught me by surprise. My brain raced for a few seconds, trying to decide what I ought to say, and then I just told him.

Jenkins sneered.

"That's not enough," he said. "I could double that."

I snorted. "You could pay five times that."

"Don't be greedy, Booker."

"I'm not being greedy, I'm just stating a fact. With the money you've got, you could pay a monthly salary five times what Blacke pays me and never miss it. You probably spend more than that on cigars."

Jenkins made a sour face. "I don't suppose you'd let me have a cigar, either."

"Nope. I saved your life, I feel kind of responsible for it. Let's see what the doctor says."

"I could triple it," he said.

"Before we go any further," I said, "let's get things all straightened out. Are you offering me a job?"

"Of course I am."

"Doing what?" I demanded. "The only thing I know how to do is write."

"You're smart. And despite your ridiculous eastern ways,

you're savvy. And you've got the guts, if only for the way you mouth off to me all the time."

"And I just saved your life," I pointed out.

"There's that, too. Nobody can say that Lucius Jenkins doesn't pay his debts."

A mad impulse led me to see just how much he admired my "bravery."

"I've been intimate with your daughter, you know."

The look that flashed over Jenkins's face made me glad that my courage had not extended to telling him this while he had access to a gun or a horsewhip, or even when he was in sufficient shape to jump off the furniture and strangle me.

He took a deep breath and calmed himself.

"I know, I know. Do you think I'm a fool? One way or another I've been able to control everyone I ever met, except Abigail and her mother. At that, I suppose you're better than some of the specimens she used to sneak around with."

I wanted to thank him, but I didn't think it would be such a good idea.

"Anyway," he went on, "if you want to work for me, you might even be able to marry her."

"I don't think your daughter has the slightest interest in me as a husband."

"Just being around me, Booker, seeing how I work, helping me, could make you a very rich man."

"If I had wanted to be a very rich man," I told him, "I could have stayed in New York and gone to work for my grandfather."

Then Jenkins asked who my grandfather was, and I told him that, too, and he was impressed.

Before the conversation could go any further, Dr. Mayhew showed up. I told him what had happened, and he went immediately to the patient, checking his eyes and his reflexes.

"Is he going to be all right, Doctor?" I asked.

"He's got a mild concussion. That's a nasty wound on the

scalp, though. He would have bled to death in an hour if you hadn't found him."

Gracious, I thought, I did save his life.

"I'm going to dress his wound now," Mayhew said. "And then I'll get him shifted up to his bed."

"All right," I said. "I'll hang around and ride back to town with you."

I had a wound dressed by Dr. Mayhew before, and had seen plenty of others, and I needed no further lessons in his technique. I left the parlor and went to the little drawing room in which Abigail and I had said good-bye less than a week before.

I had a seat and thought about Jenkins's offer. It was obvious that the "job" in question was nothing more than a bribe, but a bribe to do what?

I hadn't even to begun to think about it when noises came from the other room. Not screams exactly. Lucius Jenkins wasn't the kind of man who'd let himself scream. These were the noises of a man who wouldn't scream getting a scalp wound bathed with carbolic.

26

"GREAT," LOBO BLACKE said. "I wouldn't be surprised if you wound up with a bullet in your back now. Or
dead."

We were sharing our evening beer, alone this time, in the
Witness office. I had just reported my day's activities.

"I thought I did a fairly good job."

"Oh, you did an amazing job," Blacke said. "You were positively cogent."

"Then what's the problem?"

"I think you might have put yourself in real danger."

I put my beer down so I wouldn't spill it and goggled at him.
"And this bothers you? You, the man who sent me off to a gunfight when I'd never drawn a gun in my life? You, the man who
insisted I pretend to be the sheriff in a town with at least two
mad killers running around loose?"

"That was different," Blacke said.

"What was different?"

"The fact in neither of those cases was I putting you directly
up against Lucius. You did that all by yourself."

"Well, I couldn't just pretend not to notice. I'm not that
stupid, and Jenkins knows it."

The sour look on Blacke's face matched a couple I had seen
from Jenkins.

"I don't know," he said. "You were stupid enough to admit you'd been with his daughter."

I scratched my head.

"Yeah," I admitted. "In retrospect, I'm pretty amazed about that one, myself. I think I was testing to see how eager he really was to hire me—that is, to pay me to shut up about the Muller connection."

"Why? The fact that he tried to pay you off at all was a major breakthrough."

Blacke fell silent. He did that when he thought of something new. He dropped right out of the here and now and pursued the thought as far as he could.

"You know what else it was?" he said after a couple of minutes.

I was used to Blacke by now, so I had no trouble picking up the thread.

"No. What else was it?"

"It was a major mistake. A very basic mistake."

"I can't see that," I said. "Jenkins has probably been spreading money around to get people to do what he wants ever since he's had money to spread. Certainly works in this town, from what I've seen."

"Open your eyes, Booker, the blizzard's over."

"That's colorful," I said. "But what does it mean?"

"It means you're forgetting what *else* you've seen. For instance, who *isn't* Jenkins paying off in this town?"

"That we know for sure?"

"I'll take it that way."

"Dr. Mayhew," I said. "And you. And I suppose Big Bill Simpkins had enough of his own to stay off the payroll."

"Very good," Blacke said, one finger raised. Up until that moment, I would never have imagined there could be anything schoolmasterish about Lobo Blacke. "Now, *why* hasn't he tried to pay off Mayhew and me?"

"Because you're both men of integrity, and of real achievement. It isn't the kind of achievement that leads to great wealth, but it pays your way, and it's satisfying work."

Blacke was nodding. "That was a little flowery, but it makes the point. Mayhew and I, each in our way, would spit in his face if he tried to buy us. So here's the question, genius. What did Jenkins think was wrong with *your* integrity? Why did he think *you* wouldn't spit in his eye?"

"But I didn't."

"You didn't, huh? Listen, Booker, that crack about his daughter was a big, warm, sticky goober if there ever was one. You spit in his eye, all right."

Blacke drank some beer.

"All I'm trying to say here, Booker, is that Lucius misjudged your character. Badly. He didn't get in the position he's in by making that kind of mistake."

"Maybe he thinks any Big City slicker from the East is bound to be corrupt," I suggested. "Or maybe he hasn't been getting by on his own judgment."

"That's colorful. But what does it mean?"

"Martha Jenkins strikes me, on an admittedly short acquaintance, as a remarkably shrewd woman. . . ."

Blacke was staring at me as though I'd just grown a set of antlers.

"By God, Booker," he said, "maybe you are a genius. That woman has always supplied the ambition behind Lucius—why shouldn't she supply some of the brainpower?"

"Or even all of it."

Blacke frowned. "No, no," he said. "Remember, I've known Lucius since before he ever met Martha, and too much of what I've seen over the years is pure Lucius. The timing, the tactics, the tricks—all straight out of marshal days.

"I've been assuming all these years that Martha just said 'I want,' and Lucius sold another ounce of his soul to get it for her.

But you could be right. It could be a lot more than that. She could—and she would, by God, as determined to be a great lady as she is—lay out general campaign objectives. And she damn well could be there using her intu— What the hell do you call it?"

"Intuition," I said. "Woman's intuition."

"Yeah." Blacke showed a crooked smile. "I used to think that was all buncombe until I started living under the same roof with Becky." He nodded. "Martha may be a lot more of a helpmate than I ever imagined."

"Does this mean we're out to get her hanged, too?"

"Nice of you to say 'we,' but no. Lucius is enough of a project for now."

"At least now we can be sure he is connected with Paul Muller."

"That is something," Blacke conceded. "Of course, it would be a lot bigger something if we had our hands on Muller. But what's got me worried is that he knows we—or specifically you—know it. He's tried to win you over with money, and it didn't work. That was a huge mistake, and he knows that, too."

"What's wrong with his knowing he made a mistake? It might make him nervous," I said.

"I don't *want* Lucius nervous, dammit," Blacke barked. "That's when he gets dangerous."

27

THAT CONVERSATION MARKED the end of Louis
Bowman Blacke's vacation, or whatever it was he thought he
was doing.

From that moment on, he stopped letting me flounder around
pretending to be a lawman, and really started to work on things.
He still played the game of "Booker the Lawman" enough to
couch his orders to me as suggestions, but since I was sick of
the game, anyway, and didn't have the first idea of what the hell
I ought to be doing, I snapped up each of his suggestions like a
frog after a piece of red flannel, even if they made no sense at
all to me.

Today, for instance, I was paying a call on Junior Simpkins
with a rough script laid out by Blacke. As far as I could figure,
the plan was to find something incriminating about Junior himself, who, some wires had shown, had a cast-iron alibi that put
him in Denver at the time of his father's (and everybody else's)
death or about Harold Collier, whom (I thought) Blacke himself
had cleared pretty convincingly of connivance of the crime.

Still, I told myself, mine not to reason why.

It was a good thing I got to the rooming house when I did,
because I saw Junior in the lobby just bending over to pick up
his carpetbag and leave after settling up with the proprietor.

"Going somewhere?" I asked.

"Oh, Mr. Booker. Yes, I am. Back to Denver. Everything I needed to do here has been done, and I've got business to tend to back in Denver. Taking the ten o'clock train."

I consulted my watch, a real beauty given to me by Blacke to celebrate the success of our book.

"You've still got plenty of time," I said, clicking the lid shut. "Can you spare me a few minutes?"

"Is it important?"

"It could be," I said.

"Does it have to do with my father's death?"

"That's what I want to find out."

We went into a little sitting room off the parlor. It afforded privacy, but no comfort. Not that the place was barren, by any means. With lace and polished wood, and chintz and flocked wallpaper, it was the kind of room one expected to find only in Bellevue—and, I supposed, in Mrs. Simpkins's place, once she'd done away with the last of Junior's influence.

The trouble was that all the chairs were tiny artifacts of carved wood, shaved so thin by enthusiastic artisans that they looked as if they'd collapse if a fly lit on them. Someone my size, or someone the size of William Simpkins Jr., who was even bigger, seemed beyond the realm of possibility.

We eyed the furniture warily.

"I like your approach to this stuff much better," I said.

"Thank you." After a pause of a second or two, he said, "Well, I'll try it if you will."

Slowly, we lowered ourselves onto a couple of the toy chairs. We wound up sitting exactly the same way—with half our fundaments hanging over the edge and our feet planted solidly, ready to jump if the chair gave way.

"What is it you wanted to see me about, Mr. Booker?"

"Harold Collier."

"Harold Collier? You mean the Harold Collier I knew here in Le Four? The one I went to school with?"

"That's right," I said. "You were taught by your stepmother, weren't you?"

"She wasn't my stepmother then. But yes, we were." His face took on a distant expression. "Gosh, Harold Collier. I haven't thought of Harold for years. How is old Harold?"

"You mean you don't *know*?"

"Don't know what?" Junior asked blandly.

Once I had a chance to think about it, it made sense. Junior had been away from Le Four since before the blue man came to be, and most folks had had other things on their minds since he'd come back.

So I told Junior Collier's sad story, and how he had come to be, however briefly, a suspect in the poisonings. Then I told him of my visit to the blue man, and of the note he'd gotten luring him to the fatal medicine show.

"In fact," I said, reaching into my vest pocket, "I have the note right here." I pulled it out of my pocket, and still holding on to it, showed it to him. Actually, it was something Blacke had our artist copy when we were looking at the envelope.

"Does that look like Harold Collier's hand?" I said.

"Good God, Mr. Booker. I don't know if I could ever recognized block letters made by Harold Collier, but heavens, I haven't seen the man in fifteen years, and our school days were longer ago than that."

I tried to sound more disappointed than I felt. Disappointment was minimal, mainly because I knew that Lobo Blacke could not possibly have been such an ass to expect Junior to identify the block letters on the note.

Now, to move on to the next mysterious step. "Of course," I said, "you understand we have to try everything."

"Of course."

"Now," I went on, "if you will just do one more thing for me—"

"I can tell you one thing."

"What's that?"

"It *could* have been Harold."

"What makes you say that?"

"Well, it could have been printed by any of hundreds of people who went to school here in Le Four. But it was written by somebody who learned their letters from Miss Hastings."

"Now the widow Simpkins," I said, just to make sure.

"That's right. Look at the letter *N*. See that little horizontal line at the end of the letter, the upstroke? She used to teach us all to make that to remind us not to keep going and make an *M* out of it. She had the same thing about *V*s and *W*s. I thought everybody did it that way, until I got out of town."

"That's very interesting," I said. And it also tied in with what Lobo Blacke wanted me to obtain next.

"Would you mind printing an alphabet for me?" I asked. "In case any more notes show up. You are a good representative of the Hastings system of education, aren't you?"

He grinned at me. "Not according to the lady herself. She still has no use for me. Still, she never complained about how I made my letters."

"Very good," I said. "I have a piece of paper here," I said, "but nothing to write with."

"Oh, the lady who runs the place just made out my account. I'm sure she'd let us use a pen for a few moments."

"I'm sure she would," I agreed, "but for this to be right, it really should be in pencil."

Now, I had a pencil in my pocket, but I was under instructions from Blacke not to take it out unless I absolutely had to. Pencils, being expensive and wasteful, were not all that easy to come by in Le Four.

But Junior didn't let me down. He said, "Of course," and reached into the pocket of his coat. "I should have realized," he said. "I have a pencil right here."

It was a strange-looking pencil at that, stubby and short, and not round or hexagonal in cross section, but rectangular. The lead inside was rectangular, too.

"I never seen a pencil like that before."

He looked at it. "Oh. Of course. This is a special pencil for carpenters. Great tool to work with—short, to fit in a pocket, and square, so you can put it down on the work without worrying if it'll roll away."

"Where do you get them?"

"A company in Massachusetts makes them. I discovered them just before I moved to Denver. I had Trimble, who used to own the general store, order a dozen boxes for me, I was so in love with the idea. A lot of woodworkers still use chalk or charcoal, but the line is imprecise and sloppy."

He had now taken a small folding knife from the same pocket the pencil had come from and expertly carved the wood of the implement into a neat pyramid of brown wood topped with a tiny one of black.

"Terrific," I said. "Now, if you'd just print an alphabet, I'll let you go."

He gave me his ingratiating grin. "Out of the clutches of the law, eh?"

"Precisely." When he was done, I shoved both pieces of paper in my pocket for later examination.

"Come on," I said, "I'll walk you to the station."

But Junior was in for a major disappointment at the station. That day's train to Denver had been canceled, and there wouldn't be another until Thursday.

I told him it was a tough break and walked him back to the boardinghouse, then I stopped in at the office of the *Witness* to report developments to Blacke.

Blacke wasn't in the composing room when I came in. That was in sole possession of Merton Mayhew, who was sitting at the checker table with some paper, a pen, and an inkwell, scribbling furiously. It might have been homework, but I doubted it because of the enthusiasm and concentration with which he went about it. He had ink stains on his hands and face, but somehow the pink tip of tongue that always protruded from the left corner of his mouth when he was writing had so far remained unscathed.

"What's the story, Merton?"

"Oh, Mrs. Simpkins came by and told Mr. Blacke she's going to use her husband's money to set up an orphanage on some land she owns out of town. The place is to be run on . . ." Merton consulted some notes. " '. . . the soundest and most modern custodial, nutritional, and pedagogical techniques, with plenty of good food, light, air, and exercise for all the children. Furthermore, White, Indian, and mixed-breed children will be accepted alike, so that the more enlightened race may have a civilizing effect on the aboriginal one.' "

Merton looked up at me. "I asked her if some people weren't going to be bothered by that, she gave me a hard stare and said, 'Young man, don't you *believe* an Indian child can be civilized by the proper influences?'

"I told her that most of the Indians I'd ever met didn't need that much civilizing."

I thought of Daisy Herkimer and her dead brother. "No more than anybody needs, I guess," I said.

"Well, Mrs. Simpkins just sniffed at me and said she hoped I would learn better before I was grown."

I smiled at him and told him he was doing fine. "Where's Blacke?" I asked.

"In his office. He said he wanted to talk to you as soon as you came in." Realizing what he'd just said, Merton looked sheepish and said, "Sorry."

Just then, the door to the office opened, and Blacke bellowed, "*Booker!* Stop distracting poor Merton from his work and get your duff in here."

I didn't dawdle on my way to the office, but I didn't scamper either. A man has a certain amount of dignity he's got to maintain.

"Hello again," I said with a smile.

"Yeah, yeah, hello. What have you got?"

"Well, he had a pencil, just as you predicted. A kind of an odd one."

"Odd how?"

I described the pencil first, since he was so eager to hear the details, then I filled in the whole story of my morning with Junior Simpkins. When I was finished, I handed over the note Harold Collier supposedly received and the alphabet Junior had done.

Blacke sat musing over them for a minute or two.

Without looking up, he asked, "How did he take it?"

"Like a lamb," I said. "Wrote the letters without a word of complaint. If he had any suspicions of what I was after—not that I have any myself, you understand. But if he had any, he didn't show them."

"I don't mean that," Blacke said, still comparing the notes. "I meant how did he react to the train being canceled?"

"He took that pretty hard," I said. "He even went so far as to say 'damn,' which for him is a tirade."

I mused for a few seconds. Blacke looked up impatiently, but if he could drift off in the middle of conversations, so could I.

"You know," I said, "life is endlessly fascinating. Here's a man who could take being cut out of his father's will—or at least mostly cut out of it—with hardly a qualm, showing no rancor for the father in question at all. Then he gets more upset than I've ever seen him by the knowledge that he has a few more days to spend in our lovely little town."

Blacke grunted. I took it as a signal to keep talking.

"By the way," I said, "you'll have to fire me from the *Witness*. Since I took up being a lawman, my journalistic skills have eroded sadly. In all the hubbub at the station, I never did find out *why* the train was canceled."

"I know why it was canceled," Blacke said.

"Care to share the knowledge with me?"

"Sure," he said. "It was canceled because I sent a wire to the president of the Great Northern in St. Paul asking him to get it canceled."

I was impressed. Not at Blacke's nerve in holding up several hundred railroad passengers who had their own lives to get on with merely to help his plan—Lobo Blacke has the nerve to do just about anything. I was impressed that the railroad had gone along with it. I knew that Blacke had twice been offered a job as chief of security for the railroad, and had twice turned it down. Apparently they still wanted him. Either that, or they were so flabbergasted by his gall that they said yes under a kind of mesmerism.

"I thought it would be best," Blacke said unnecessarily, "for young Simpkins to be handy to us for a while. Things are coming to a head, and he'll want to be around for the finish."

"They are, are they?"

Blacke took a deep breath, slapped a hand on the table, and said, "Yep, they are."

"You don't sound especially pleased by the prospect."

"No, by God," he said. "I am not. There's still too much going on, too much up in the air, too much that can go wrong. These letters, for instance—"

"Yeah," I said. "What about them?"

He shoved them across the table to me. "Look for yourself," he said.

I held the note and Junior's alphabet side by side and compared them.

"Well," I said, "the printing is nothing alike, except that idiosyncratic *N* and *W* that Mrs. Simpkins taught them in school."

"When you get a chance," Blacke said, "tell me what 'idiosyncratic' means."

"It means—"

"Not now. Take a closer look."

It took me a moment, but I saw it. "Thick and thin strokes," I said. "On both of them."

Blacke was nodding. "It had to be. You see, once I remembered Junior was a carpenter, I remembered carpenter's pencils."

"What do you know about carpenter's pencils?"

"I've had quite a bit to do with carpenters in my time," Blacke said. "For one thing, whenever I'd ride back into town, it was usually time to build a gallows."

I admitted I hadn't thought of that.

"Anyway," Blacke repeated, "I thought of carpenter's pencils. And it occurred to me that after the first stroke or two, when the point wore down even a little, you were writing with a lead that was wider one way than it was the other. What did Henry call it?"

"Broad nib," I said.

"Yeah. Like that, so you'd have to look more closely to see it. So you established that Junior uses the things and has for years."

"Are you saying Junior wrote the note after all? That he might be the killer? It doesn't make any sense. If he wrote the note to Harold Collier, he disguised his printing, either then or today."

"So?"

"Why would he do that, and keep those *N*s and *W*s there? And then call my attention to it?"

"I can't answer that," Blacke said. "I didn't say anybody disguised anything, did I?"

He made a face. "Anyway, that's not what I'm working on at the moment."

"What are you working on?"

"I'm working on a way to get you face-to-face with Paul Muller."

28

DAISY PUT MY hand on her breast and let me feel it swell as she breathed in.

"I'm glad you came here," she said. "A girl doesn't like to be a one-time thing, you know." She giggled.

I kissed her, then smiled back. "I didn't want to take advantage of your grief."

"Hell," the princess drawled. "I've had my grief. Grief is about dyin'. Bein' a man and woman together is about livin'."

About living, yes. That's why I was there. In a little while, I was going out to face Paul Muller. Lobo Blacke had arranged it, and he had a plan.

I had a conviction I wouldn't survive the night. So if I was going to die, I decided, I wanted the memory of a woman's embrace fresh in my mind at the end.

I didn't share these thoughts with Daisy Herkimer, but I don't think I imposed on her, judging from the enthusiasm of her embrace, the warmth of her sweet brown mouth, or the magnitude of her shudders when the climax came.

"Oh, golly," she said, "it just gets better, doesn't it?"

"Daisy," I said, "don't let anybody ever civilize you."

She scowled at me. "You sayin' I ain't civilized?"

"No, no. I used the wrong word. Never let anyone refine you.

Don't let contact with any kind of people change you from the way you are."

"If you don't want me to, Quinn, I won't."

"Good."

"How soon before we see if we can make it even better?" I kissed her throat. "I don't know, Princess. Not tonight. I've got something to do."

"Dang," she said. "You hurry back when you're done."

"If I can," I said.

I rolled off the bed and dressed slowly. I bent to kiss her one more time, then left the room.

I got my badge and my gun from the office. Dr. Herkimer was asleep, and I left him that way. The jail would be guarded tonight, but from the outside. Stick Witherspoon was already planted on a rooftop across the street, just in case Blacke's big rendezvous should be used as a decoy.

I left and locked up behind me and made my way to the *Witness* building, through the alley, and around to the back.

There was a low porch back there, and Blacke was on it in his wheelchair, tapping his finger on his knees and grumbling to Merton and Rebecca, who were waiting with him.

"You're late," Blacke growled.

"I am not," I replied. "You said sunset, and more than half the sun is still up."

"Any fool knows that sunset starts when the sun first touches the horizon."

"And it isn't over until it disappears completely."

"Stop arguing," Rebecca said. Her voice was quiet, but she demanded attention. If the circumstances of her life had worked out differently, she might have made an excellent schoolteacher.

Blacke and I shut up. It was a stupid argument, anyway.

Merton, as evidenced by his barely suppressed grin and the involuntary bouncing on the balls of his feet, was, as usual, vicariously excited by the possibility of impending violence. One would think that Merton, being the son of his father, would be more aware than most boys his age of the consequences of bullets and blades, and therefore less bloodthirsty than was usual for someone his age. In Merton's case, however, nature never failed to conquer experience, and usually without a struggle.

Rebecca wasn't taking the trouble to conceal anything of her emotions. Her blue-green eyes flashed apprehension, and anger at us for making her feel it.

"Do you insist on going through with this nonsense?"

"Mind your manners, Becky," Blacke said, with some asperity.

She ignored him and looked up at me. "Mr. Booker. Quinn. It's useless to argue with Uncle Louis about this, I know. When he gets an idea in his head, he is little better than a madman."

Merton Mayhew gave a snort of laughter, which he managed to turn into a coughing fit. A fairly convincing one, too. Apparently he had learned *something* from being the son of a physician.

Rebecca ignored him, too.

"You, on the other hand," she said to me, "are young, educated, and still retain, perhaps, a vestige of sense. You are riding out to meet the most dangerous man in the territory, on his terms. And one of you probably won't even be able to remain on the horse."

That last remark was unfair. We'd spent a good part of the previous day trying various ways of getting Blacke on the back of a horse so he'd stay there, and at length, we'd come up with one that worked pretty well. Of course, since the notion that a cripple would be riding anywhere was our ace in the hole according to Blacke's plan, we'd been limited in our experimentation to the area in back of the *Witness*. Still, while I had plenty of doubts about the rest of the proceeding, I was fairly sure he'd stay on the horse.

I stepped onto the horse and took Rebecca's hand.

"Rebecca," I said. "I know we're taking big risks, and I'm scared to death."

"Bah," Blacke spat. "You'll be safe as a church."

This was Blacke's night for being ignored. Or maybe it was just the night he had decided to stand for it. Maybe he was a little scared, too.

"But so far, fifteen people are dead, and even though there hasn't been any mob action for a while, the town is getting ugly. I'm not happy about wearing this badge, but I've got it, and I've got to do something to bring the situation to a head, and Blacke is the only one who has even a glimmer of a plan to bring that about."

"Why the blazes do you keep talking about me like I'm not here?" Blacke demanded.

"Because this would be an easier conversation to have if you *weren't* here," I explained. "Now, shut up."

Blacke's mouth dropped open. He wasn't used to being told to shut up, and he was going to blast me for it, but when he saw the tiny smile flit across Rebecca's lips, he let it go. One aspect of Blacke's genius was his ability to gauge when a man knew what he was doing.

I possessed no such gift. I had to get by on faith.

I tried to explain as much to Rebecca, concluding with "When you come down to it, wheelchair or not, Lobo Blacke is the most dangerous man in the territory."

"Dangerous enough to get you both killed!" she cried. Then she virtually jumped into my arms and embraced me. She broke loose a second later, bent over Blacke, enfolded him in her arms, and gave him a very thorough, un-niecely kiss on the mouth, then ran inside as tears began to spill from her eyes.

"Wow," Merton Mayhew said, scratching his head.

I could find very little to add to that observation.

Blacke sat for a second rubbing his mouth, as though it tingled.

He looked up at Merton. "Son," he said, "do you understand what just happened here?"

"No, sir," Merton said earnestly.

"Well, boy, no matter how long you live, you never will." Blacke shook his head as though to clear it. "We'd better get going, Booker. Merton's already saddled the horses. Would you get them, please?"

I went to the small stable behind the yard and led Posy and a stallion named Domingo near the porch. Merton, meanwhile, had fetched additional help in the form of Clayton Henry and Mrs. Sundberg.

Together, the four of us lifted Blacke up to Posy's back and into the modified saddle there. Peretti, the cobbler and saddler, had made a high back to the saddle and had bolted a belt to it. Blacke strapped himself in and pronounced himself happy with the arrangement.

"Oh, no," I said. "Not until we take care of your legs."

I handled that part of it personally, tying short lengths of rope that bound his ankles into the stirrups and his knees to loops Peretti had added to the saddle.

It was the first time I'd touched Blacke's legs, and it was amazing, considering how heavy and robust the top of him was, to feel them thin and stick-fragile under my hands.

The idea of a man with no feeling in his legs or rump sitting a horse is, of course, ridiculous. With any other man than Lobo Blacke, and any other horse than Posy, I should have refused to have anything to do with it. But I had seen it work earlier, and I knew Blacke would bring it off. I knew we'd get to where we were going. It was what was to happen after we got there that made me nervous.

Which reminded me of something.

"Make sure you can reach the ties on your ankles," I said.

Blacke was getting irritated. He was enjoying being up on Posy, and he didn't want to be reminded of his infirmities.

"I can reach them."

"Humor me," I said patiently. "Try it."

He did, and he was right. Good. One less thing to worry about.

"Hand me the rifle," he said.

Without a word, Clayton Henry handed the Winchester repeater to him. He seemed glad to be rid of it. Blacke stuck it in a scabbard on the right side of the horse. Peretti hadn't had to add that. It was a relic of Blacke's lawman days.

I wasn't used to looking up at Blacke's face. He was commanding enough in a wheelchair. Now he was positively imperial.

"Well?" he demanded. "What are we waiting for?"

I mounted Domingo, and we rode out.

29

I'M NOT SURE I have ever fully understood how Blacke managed to arrange that night's rendezvous in the first place. His years as a lawman provided him with a network of friends, spies, and informers that he still somehow managed to retain. I have asked him to make me more fully aware of the workings of these people, but he has always refused, for two reasons—to protect the people themselves, and to protect me from having to associate with the likes of them.

When I consider the persons he *has* thrown me together with, that second reason becomes laughable, but I have never been able to budge him.

Roughly, though, it worked like this.

Blacke learned from one of his shadowy informants that Paul Muller had an informant of his own in town, not an accomplice exactly, but someone who could get messages to the man for a certain fee. Blacke's man said he didn't know precisely who this person might be, but he could think of four or five possibilities.

Fine, Blacke had said. You get around and whisper to each of the possibilities that Booker is willing to give him a clear shot at the prisoners if he can figure out how to do it without getting his ass in a sling. He's getting tired of trying to hold this town together, and I don't blame him.

Blacke's informant said he would whisper in a few appropriate ears.

"Wouldn't it be interesting," I said when Blacke had told me this part of the story, "if your informant and Muller's informant turned out to be the same fellow?"

"Mind your business," Blacke said. "I told you you don't want anything to do with these people."

Interesting or not, I received what I considered confirmation for my guess when less than five hours later, a note was stuffed in the door of the jail. It read simply:

9 P.M. BISHOP'S ROCK. ALONE. M.

Bishop's Rock was an outcropping on the prairie east of town, not far from where Lucius Jenkins and I had been ambushed.

When I showed the note to Blacke he said, "Written in ink."

"You weren't expecting more carpenter's pencil, were you?"

He smiled. "Not this time, no. But I was expecting him to choose a meeting place something like Bishop's Rock. You'll get there early and wait on the south side of it. Don't let yourself get moved from there."

"Why?" I demanded. "Is there something lucky about being killed on the south side of Bishop's Rock? An old Indian superstition, or something?"

"No," Blacke replied. "There's something lucky about having me on the top of the hill that faces the south side of Bishop's Rock, covering you."

"You?"

"Sure. You didn't think I was going to send you out there alone, did you?"

"As a matter of fact, I did."

Blacke shook his head.

"Booker, as a town lawman, you're pretty adequate. As a writer, you are downright cogent. But as a strategist, you stink."

"But how are you going to get out there?"

"I've got it all worked out. But it has to be me, don't you

see? I'll be the last person in the world Muller would expect to be out there. His informant will have told him the whereabouts of everyone else who might help you, but even if he sees me leaving town, he'll never get word to Muller in time. So you'll meet Muller, and you'll talk to him."

"Um, not wishing to sound bloodthirsty or anything, as long as you've got him covered, why don't you just plug him as soon as he shows up? He is a killer, you know."

"Because," Blacke said patiently, "I want you to talk to him."

At this point, things seemed so fantastic I almost forgot to be afraid.

"What," I said, "do you want me to say?"

And he told me.

If Muller was as good as his word, I had only a short time now before I'd be saying those words. I split up from Blacke some miles back, since he wanted to ensconce himself on the hilltop unseen. One thing I was worried about was the fact that Blacke would have to undo his ropes and belt and simply fall to the ground from Posy's back. Another was that he would never be able to get remounted by himself.

Typical, I thought. Here the man was sending me out to get killed, and I was worried about him.

I checked my watch. Five minutes to nine. I clicked the cover shut and put it back in my pocket. Maybe, I tried to tell myself, he wouldn't show up.

That delusion lasted about thirty seconds.

A voice came from the darkness, a strangely soft one. "Take off your gun belt and throw it away."

I was loath to do it, but Blacke had told me to go along with Muller as far as I had to.

It occurred to me at this point that Blacke could be up on that hill with a Gatling gun and a regiment of cavalry, commanded by my father in person, and it would do me not the slightest bit of good if Muller took it into his head to shoot me

manded by my father in person, and it would do me not the
slightest bit of good if Muller took it into his head to shoot me
from behind the rock. He must have ridden up so as to be
blocked from my view by it, no doubt the reason he picked it for
a rendezvous in the first place.

I knew he hadn't been lying in wait for me, because I had
walked around the whole thing when I first arrived.

I went for the buckle of the gun belt.

"Slowly, now," Muller said.

I did it very slowly. I raised it out to arm's length so he could
see it in the moonlight, then tossed it away.

"Good," came the voice, and it sounded as if it honestly
approved of me, at least so far. "Now turn around and take off
your coat."

"It's going to get chilly now that the sun's down," I protested.

"You'll be a lot colder with holes in you. I just want to make
sure you've got nothing up your sleeve."

I certainly *hoped* I did, but in the more literal sense in which
Muller meant it, I was perfectly happy to humor him.

In my white shirt and silver vest in the moonlight, I must
have been a truly superb target.

"All right," I said. "Do I get to see you now?"

"You get to see more than that," he said, and to my surprise,
out of the darkness flew the stumbling figure of a woman. Jennie
Murdo had been flung from behind the rock and fell at my feet.

I bent to help her. She looked up at me with a face that
showed more misery than any I had ever seen. Whiter streaks
in the grime that covered it made it look as if a constant flow of
tears had eroded channels for themselves.

She said nothing, and as soon as I helped her to her feet,
she stood away from me, backing away until her husband told
her to stop.

"What is she doing here, Muller?" I asked. "I thought our
talk was supposed to be private."

"Don't worry about that," he said. "This is decision night for me."

With that, he made his first decision, to step out from behind the rock. At last, after having read, heard, and written about him, after having seen a corpse of his making and almost been killed myself by him, there he was.

My first reaction was to be shocked at how short he was. He was *tiny*. A foot shorter than I was, an inch or two shorter than his wife. This was not the sort of man to terrorize the West.

But that first impression held only for a second. Because however small, the buckskin-clad figure before me radiated power. It was there in the broad shoulders, in the aggressive, forward-leaning stance, and in the eyes that were visibly blue even in the pale light of the moon. Those eyes held anger and a trace of madness. They were the eyes of a man who had already done much, and who might do anything.

I had been doing my best to convince myself that the proposition Blacke had told me to offer the man was logical, reasonable, and the best Muller could expect from the rest of his life, considering how he had lived it so far.

Now I knew that none of those things mattered a damn to the man. Except while setting up and executing a crime, I doubt the man had ever looked forward more than five minutes.

"This is decision night," he said again. "This is the night I work it all out. What I do about the rest of the bastards who killed my son. What I do about my pretty little whore of a wife."

"Ben, I swear I never—"

"Shut up," he said. There was no rancor in his voice. He kept talking to his wife, though he never looked at her. "Maybe I even believe you. Who knows? That's another one of the decisions I have to make. Along with what I'm going to do with Sheriff Booker here."

"Deputy," I said.

Muller grinned. "Doesn't make any difference. Lobo Blacke was only a deputy U.S. marshal, and he's the one put me in jail."

Keeping his gun aimed steadily at my midsection, he scratched his jaw with his other hand.

"You may have noticed," he said, "that I'm not pondering anything with regard to Blacke. You might be wondering why that is."

I was willing to play along.

"Perhaps because now that he's a cripple, he's not worth the trouble," I suggested.

Muller shook his head in disappointment. "Hell, no. I'd dig up a corpse and shoot him if I had cause to. No. The reason I've got no quarrel with Blacke is that he played fair with me. I robbed the banks, and he tracked me down fairly, faced me, and caught me.

"Not like the cowards who killed my son. You know, in the time I was around, I never had to whip that kid? He was a good little boy, he had a good ma, and he would have grown up to be something. Maybe I could be remembered as his daddy instead of as 'the ace of bandits.' Isn't that what you called me?"

The gun seemed to jump a little.

"I made up a character," I said. "I just had him do a version of some of the things you did."

Muller laughed. It was low and smooth like every other sound he made.

"Don't worry, Deputy. I kind of enjoyed it."

It occurred to me that he was "kind of enjoying it" right now; that he wouldn't mind if we stood there chatting all night. I, on the other hand, hungered and thirsted to get to the point. I thought I ought to try to guide the conversation into the proper channel before Blacke went to sleep up there on his hilltop and this whole thing blew up in my face.

"Well," I said, "I know one decision you've made."

"What's that?"

"You've decided what to do about Lucius Jenkins."

"Oh, yeah. I decided that long ago. And you saved his life. I'm a mite unhappy about that."

"Why did you want to kill him?"

"Never mind about that."

I shook my head. "You're not making any sense, Muller. You're determined to kill him, and you're still protecting him."

Muller pursed his lips. "Maybe you better keep talking."

"Glad to," I said. "Jenkins has been the brains behind hundreds of crimes. Payroll jobs, bank robberies, stagecoach hijackings, train robberies. For a cut, he plans the action, arranges for bribes and other expenses, and helps the men who pull the jobs get rid of the loot."

"You seem to know a lot," Muller observed.

Out of the corner of my eye, I saw Jennie Murdo's hand steal to her mouth. After all she'd been through, there was still something that could shock her.

"You worked for him, too—"

"Not *for* him," Muller interrupted. "*With* him. I made my own plans. He helped with some inside knowledge. And as you say, he could turn certificates into hard money faster than any of us could."

"When you got caught, you could have sold him out—with evidence—and probably have gotten a lighter sentence. But you didn't."

"No, I did not. Jenkins said he'd see that Jennie and little Buck never wanted for anything. He said he'd see the boy set up in business, or put through a fancy college back east, if he had it in him to go. He said he'd look out for both of them. Instead, he let some bastard trick my wife into giving poison to my son."

Jennie Murdo made a sharp intake of breath, like someone who's just been stabbed.

"For that," Paul Muller went on, "he's going to die."

"Maybe," I said. "But he's got an army surrounding him

now, and lawmen from all over the territory are searching for you. There's only one chance for you to get him now."

Muller grinned. "Oh. So *you're* the mastermind now, huh?"

"You don't need to be a genius to see this, Muller. The one and only way for you to get your revenge on Jenkins is to turn yourself in and testify against him. You know enough about what he's done to make him die at the end of a rope, money or no money. I'll bet you do."

"Oh, I've got plenty enough for that, and I can tell you where to find evidence to back it up. There's just one trouble with your plan, Deputy. *I* die at the end of a rope, too. I don't hanker after that."

"Maybe you wouldn't. I can recruit a lot of influence in this territory. Could probably get it commuted to life in prison."

"As if that would be any better. Hah."

"Would you rather be backshot by some posse member out after a reward?"

He ignored that. Instead, he said, "This influence you can recruit. You talking about Lobo Blacke?"

"Him and a few others."

"Blacke. And you work for him. I'll bet this was his idea."

"I'm the law in Le Four just now," I said. "This is my responsibility."

"Bull. Blacke is calling your tune. I guess now that he's only half a man, he's got to play tricks, not face a man square like he did before." He sighed. "I guess I'll have to add him to my list after all. I'll leave a note on your body that says so."

Before he could do anything about it, though, Jennie Murdo said, "No!"

Again, he spoke to her without ever taking his eyes off me. "Don't tell me no, little darlin'. I'm still torn about what I'm going to do about you."

"I know," she said. "I know. I've been crying and weeping and so weak, you're afraid to take me along, and you won't leave me behind, so you figure you have to kill me."

"And you gave the poison to my son, don't forget. Accident or not, a ma's not supposed to do things like that."

"Yes, Ben, you're right, of course, but at least let me show you I won't be weeping anymore; let me show you I can be strong."

"How?"

"Let me kill Booker."

30

S H E   H E L D   O U T her hand and took a step in the direction
of her husband.

"They hang women, too, you know," Muller said.

My sentiments exactly. I decided that it was time for Blacke
to use his Winchester, but apparently he didn't. Of course, he
couldn't hear what was going on, and there was nothing about
the tableau we made that would *look* any more dangerous to me
from a distance.

"I know, Ben—Paul. I know that. Once I shot Booker, I
would hang if they caught us. You'd know you could trust me.
I'd have to stay with you forever and ever, and whatever crazy
things I've said from hurt and grief, that's where I've always
wanted to be."

Muller made a face, then shrugged. "All right, you shoot
him. But I'll hang on to this gun. You use his. It's over there
behind you."

She went and picked it up, held it in two hands, and stepped
toward me.

Would Blacke shoot a woman? Could he get two armed
people before one of them shot me? I had trusted in the man's
genius, but the genius seemed to be slipping.

She took another step.

"Don't get too close," Muller said in a tone of friendly advice. "You don't want him grabbing you, or I'd have to shoot you both. You can't miss him from there, anyway."

She took a tighter grip in the gun and said, "I'm sorry." For a second, I was looking down the barrel as it came past my face, then spun around rapidly and fired at Muller.

Hit him, too, in the gut, just below the sternum. From the way the blood gushed out, I knew he'd be dead in seconds, but in those seconds he could do plenty of damage with the gun he still clutched in his hand.

In fact, with his rapidly glazing eyes, he was trying to draw a bead on his terrified wife, who could now be a statue entitled *Horror*.

I ran over and knocked her down, and Paul Muller's last bullet roared over our heads.

When the echo of the shot died away, Muller snarled, "Bitch," and collapsed for the last time.

I left Jennie Murdo sobbing on the ground and went over to check Muller, just to make sure the ace of bandits didn't have one last trick up his sleeve.

He didn't. I got there just in time to hear his death rattle. I took the gun from his hand (even the grip was astonishingly tight) and turned back to his wife.

I'd made another mistake, one that, under different circumstances, might have killed me. I had forgotten to take the gun away from her.

She was on her feet now, still holding the gun. She was pointing it at her head.

Fatigued from a night of tension, fear, and violence, I was reacting now with exasperation.

"Now what?" I demanded.

"Stand back," she said. "I don't want to hurt you, Mr. Booker. I know you've been doing your best for all concerned."

"I appreciate your saying so, but why are you pointing a gun at yourself?"

She spoke to me between sniffles and sobs. "I've killed my son and my husband. Everyone I loved. Why should I live?"

I try to make a policy of not answering rhetorical questions, so I addressed myself to the first part of her utterance.

"Your son died by accident, Mrs. Murdo. You didn't kill him, whoever poisoned that medicine did. As for shooting your husband, you did it to save my life. And the Lord alone knows how many others."

"Yes," she said. "He was a monster. I have come to know that. But since he dragged me from my cottage the night he dropped that body in front of the sheriff's office . . . Seeing him again, I realized I still love him."

She was suddenly screaming. "What sort of woman can degrade herself enough to love someone like that?"

"All kinds," I said. "The reason we know that love is divine is that it makes no earthly sense."

"My love has not been divine," she said. "It has brought evil and misery, and the only person who could have redeemed it is dead. As I deserve to be."

She squeezed her eyes shut and touched the barrel of the gun to her head.

Absurdly, I wanted to point the gun I held at her and order her to stop, and I might have done that if the shot hadn't rung out.

In the event, I was aware of the effect of the shot before I heard the report. The arm crooked toward Jennie Murdo's temple straightened, and the gun went flying away. She was collapsing to the ground when the sound of the shot made its way to us. I was by her side before the echoes died away.

Kneeling beside the woman, I heard the voice of Lobo Blacke, faint with distance, but unmistakable, screaming at me.

"Dammit, Booker! Is she all right?"

I didn't answer right away because I still didn't know. She was bleeding profusely from just above the elbow. The bone didn't seem to be broken. I fixed my necktie above the wound for a tourniquet, then used my handkerchief to wipe blood away from the arm itself. I tore her sleeve away and saw that the bullet had passed right through.

Mercifully, she had fainted. I checked her pulse, heartbeat, and breathing, and they seemed to be fine. Another customer for Dr. Mayhew. Maybe she'd be lucky and remain unconscious through the carbolic.

"*Booker, God damn you to hell! Answer me!*"

I stood, cupped my hands to my mouth, and yelled in the direction of the hill, "*She'll be fine!*"

"*Good! Come and get me!*"

"*Right!*"

That ended the conversation between us for a while, which suited me fine because all this yelling was straining my throat.

Still, going to get Blacke was easier said than done. The first thing I did was to make sure I had both guns. Next, I went to where I had tethered Domingo. I was surprised for a second to see another horse, big and black, tied nearby. Then it occurred to me that Muller hadn't come here in a hansom cab, tipped the driver, and told him to pick him up in an hour or two.

I led Domingo around the rock, lifted Jennie Murdo up to the saddle, then climbed on behind her, much as I had with Lucius Jenkins the other day. I had the horse walk slowly up the hill to where Blacke waited.

Blacke waited.

"About time," he said as I carefully laid the wounded woman on the ground. "What's the matter with her?"

"You shot her," I said. "She's fainted."

"I'm sorry," Blacke said. He didn't sound all that sorry. "Shooting a gun out of a woman's hand at this distance, by moonlight, would take a better marksman than I am."

"I'm not complaining," I said. "She was on the verge of blowing her head off. A wounded arm is a small price to pay."

Blacke grunted. "She was about to blow her head off with *my gun*. I mean, the one I gave you. That gun never killed a woman yet, and I wanted to keep it that way."

Then he chuckled.

"But she's something, at that, isn't she? What did she do, tell Muller she'd kill you to prove herself to him?"

"Exactly."

"Then she turned around and let him have it. Clever woman."

"She doesn't think it's so wonderful as you seem to."

"You're wrong there, Booker. The whole reason she's as upset as she is, wanted to kill herself, is that she knows *precisely* how wonderful and clever she was, and she's ashamed of the pride she feels over it. And way down deep, Booker, everybody has a tiny part of his soul the devil never lets go of. That part might even have enjoyed it."

"How can you possibly know this?"

"Because it's just the way I felt the first time I killed a man."

Using his arms, Blacke forced his body around and up into a sitting position. "Now, will you please get Posy so we can get out of here?"

That was easy enough; all I had to do was whistle and Posy trotted up the hill. The hard part was getting the bulk of Lobo Blacke back up into the special saddle, but I managed it. By the time I had him tied in, Jennie Murdo was stirring.

"Take it easy, ma'am," Blacke said.

"My arm hurts."

"Yes, ma'am. You tried to shoot yourself."

"But I was aiming at my *head*."

"I've been around guns all my life," Blacke said, "and I know some strange things can happen."

And there *you* have it, I thought, the answer to the burning question of earlier in the evening. Lobo Blacke would indeed shoot a woman; he just wouldn't want her to know about it later.

I pictured Jennie Murdo whiling away the boring hours of her recovery trying to figure out just *how* she could have shot herself in the elbow of the arm that held the gun.

"Now," Blacke went on, "have you got that foolishness out of your head?"

She was too fuddled by pain to answer. I appropriated Blacke's neckerchief to make a sling for her, assured him she wouldn't try anything, at least for a while, and lifted her once more into the saddle.

A stop back at Bishop's Rock to sling Paul Muller over the back of his horse, and then we went back to town.

31

"SON OF A BITCH," Blacke breathed. "God damned son of a bitch."

"We certainly are being profane this evening," I said.

"Go to— Oh, put a sock in it, Booker. I've had a tough night, you know?"

"Yes," I said. "I think I was there. I think I was the one Paul Muller was about five seconds from shooting to death before his wife saved my life. Not the hero on the hilltop, mind you. His wife."

"I had a bead on him all the time, Booker. I never saw such a man for worrying as you are."

"Maybe you just never saw such a man for admitting it," I suggested.

Blacke ignored me.

"Oh, Lord, if we could have just taken the bastard alive. I could have gotten the location of the evidence from him, I know it."

We'd been back in Le Four for about an hour. Stick Witherspoon was back on duty inside the jail, Jennie Murdo had been left in the care of Dr. Mayhew ("You have done something I would never have dreamed possible, Mr. Booker—you are beginning to make me long for the days of Asa Harlan as sheriff"), the horses had been taken care of, and I had changed my clothes and washed various blood spatters off my hide.

Rebecca had taken Blacke away and tended to him as well. It is not, it seems, good for a paralyzed man to spend too much time prone, and Rebecca wanted to see if there had been any ill effects.

I wondered if the kiss she had given him earlier had been a topic of conversation between them.

If it had been, there was no indication of it when I joined Blacke in the composing room. Mrs. Sundberg had prepared a tray for us before going to bed, and we both dug in gratefully as we talked.

Blacke had just taken a large bite of a steak pie when I told him what Muller had said to me about Lucius Jenkins and his role in criminal activities throughout the West. That had brought forth not only the flow of profanity but a fine spraying of golden pastry crumbs.

"That close," Blacke went on. "That close to making some real progress in bringing Lucius to justice, and now it's gone. Why did you let her shoot him, Booker?"

I looked at the ceiling and cupped my chin in my hands.

"Hmmmm," I said. "That *is* a poser. Why did I let her shoot him? Let's see. He had a gun. She had a gun. I, following your instructions to the letter, did not have a gun. He, having heard me pass along the proposition you suggested, was about to ventilate my liver, and, incidentally, embark on a mission ending with your death immediately after. Golly, I give up. Why *did* I let her shoot him."

Blacke was smiling in spite of himself.

"All right, all right, I just get frustrated, is all."

"Things might not be as hopeless as you think."

"Why not?"

"Because before this, you've been hoping to find some evidence that Lucius Jenkins is the criminal mastermind you're sure he is. Now you *know* it exists."

Blacke nodded. "That's a fact, isn't it?"

"Not only that," I went on. "You know the evidence is something—or someone—that Paul Muller knew about and could produce if he wanted to. So all you have to do is imagine what and where that might be, then ask me nicely to go bring it back for you."

"Yeah," Blacke said. "That's all." He grunted. "Still, it's a place to start. Shouldn't be impossible. I know Lucius, and I know Muller. What kind of evidence could there be . . . ? Evidence that Muller would recognize as evidence, I mean. . . ."

His voice drifted off the way it did. Usually, I just let him muse, but this time I interrupted.

"Excuse me. Blacke?"

He jumped. "Yes, yes, what is it?"

"Well, the Lucius Jenkins hunt is all well and good, but we had fifteen murders in this jurisdiction—*my* jurisdiction, God help me—and we've cleaned up one of them. We still have all the poisonings to deal with. Or should I not say 'we.' "

Blacke pushed his hands flat down on the table to straighten his back, then gave a huge sigh.

"No, it's okay to say 'we.' In fact, I guess you're right. Now that Muller's taken care of, we might as well get this taken care of as soon as we can."

"We can?"

"We can what?"

"We can take care of it?"

He shrugged. "As well as we'll ever be able to. It depends how people react, and it's going to be a lot of show for damn little substance. We'll have to take a chance."

"You scare me to death when you say that."

He grinned at me. "You're the sheriff. Practically everything that has to be done has to be done on your authority. You can always say no."

"This is just your subtle way of telling me that if whatever it is you're planning ends in tragedy or disaster, I'm the one holding the bag."

Blacke sighed. Suddenly he looked very old.

"It's a tragedy already, Booker. All we can do is clean up after."

He slumped in his wheelchair for a few seconds, then gave a quick sharp nod to rouse himself.

"So let's get going," he said.

"As soon as you tell me what needs to be done. And why."

And he told me. Until then, I hadn't really believed that this thing was ever going to end, not in my heart. Now, though he had convinced me he had the answer, I didn't think anyone else in town was going to believe it. Was there, I wondered, such a thing as an anti–lynch mob?

Fortunately, there was enough work to do to keep my mind off the problem. Once again, I spent the night going through town, waking people up, though not on the scale, or with the degree of panic, as on the night of the poisonings.

I woke Clay Becker, the town carpenter, in his shop near the livery stable, and told him I wanted a platform put up in front of the sheriff's office.

He grinned at me. He grins quite a bit, though he lacks a sufficient number of teeth to make seeing him grin a truly pleasant experience.

"With a trapdoor, Cap'n?" He called everybody "cap'n." "You fixing to hang somebody?"

"A trapdoor won't be necessary," I said. "But I want a ramp."

"A ramp?"

"Yes, a nice, shallow ramp, so that Lobo Blacke can get up on the thing without being carried."

Clay rubbed an unshaven cheek. "When do you want this by?"

"As early as possible. Before noon."

He shook his head. "Can't do it," he said. "Not without help."

"I'll get you help."

"I don't just mean two hands and a body, Mr. Booker. I mean somebody as knows what he's doing."

"I'll get one. Where do you want me to have him meet you?"

"Right here. He can help me load lumber on the wagon."

Then we haggled over the price for a minute or two, ending up at the price we'd both known from the start he was going to get.

I was just turning to go when I thought of something that gave me a chill.

I turned back to the carpenter.

"Clay," I said, "when you measure a piece of wood, and you want to mark it, what do you use?"

"I generally score it with a nail," he said, "and cut along the scratch. Unless I'm measuring on a surface that will show. Then I use chalk. Why?" I saw the toothless grin again. "Thinking of 'prenticing out to me?"

"Do you ever use a carpenter's pencil?"

"Naw. Chalk is cheap, and I got to buy nails, anyway. Why should I spend money on something fancy I don't need?"

I breathed a little easier. I knew Clay hadn't been getting them through the general store, but it was best to make sure.

"All right. I'll have Junior Simpkins meet you here as soon as he can."

"Little Billy Simpkins? He used to hang around here all the time. He knows what he's doing all right."

I had to rouse half the boardinghouse before I got a chance to talk to Junior Simpkins. Finally, after the porter, the proprietor, and several guests had angrily asked the noisy visitor what he wanted (one teatotaling Methodist circuit rider nearly threw a chamber pot at my head before it sank in that I was the Law, there on official business), I was ushered into Junior Simpkins's room.

He was sitting up in bed, blinking sleepily, still too tired to realize that the thing in his left eye he couldn't seem to blink away was the tassel of his nightcap. His big white feet protruded from the bottom of his nightshirt and rested on the oval rug alongside the bed.

"Sorry to bother you, " I said. "But I need your help."

"Booker?" he said. The fog had lifted sufficiently for him to push the tassel away from his eyes. "What? What is it?"

"I've just come from Clay Becker's," I said.

Sleepily, Junior showed me a grin very similar to that of the old man's, except that it had more teeth.

"Clay Becker," he said. "How is he?"

"I've been here less than a year, but I'd venture to say he's the same as ever."

"I've been so preoccupied here, I never got around to visiting him."

"Well, if you're willing to help, you'll be working with him."

"What do you mean?"

I told him about the platform and the ramp.

He thought it over. "The ramp will be the tricky part. What do you want this thing for?"

"I've got to talk to as many people in town as I can reach. Show them a few things. Lobo Blacke wants to speak to them, too. We figure building the thing through the night and morning will attract the crowd, and the platform will give us a good spot to speak from."

"Oh, I thought . . ."

"Can't hang anybody without a trial," I said.

"No, no. Of course not."

"Will you help?"

"Sure I will. If only for the chance to work on a project with old Clay again."

I told him how much I was paying Clay Becker, and asked if he'd be happy with the same.

"I'm not doing this for money," he said. "Keep mine. No. I've got a better idea. Give my money to my stepmother, for her orphanage fund." He started to laugh. "That ought to confuse her."

I told him it would be the way he wanted it.

The next stop was the livery stable. I woke up Jackson Watford and asked him if he could send one of his helpers with a note from me out to Bellevue. He was all business, and instantly named a price for himself, plus a bonus for the rider. There would be no haggling. I often thought Watford spent all his spare time imagining anything that might possibly happen to him and putting a price on it.

It was a fair price, and I paid it—or rather, the town did. It was sort of intoxicating, spending money that didn't belong to me. I was beginning to understand why people went into politics.

I scribbled a note while Watford summoned one of his men. I told Lucius Jenkins that Paul Muller was dead and that I had spoken to him before he died, and some things would be declaimed in front of the sheriff's office in the morning that he might be interested in hearing if he were well enough to travel.

There, I thought, that ought to fetch him. A string of truths that added up to a barefaced lie. Still, though he might have lucked his way through Blacke's clutches this time, Lucius Jenkins should still be around for the finish of the case that had brought him so close to disaster.

I handed the note to Watford's assistant, a young Negro lately out of the cavalry, then left the stable.

I saw a fire roaring away, well down Main Street.

"Now what?" I yelled, and ran down the street.

As I got closer, though, I saw that it wasn't a building that was on fire, it was a huge pile of scrap wood out in the middle of the dusty street, directly in front of the sheriff's office.

Clay Becker and Junior Simpkins were there, sinking a stout piece of lumber into the earth.

"What the hell is *that*?" I yelled over the crackling of the flames.

"It's light to work by," Clay said. "I can't build no platform in the dark, let alone a ramp."

Junior was almost apologetic. "You said you wanted to attract a crowd."

I looked around and saw that there were already faces in the window, looking at the fire and at the construction project. And, I sheepishly admitted to myself, it had never occurred to me that the men would need light to see by.

"Good," I said. "Carry on."

I went to walk on, but Junior asked me to wait a minute.

"I want to talk to you about that ramp. I've got an idea about that. . . ."

By the time he finished telling me, I was grinning. I told him to go ahead, then I went to tell Blacke that everything was in hand.

32

BY TEN O'CLOCK, when the platform was finished (there was not ramp), a crowd had gathered that was so large, I almost wished I had something to sell them. Enterprising merchants were moving among them, selling pies, lemonade, and parasols against the sun, and anything else they could turn a profit on. It was something to see.

From my vantage point from my third-floor window, I could see all the milling around. If I opened the window, no doubt I could hear a choice selection of rumors, too, but I didn't want to show myself.

Every few seconds, I looked down the street toward the *Witness* office, waiting for the signal that Blacke had decided it was time to start.

As usual, Blacke was delaying long enough to drive me crazy. He always said he did it to unsettle his opponent, but all I know for sure is that he unsettled me.

I scanned the crowd for familiar faces, and they were all there. Lucius Jenkins was sitting on a buckboard on the far side of the street, still too dizzy to stand for a long time. Junior Simpkins was talking to him, and Lucius looked sour. Stu Burkhart was wandering, whispering in ears. He looked as if he hoped he'd get another chance to lynch somebody. And, I was glad to see, Harold Collier had heard about this and had come to town to see the end of it. He had decided to brazen it out, his blue face and hands quite pretty in the sunlight, if you could forget what color they were supposed to be. Harold was eating a piece of pie and talking to old Mrs. Simpkins, who was smiling benignly at him.

She wasn't the only relative of a poisoning victim in the crowd; they were all there, as far as I could tell, even a grim-faced Jennie Murdo, who had either fled or been let out of Dr. Mayhew's house. I could ask him; the doctor was in the building, pressed into service once more, but I decided it didn't matter. If anyone should be there for the finish, it should be Jennie Murdo.

I checked the *Witness* office again. Merton Mayhew came out, looked at my window, and waved his cap.

"All right," I said to the emptiness of the room. I took a deep breath and turned away from the window.

At Daisy Herkimer's door, I knocked and said, "It's time." I unlocked the door, and she came out, demurely dressed in one of Rebecca's frocks.

"How do I look?" she asked.

"You look wonderful. Let's go."

"I'm a little scared," she admitted.

So was I, but I didn't say so. Instead, I said, "There's nothing to worry about," and reminded myself of Lobo Blacke. "After this morning, it will be all over."

"I hope so." She gave me a little kiss, and off we went.

Theophrastus Herkimer was shaved pink, and his clothes had been brushed, and instead of the frightened little man he'd been over the past few days, one could almost see the "miracle worker" who'd first come to town.

He and Mayhew were discussing various ways of reducing a fever when Daisy and I appeared, and Herkimer broke off the discussion to run to his daughter and take her in his arms.

"Darling, the doctor says we are to have complete confidence in Mr. Blacke and Mr. Booker; that they are geniuses in their way, and will not fail."

I looked at Mayhew. "Laying it on a bit thick, aren't you, Doctor?"

The cadaverous face was impassive. "I am a man of science. I report what I see."

Stick Witherspoon was standing by the door, looking at his nails. A Winchester, twin of the one Blacke had used last night, was leaning against the door frame. It was Stick's assigned task to start the show, but if he felt nervous about it, it wasn't evident.

"Ready, Stick?"

"Been ready," he replied.

"Go ahead, then."

He began to unbolt the door as I came to join him. I handed him the rifle, then let him out, quickly closing and relocking the door.

Stick walked quietly to the side of the platform where the stairs had been built, and mounted to the top. From behind, I could see him standing there, rifle in the crook of his arm, looking at the crowd, ready and formidable without being overly threatening.

Stick's appearance on the platform changed the nature of the crowd noise, but the appearance of Lobo Blacke hushed them completely. Blacke wasn't wearing his usual business garb, suit jacket, vest, and tie. He was wearing a gray shirt and a battered black hat on his head. Even with the gray blanket across his legs, it was easy to imagine the lawman who had brought to justice some of the West's worst outlaws.

Rebecca pushed the wheelchair through the crowd, which parted for him like the Red Sea before Moses. Blacke paid no attention to anyone, but stared grimly straight ahead.

Seeing the deadly dignity of that stare and the effect it had on the crowd, I began to worry about the little trick I'd pulled about the ramp.

Junior Simpkins's idea had been to build, instead of a ramp, which would take metering and sanding and many other things

I did not understand and that were difficult to do by firelight, a platform hoist to majestically *elevate* Blacke to his speaking perch.

And in practice it worked out that way. Blacke understood instantly, had Rebecca wheel him onto the lift, and sat like a sultan while Clay Becker and Junior winched them smoothly to the top and held them there while Rebecca wheeled him onto the platform proper. Then she went down the stairs and took her station there.

And once again, Blacke waited. We could only see him from behind, but I knew he was staring out at the crowd with that look he had that made you wonder what you ought to be afraid you did. The silence was deafening, and the tension immense.

Then, at the point at which it was taking all my strength not to open the door and scream *"Get on with it!"* he began to speak.

"What brings you out here today?" he asked conversationally. "Curiosity, or bloodlust?"

Blacke had the kind of voice that could fill whatever amount of space it needed to. It not only filled Main Street, it filtered through the doors and windows of the jail with no trouble at all.

There was a murmur from the crowd.

Blacke cut them off with a wave of his hand.

"Don't bother to answer," he said. "It doesn't matter. This morning, Mr. Booker and I are going to satisfy both. And in the process, change this town back from a pack of nervous animals to the decent place it was before this tragedy happened.

"Now, I'm going to bring out to this platform the people you tried to kill the other night, two people I can now prove are perfectly innocent. So at least you don't have that on your consciences.

"Booker! Bring out Herkimer and the princess!"

I was already opening the door. I had my gun out of my holster and into my hand. Dr. Mayhew had a spare in his hand. He looked ludicrous with a gun, but he assured me he knew how to use it, and would, if necessary. I expected some more sarcasm, along the lines of what I'd heard last night when I brought him the corpse of Paul Muller for autopsy, but apparently the seriousness of the current situation restrained him.

As soon as the door swung open, Stick, on the platform, snapped the Winchester to his shoulder and scanned the crowd through its sights.

As the four of us walked the short distance from the door to the platform stairs, I looked around for Stu Burkhart and found him whispering urgently to a couple of his neighbors, who were simultaneously ignoring him and trying to edge away from him. That was a good sign.

At the bottom of the stairs, Rebecca came forward and pressed Daisy's hand encouragingly. Daisy gave her a little smile in reply, and then the doctor stayed at the bottom of the stairs looking vigilantly for someone who needed to be shot, while Herkimer, his daughter, and I joined Blacke.

We stood off to Blacke's left while Stick, on his right, slowly lowered the rifle to its previous position.

"These are the people," Blacke said, "that you wanted to string up without a trial. Wanted to hang them, even though five minutes of thought would have shown you they were the *least* likely people to have poisoned the medicine."

He went on to explain how Herkimer had never been to Le Four before, could have no grudges against the place or anybody in it, and how it would be total stupidity to put the poison in his own elixir.

"But suppose he did. Suppose he poisoned the mixture, knowing that before the night was out people would begin to start dying of it. What would he do then? Run for his life? Or calmly eat a meal, and go to sleep in the exact spot he'd doled out the poison from?"

Blacke leaned over the arm of his wheelchair and spat on the fresh clean wood.

"But you people didn't want to think. You just wanted to do something to make yourselves feel better. I don't blame the bereaved as much as I blame the bloodthirsty fools who led the mob. As much as I blame, say ..." Blacke's voice was suddenly a lash. "*You*, Stu Burkhart!"

I could actually see Burkhart's legs begin to quake. "You got—"

His voice was a squeak. He swallowed hard and tried again. "You got no call to talk to me like that, Blacke." It was a little better that time.

"I'll talk to you any way I damn please," Blacke told him. "Not only are you a bloodthirsty coward for leading a lynch mob, you're a fool. You *saw* the actual killer sneaking out of Herkimer's wagon, but you didn't care a damn about that. You just wanted somebody hanged."

"I just wanted justice," Burkhart said.

"You keep your mouth shut, little man," Blacke said, "or you may get it someday."

That brought a nervous laugh from the crowd.

"I don't know if Burkhart ever got around to telling any of the rest of you, but he told Deputy Booker even before anyone was poisoned that he saw a small figure in a long, hooded coat, slipping out of Herkimer's wagon and into the shadows of the grove."

A voice came from somewhere on the far side of the street. "Stu would tell anybody anything if it made him look like a big man."

"He could be ten feet tall, and nobody would mistake that pissant for a big man," Blacke said. "But in this case, we can believe him, because another witness claims to have seen the same thing."

He let that sink in for a few seconds, then said, "Isn't that right, Mrs. Simpkins."

The old woman blushed and murmured something about not wanting to be singled out.

Blacke gave her a big grin. "Nonsense," he said. "Just think of all of us as a big class. Dr. Mayhew, help her up on the platform so everyone can hear her."

She tried to demur, but no one would have any of it, so to the sound of applause, the ex-schoolmarm climbed up to the platform.

33

IN DEFERENCE TO Mrs. Simpkins's age, a chair was produced for her from somewhere, and she sat down next to Blacke. At his urging, she repeated her story of the figure leaving the wagon, confirming in every detail Stu Burkhart's story.

"So," Blacke concluded, "Stu may be a blowhard, but in this case I'm sure he's telling the truth. Mrs. Simpkins, please stay right there, because I'll have to ask you another question later."

Blacke took off his hat for a second and mopped his brow on his sleeve. He put the hat back on and addressed the crowd again.

"Next, we come to Harold Collier. Mr. Collier!"

While Blacke was talking, the blue man had been relatively free from the curious stares of his neighbors. Now, with the mention of his name, *all* eyes were on him, and he seemed to shrink away from them.

"Mr. Collier," Blacke said again, "we've not met before, and I want to tell you what a pleasure it is for me. There are many kinds of heroism, and you're showing us one kind today, and not the easiest kind, either."

"I just got tired of hiding," Harold Collier said. His tone and gestures would have gone perfectly with a blush, but of course that was impossible to tell.

"That's all right," Blacke said. "Practically everything that gets done in this world happens because somebody gets tired of something or other. This little gathering is taking place because Deputy Booker got tired of watching his back in case the hopped-up fools in this town got violent again, and we're all tired of breathing the same air as the killer, aren't we?"

There was a murmur of assent.

Blacke led Collier to tell about the note, and how curiosity and pent-up anger led the blue man to come to the medicine show.

"But it wasn't the one who'd sold you the tainted medicine, was it?"

"Hell, no. Never saw this one before. Or since, until this morning."

"All right. I want to talk about the note you got. You people listen carefully."

He hadn't had to tell them that. They were so silent, you could hear the horses whicker and the birds sing.

"For one thing, it was an out-and-out lie. And the only thing it achieved was to get Harold Collier out to the grove. Why go to the trouble? Just a precaution. Someone else for you to suspect—and possibly lynch—if for some reason the innocence of Dr. Herkimer was obvious."

Blacke let them think about that for a minute.

"The sending of that note shows that this murder was already planned. It was planned at least as soon as it was known that the medicine show was coming to town. Most probably, it had been planned weeks before, and was just waiting for a medicine man to show up."

"But *why*?" It was Jennie Murdo. Mindless of the bumps and jostles to her injured arm, she was fighting her way through the crowd to get closer to the platform.

"*Why*?" she demanded again. "My boy never hurt anybody in his life. He was a good boy, and friendly. Why would someone plan for weeks to kill him? And all these other people? What could somebody possibly gain by killing my boy?"

"Confusion," Blacke said simply. "I'm sorry, ma'am, but like thirteen of the deaths, your boy was killed by chance, more or less at random, to provide a smoke screen for the murder the killer really did want to commit."

"My God," Jennie Murdo breathed, and staggered back. Dr. Mayhew ran over and caught her and had her sit down in the steps.

Blacke wheeled himself forward a foot or two to make sure she was all right, then resumed his prior position and went on.

"Thirteen killed so that a fourteenth could safely be killed. Early on, Booker realized he was dealing with a monster without conscience, and it would take all his efforts to bring this monster to justice. He could have used more help and trust from the town, but forget that for now."

He certainly was rubbing it in, I thought. Still, maybe if he did it enough, the lesson would take. I also liked his reconstruction of my mental processes. I hadn't realized I was so brilliant.

"But," Blacke said. "I'm getting ahead of myself. I'm still talking about the note. There are a couple of things you'll have to take my word for, but the jury will get a good look at them at the trial.

"First of all, the letters are made the way Mrs. Simpkins taught children to print around here for years. That means the killer has to be at least thirty years old, and someone who's been around Le Four a long time.

"Second, the note is written in pencil. Now, pencils aren't *unknown* in our fair community, but they're rare. But there's more. By careful examination, Booker decided that this note was written with a special kind of pencil, rectangular instead of round, or, you know, with six sides. Makes a special kind of mark, you see, when you use it to make letters.

"Of course, the killer wasn't used to making letters with it."

There was a bit of a commotion behind the platform, nothing much. I was sure Junior and Clay Becker would call for help if they needed it.

Blacke must have been thinking the same way, if he heard it at all, because he kept right on.

"Now, it so happens that there's somebody in town who knows all about this kind of pencil—"

"*You son of a BITCH!*"

I turned to see Junior Simpkins clambering over the edge of the platform, his eyes red with anger, riveted on Lobo Blacke.

Quickly, I stepped in front of the charging carpenter. He reached out a hand to my chest, as though he were going to push me aside like a swinging door. I grabbed the hand, stepped sideways, and yanked hard.

That pulled him off balance, and got his attention. He looked at me dully. All right, his eyes seemed to say. If he had to deal with me before he tore Blacke limb from useless limb, so be it.

He pulled back a hard right hand and aimed it for my face. Big as Junior was, it might have killed me if it had landed, but it took longer to get there than the Prairie Comet takes to get from St. Paul to Le Four.

I ducked the first and sent a right hand into his stomach. It went in a long way, but it didn't seem to affect him very much. I planted one on his nose that did better.

It was in moments like these (and very seldom otherwise) that I was grateful for my father's incessant training in boxing and other forms of fighting, clean and dirty.

For his part, Junior's smarting nose convinced him that boxing wasn't the way to go, and growling something about being set up and trapped, he wrapped me up in a bear hug. He didn't, however, pin my arms, and I was able to give him an open-handed slap on both ears, forcing air in against his eardrums. He shouted in pain and twisted around, just before, still holding tightly to me, he fell backward off the platform.

It was a good eight-foot fall. He landed on his back with my weight directly on top of him, and that was the effective ending of the fight.

Junior was making terrible wheezing noises as I peeled his now limp arms from me and stood up. His face was red, and his eyes were popping. He'd obviously had the wind knocked out of him.

I resisted an impulse to kick the fool a few times while he was lying there. Instead, I went over to him, grabbed his belt buckle with two hands, and pulled. That in turn changed the shape of his chest cavity and let air into his collapsed lungs. Junior was beginning to recover even before Dr. Mayhew could tell me not to do what I'd already done.

"He might have had a broken rib. You might have injured him badly."

"He still has to breathe," I pointed out. I turned to Junior, who was regaining some interest in the world beyond his lungs. "Any pain? Think you've got a broken rib?"

Junior shook his head and made motions as if he wanted to get up.

"Just lie there for a minute. Catch your breath. Avoid getting kicked or shot. Just listen carefully to the following question: What the hell was that all about?"

Junior had enough breath by now to sound hurt. "He was about to accuse me of killing all those people. Of killing my *father!*"

"He was not, you idiot!"

"He wasn't?" Junior sounded suspicious.

"Were you, Blacke?"

"No," Blacke said. "I wasn't. Never crossed my mind. You didn't do it. You were in Denver. That's been triple-checked."

"Oh," Junior said. He looked about him sheepishly. "Golly. I'm sorry."

"That's all right," Blacke said gently. "May I go on with what I wanted to say?"

"What? Oh. Sure. But all that stuff about carpenter's pencils made me nervous. . . ."

Roaring physical aggression was an interesting definition of "nervous," but if Blacke was willing to let it pass, I would go along.

Blacke was being (for him) supernaturally patient. His voice was calm as he said, "I'll make everything clear in a moment."

He raised his head once more, to take in the whole crowd.

"As I was about to say, Junior Simpkins is a master carpenter and furniture smith, with a thriving business down in Denver. He swears by carpenter's pencils, and used them in Le Four before he left, then he was learning his craft. He told Booker that he used to buy dozens of them at a time."

He fixed his eyes on Junior. "Now. Mr. Simpkins, when you left town, you were in a bit of a hurry, weren't you?"

"Uh, yes. There had been family unpleasantness. I don't want to talk about it."

"We don't need any details," Blacke assured him. "I just want to know if you took the time to pack all the carpenter's pencils you'd accumulated when you left."

"No. I threw some clothes in a suitcase and went to the train station."

"Any idea what happened to the ones you left behind?"

"Sure. There's three boxes on the shelf of the closet of my old room. It's been a storeroom since I left. I thought of taking them along this time, but I was afraid it would have caused trouble with my stepmother."

"Not this time," Blacke said. "She would have urged you to take them with you, if she'd known you were thinking about it. It would have helped her in setting you up as another potential murderer. And it would have removed evidence, since she undoubtedly used one of those pencils to write the note to Harold Collier.

The crowd gasped. Gloria Simpkins, who had been sitting quietly through all this, shot up from her chair.

"Disgusting!" she snapped. "I'll not sit still for this."

But she had nowhere to go. She was too old and brittle to jump down from the platform, and I was sprinting up the stairs to cut her off there.

I took her firmly by her thin wrists and looked into the deceptively mild blue eyes.

"Gloria Simpkins," I said. "I arrest you for the murders of William Simpkins, Buck Murdo, Jack Hennessy, Beatrice Dixon, Amos Jacobs . . ."

34

"NONSENSE!" MRS. SIMPKINS snapped. Very confident, very schoolmarmish. "You should be ashamed of yourself. Had you been in my class, young man, I would have taught you better. You must apologize right now to the good people of the town for wasting their time on such malicious foolishness. Both of you."

Blacke was unimpressed. "Tell me again about the figure you saw near the wagon," he said.

"I have said all I am going to say until I instruct my attorney to sue you for slander." Mrs. Simpkins folded her hands across her thin chest and raised her chin in the air.

"It doesn't matter," Blacke said.

It mattered to me. A crowd is a high-strung animal, and this one was getting restless again, on the verge of getting ugly. This sweet-looking little old lady, the one who had taught them to read and write and figure, a murderer?

"You told Booker you saw what Stu Burkhart saw—the silhouette of a small, hooded figure in a long coat.

"That was even before we knew anyone had been poisoned. But when the dying started, and we were thinking of a vicious killer, we didn't think of a woman. Didn't want to, at least not at first. But the description of a silhouette works just as well for a small, slight woman with her shawl up over her head."

The animal that was the crowd stopped to listen.

"And when Booker talked to you the next day, and you knew that you'd been seen, you did something brilliant. *You said you'd seen the figure, too.* With one subtle touch, you changed yourself from a suspect to a witness."

She sniffed. "I will own your newspaper before the summer is out, Mr. Blacke. You will be living on charity."

"Maybe so," Blacke said. "But if we're going to do this, let's do it right."

He continued to address his words to Mrs. Simpkins, but he was looking at the crowd, fixing them, one after another, with a particularly intense stare.

"But it just couldn't last, Mrs. Simpkins. You tried to be too thorough, too subtle. That note to Harold Collier was printed in the unusual style you developed. The natural assumption was that it was written by one of your students—but why not by you, personally?

"Again, the note was written with that special carpenter's pencil—do you generally use a distinctive color ink?"

"Purple," Junior Simpkins said. "Usually purple ink."

His stepmother shot him a look of purest hatred. A lot of people in the crowd saw it, and now Blacke had another card to play.

But the note was still unfinished business. "You didn't want to use the ink that might point to you. You didn't want to be seen buying a kind of ink that would match the note. You didn't want to be seen buying a pencil. But you did want to get that note to Harold Collier."

"But as we've seen, you had access to a number of pencils, the rectangular kind, left behind by your stepson. You simply used one of those, never thinking of the distinctive mark it would make."

"And now, we come to why." Blacke's voice had dropped low when he said that, and the townspeople were straining to listen. "The answer is that you wanted to kill your husband."

Mrs. Simpkins continued to look at the sky.

"Big Bill Simpkins was a sick man," Blacke said. "Do you agree, Dr. Mayhew?"

"Examining him in the throes of the poison, and during the autopsy later, I found two cancerous tumors, either of which would have killed him within a year."

Addressing God or the world at large in a breezy voice, the old woman said, "Then I had no reason to kill him, did I?"

Blacke shrugged. "*Within a year*, the doctor said. A lot can happen in a year. For instance, a dying man can start to miss his son. The son you hated and drove away, years ago. They might exchange letters; they might become reconciled."

Down below, I could see Junior Simpkins's mouth form the words "Oh, Dad."

"He might," Blacke went on, "start talking about changing his will so that his son inherited his estate, or a goodly portion of it."

Blacke wheeled his chair around so that he was facing Mrs. Simpkins, even if we wouldn't look at him.

"Who was the very first to die of the poison? Big Bill Simpkins. Who benefited from his death? Just his widow. Who watched him, and thirteen other innocent people in this town, including an innocent little boy, die without shedding so much as a tear? *You* did, Mrs. Simpkins. Who, thinking herself smarter than all the people she'd taught over the years, left a trail a mile wide the moment anybody thought to look for it? *You.*"

Mrs. Simpkins refused to look at him, but her small frame was starting to shake, and her face was dark with anger.

"And why did you kill your husband and all these innocent people? Greed. Greed and spite. You couldn't stand to see a man reconciled with his son. You couldn't stand the thought of the son getting hold of more than a tiny bit of all that lovely money. So you killed, and killed, and *killed* so that you could have it all.

"And did it touch you at all, Mrs. Simpkins? Maybe late at night, when you're gloating over how rich and powerful you're going to be; about how you're going to have children to rule again, a whole buildingful, with no parents to look out for them. And if you take a dislike to one of them, the way you did to Junior Simpkins, why you can just poison them, too.

"In those times, do you ever hear the screams of the people you poisoned, or the sobs of their loved ones? When the voice of little Buck Murdo asks you why you killed him, is he happy with the answer 'I wanted the money'?"

By now, I thought Mrs. Simpkins was going to shake herself right off the platform. Instead, she finally looked at Blacke.

"No!" she shouted. "No, no, *no!*"

"He's not happy with the answer?" Blacke said softly. "I wouldn't have thought so."

"I hear no voices! I didn't kill those people! It was Destiny!"

"Destiny?"

"Yes, you fool Destiny. My orphanage was destined to be, and Simpkins had promised! When he decided to break his promise, he had to die, so that destiny would be fulfilled! And I knew others had to die, so that I'd be free to fulfill it.

"But I killed no one, and marked no one for death. I simply added the poison to that miserable charlatan's mixture. *God* chose the victims, don't you see? That way, only those *destined* to die would be taken, and I could carry on my work."

Jennie Murdo began to scream and try to get up the platform. One-armed as she was, if she'd made it up there, she would have made any lynch mob superfluous. Dr. Mayhew wrapped her up in his long arms and spoke soothingly to her.

He looked up at Blacke and me. "Do you need me anymore?"

"No, I think it's under control here," I said. "Take care of her."

"I'll help you," Junior Simpkins said simply, and the two of them led the woman away to the doctor's office.

"I guess," Blacke said rather superfluously, "that's about it. We're going to lock her up now. You can all go home."

But they didn't, not quite yet. They watched as the princess came over and gave me an enthusiastic kiss, in front of God and everybody. Her father shook my hand vigorously, decided that wasn't enough, and embraced me.

"Mingle with the crowd," I suggested. "See if anybody around here is man enough to apologize."

It could be Herkimer didn't want to have his faith in mankind shaken any further than it already was, but he didn't take me up on my suggestion. Instead, he and his daughter followed quietly as Stick and I, each holding an arm, escorted a proud and defiant Mrs. Simpkins to her destiny in the town jail.

The crowd melted away almost before we had the door closed. I was about to tell the Herkimers they were free to go when I heard Lobo Blacke's voice calling from outside. "Hey! Hey! Booker, goddammit!"

Sheepishly, I went outside and winched him down from the platform.

35

"PAPERS ARE SELLING like lemonade on a hot day," Merton told me.

"Good," I said.

He scratched his head. "I don't get it, though. Everybody was right there and saw what happened."

"That's just it," Blacke said. "They were part of it, they want to see it all written down for the ages. They feel like the story's about them."

"I hope nothing like this ever happens around here again," Merton said. He got enthusiastic amens from Blacke, Rebecca, and me.

A lot had happened over the last couple of days. I, with absolutely no reluctance whatever, had hung up my badge for good. Not only had the marshal arrived, but Asa Harlan was back on his feet. Jennie Murdo had made herself a black dress and gotten on the train to go back to Denver. She had a large draft on a Denver bank to take with her, provided by Lucius Jenkins. It was seen as generosity and maybe it even was, but I think it was a gratitude payment for her having gotten rid of her husband and all the potential embarrassments he could have caused Jenkins.

Jenkins had another talk with me, too. Once again, he offered me money, land, power, and his daughter's hand (and any other body parts I might take a fancy to) to leave Blacke and come work for him. I found the whole thing vaguely distasteful, but I told him I'd think about it.

And I had been. The role of spy does not exactly appeal to me, but it might be the only way to bring Jenkins to justice, a cause that was beginning to obsess me as much as it did the man in the wheelchair. I'd have to talk it over with Blacke.

And now, it was time to say good-bye to Dr. Theophrastus Herkimer and the princess. The colorful wagon, looking somehow duller and smaller after its days locked up, was standing in front of the sheriff's office. The Herkimers, having at last completed the legal requirements, were loading belongings into the wagon.

They attracted no attention whatsoever from the people of the town, except for an occasional furtive, guilty glance.

I held the door for Blacke and Rebecca; Merton followed.

Daisy met me halfway across the street and gave me another resounding kiss. I could feel waves of disapproval coming from Rebecca and Blacke.

"I'm gonna miss you," Daisy said.

Merton goggled. "You can *talk!*"

"How about that?" she said playfully, and kissed him, too. I thought the boy was going to melt. I had not known a human being was capable of turning quite that color.

"The medicine show circuit is gonna seem awfully dull after this," she said.

"The dullness will be welcome," her father said. "In a year or so, we'll have enough to settle down. If you didn't already have such a magnificent physician here already, I might come back."

"Heck," Merton said, in a voice that was still slightly hoarse. "Dad's always complaining he's got more work than he can handle."

The medicine man smiled at him. "You're a generous lad,

and your father is a great man. Perhaps I shall correspond with him. I find I've missed talking to medical colleagues."

"I'm glad to be going, in one way," Daisy said.

"What's that?" Rebecca asked. All her scorn of Daisy's displays of affection seemed to be reserved for me. For Daisy, she had nothing but indulgent friendship.

"Gettin' out from under the same roof as that crazy woman. All she does is read the Bible out loud and say nobody can do anything to her because of her Destiny."

Blacke grunted. I said, "Well, you can write about it in your book."

"What are you talking about, Quinn Booker?" Daisy said.

"When you settle down, you should write a book about your adventures. You could call it *Princess Daisy*."

Bewildered, she looked at me for a few seconds. Then she laughed.

I told her I supposed she was right. Then, with handshakes and more kisses all around, Daisy and her father boarded the wagon and drove off.

We stood there in the road watching them go.

Blacke grunted again.

"Are you in pain?" I asked him.

"Just from you," he said.

"Then why are you grunting?"

"I'm thinking about Destiny."

"What about it?"

"I don't believe in it. It's too easy. If things happen because they *have* to, what's the point of doing anything? Do you agree?"

"I sure do. If I believed in Destiny, I'd be a lieutenant in some godforsaken army fort somewhere."

"Things happen because of what we do. Or what we don't do. That's the only way life makes sense."

"Every once in a while," I said, "I'm reminded why I put up with you."

"Why you put up with me? Hah!"

He cut me off before I could continue the argument.

"Anyway," he said, "there's something I've got to do right now."

"What's that, Uncle Louis?" Rebecca asked.

"Have dinner. I've been smelling Mrs. Sundberg's cooking all morning, and I'm starving. Any takers?"

It was unanimous. Smiling, the four of us went inside to eat.